BEAUTIFUL POTENTIAL

J. SAMAN

Prologue

GIA

"You ready for this?" My best friend Chloe asks me as she leans forward, and slightly across the girl sitting in between us. "I mean, holy shit. Like any second they're going to call our names out and we're going to walk across that stage and they're going to put those things that have a name—that I don't remember—over our necks and then we're going to be midwives."

I laugh at my overly dramatic friend, shaking my head lightly. "Thanks for giving me the play-by-play. I was a bit nervous how this would all unfold."

She winks at me. "But not anymore."

"Not anymore," I concede, glancing around the room for the twentieth time in the last half hour. "Have you seen my parents anywhere?" I ask.

"No, I haven't. And I thought for sure when you went up to accept your Academic Achievement Award, your father would have screamed at the top of his lungs." *Me too.* "Did you have to go and get freaking 4.0 and show us all up?"

I shrug, just a little put off that my parents don't seem to be here. And it's not like I have my cell phone on me because I don't. I'm wearing a black graduation gown which obviously has no pockets, and under that, a dress which also has no pockets. I didn't bother to bring my purse because I didn't want to carry it and now I'm regretting that decision.

Maybe the traffic getting into the city was bad, but my parents aren't the sort to be late, especially for big occasions. And I consider graduating with my doctor of nursing practice as a certified nurse-midwife to be a big occasion. I mean, it took years to get here. And though my father would have been thrilled for me to have joined him in the long line of doctors our family is comprised of, I know he's proud of me.

He's told me so a thousand times over.

Ten minutes later, after enthusiastic people are done talking enthusiastically about all the remote, Third World countries they've delivered babies in—and all the ways they've changed the world to make it a better place for birthing said babies—they call my name. As I walk across the stage, I get the requisite amount of cheers. I get the friends' cheers. But I don't get the parents' cheers.

Because my parents aren't here.

Because they didn't make it to my graduation.

Walking down the steps on the opposite side of the stage from where I came up, I don't bother going back to my seat. Something is wrong. My parents wouldn't do this to me. They wouldn't.

The heavy-as-hell wood doors of the auditorium slam shut behind me and I take off at a sprint.

My apartment isn't far from here, only a few blocks and then I'm at the front door of my building. Running up the four flights, I frantically unlock the door to my studio apartment. My phone is exactly where I left it on the tiny counter, in my kitchen.

I have six missed calls.

All from my mother.

Swiping my finger across her name on the screen, it instantly calls her back. It takes half a ring before her voice fills my speaker and I can honestly say, I've never felt this sort of panic before. My heart is exploding out of my chest and I can't stop myself from pacing around in a small circle as I chew relentlessly at my cuticles.

"Gia?" My mom cries as she answers. "Oh my god, honey. We're at Mount Sinai."

Mount Sinai? Hospital, I realize a half beat later.

"What happened?" I can barely breathe the words as my knees give out and I drop to the floor.

"It's your father," she sniffles. "They think he had a heart attack, honey. It's not good. I need you to come here, now."

My face drops into my hands as silent tears begin to pour out of my eyes. I don't want my mother to hear how distraught I am. I can't even seem to ask if he's okay. If he were okay, he wouldn't be in the hospital and my mother wouldn't sound the way she does.

"I'll be there as soon as I can."

Ordering myself an Uber, I fly back down the stairs and out the front door, with my purse this time, and the second my heels reach the sidewalk, that Uber pulls up for me.

The ride is longer than I would like and by the time I reach the emergency room, I'm a wreck. Even more of a wreck than I was in my apartment, because I've had this entire twenty-minute ride through traffic to ruminate and obsess over every single what-if. Bursting through the automatic doors, I run over to the triage nurse, tell her my name and then she gives me the look. I know this look. I've given it to patients.

It's trying for placidity but it comes off as pitying.

I don't say anything as she leads me back through the huge double doors and into the patient area. She's talking to me like I know nothing and right now, I'm not as annoyed with that I as typi-cally am when people think I have no medical knowledge.

"I'm sorry, dear," she says, lacking any emotion in her tone, her eyes focused ahead, "but your father had a pretty big heart attack. It's an ST elevation myocardial infarction," she goes on, which actu-ally surprises me. Usually triage nurses aren't so forthcoming about a patient's medical condition or diagnosis, and right now, I sort of wish she wasn't so vocal. I wish she had stopped at heart attack instead of being as specific as she is. Maybe she's just trying to show off with her big words, but I know exactly what kind of heart attack that is.

It's a STEMI. Those are the kinds of heart attacks which have people dropping dead on their lawns. The types where people are dead before they even hit the ground. Widow Makers, they call them.

That's the type my father just had.

"Is he alive?" I manage as we weave our way through the emergency department. When I was in nursing school, I did an eight-week rotation in the ED. I hated every single second of it. Right now, I hate this place a million times more than I ever did then.

"He's—" she starts and then pauses, because we've reached our destination and there is a team of doctors hanging out, just sort of loitering around while one of them talks to my mother.

My father is not in the room, but my mother is.

And she's sobbing.

Not just crying, but hysterical while a tall thin man with dark skin and kind eyes tries to comfort her. I stand here, frozen on the precipice of the doorway, listening to him tell her, he's up in the cardiac catheterization lab and they're trying desperately to open the blockages from his carotid arteries by threading a catheter into the vessels and place a stent. That his heart attack was severe and he's in critical condition. That they're doing everything they possibly can for him.

I want to throw up everywhere. Bile climbs its way up the back of my throat, but I swallow it down, knowing I'm the one who has to be strong here. Right or wrong, my mother will look to me.

I step into the room and a dozen eyes turn to me. I glance past them, one by one, getting stuck on one of the doctors who happens to be remarkably handsome and then moving on. I reach my mother—and at the sight of me—she loses her last shred of composure and breaks down completely.

"They're operating on him," she chokes out through her tears. My mother doesn't understand the difference between the cath lab and the OR. She may be a doctor's wife, but she has absolutely no medical knowledge to speak of. That, and I think she's understandably too upset to focus on what they're saying to her.

The doctor who was just speaking to my mother looks at me,

then my outfit and back up to my eyes. It takes me an extra minute to realize I'm still wearing my stupid graduation gown.

At least I took off the cap.

"So he's up in the cath lab," I say, letting my mother cry into my shoulder with my arms wrapped around her. "Do you believe that will be enough to open the obstruction or is bypass going to be necessary?"

He examines at me for a second. Blinks. And then asks with an inquisitive air, "You're in the medical field?"

"Yes," I say with an edge, because I do not want to be treated like I'm naïve, by this man. "I'm a CNM, but I was a nurse before that so I'm not as clueless as this black gown would let you believe."

The doctor nods at me, those eyes which I thought were kind are now appreciative. "Well, then, CNM, I can't say for sure. We're hoping he makes it through the cath lab first..." he trails off because he doesn't want to say that he's not sure that he will.

Oh, god.

"Your father was in critical condition upon arrival–"

"So it's a wait-and-see game now," I interrupt.

He nods at me. "Yes. That's exactly right." He looks over his shoulder at one of the other doctors–the one who I thought was attractive–and then back at me. "May we speak to you out in the hall for a moment, please?"

Giving my mother a kiss and telling her I'll be right back, I follow them out into the hall. I don't like this. And I feel really fucking stupid and undermatched by the fact I'm still wearing this black gown. It makes me look like a novice despite what I just told him.

I stand there, in the middle of the hall with the entire ED going on around us. I fold my arms across my chest. "What's your name?" I ask the main doctor.

"I'm Doctor Sanders," he says. "Michael," he adds in a softer note. "And this is Doctor Finnigan Banner. He was the doctor who worked on your father when he first arrived." I nod at him, trying to ignore the second doctor's bright-blue eyes and piercing stare.

"Doctor Banner, would you care to walk Miss Bianchi through everything?"

Dr. Banner nods, stepping forward and into my personal space a bit. He's tall. Imposingly so and broad. I can tell he's built even though he's wearing a white lab coat and a baggy, blue scrub top. His chiseled jaw is lightly lined with brown stubble, which he reaches up to rub absentmindedly before his hands drop to his sides, and he gets into doctor mode.

"Your father presented in cardiac arrest—" *Jesus Fuck!* "We were able to cardiovert him back into sinus rhythm and after the EKG, we determine the extent of the MI he was having. We felt there wasn't enough time for further testing or imaging, other than some lab work, and he was sent up for stat angiogram. His rhythm wasn't holding well even with the medications we were giving him."

"I have so many questions," I start, unable to meet this guy's eyes, because even though this situation is overwhelming, his eyes are too. I glance down at my hands instead, even if it makes me feel weak to do so, and swallow hard. "But I don't want to ask them."

"Take your time, Miss Bianchi—" Dr. Banner says.

"Gia," I interrupt. "My name is Gia."

"Gia," he says in a tone I can't determine. "Both Dr. Sanders and I are here to answer any of your questions at any time."

"Thank you." I nod.

"We will update you as soon as we know anything," he promises and I feel his warm, strong hand on my shoulder, giving me a squeeze. "Right now, he's in very good hands."

I nod again. It's all I seem to be able to do.

"Thank you," I manage, bringing my gaze back up to his. "I appreciate that."

"We tried to explain everything to your mother," Dr. Sanders interjects, his tone kind regardless of the fact that I snapped at him before. I might have been a bit out of line back there. "But I'm not sure how much she understood."

More nodding. "I'll talk with her."

Walking back into the room, I'm in a daze. All of this just feels so surreal. So impossible. I've seen it with patients. I've watched as it happened to others. But you never expect it to happen to you.

My mother is still crying and once again I wrap my arms around her. She looks at me with red eyes and says, "I'm so sorry we missed your graduation, Gia. Your father is going to be so disappointed when he realizes. He was so excited, honey. So very proud." I wish she wouldn't tell me that right now. All it's doing is making me cry. Making my gut twist and knot up. "The moment we hit the FDR, he began complaining of chest pain and asked me to take him here. To this hospital." She points to the floor. "But maybe I should have taken him to the closest one instead." She shakes her head, like she can't believe any of this is happening either. "He knew he was having a heart attack," she tells me just as that doctor—Dr. Banner or whatever his name is—enters, standing tall and rigid.

I see it on his face. He doesn't even have to tell me.

My father is dead.

He looks at me, those eyes lingering on mine for a few extra seconds and then he turns to my mother. Dr. Sanders joins him and they proceed to gently explain that he is in fact dead. That my father is dead.

They apologize. Tell her how sorry they are for our loss and blah, blah, blah. All I can think about is the fact that my father is dead. That my mother is a widow. That he never saw me walk across that stage tonight, and while he was having a heart attack, I was pissed off they weren't there.

A nurse comes in and takes my mother out of the room. They lead her somewhere else. Somewhere where she can speak to people and make arrangements and see my father and do whatever people do when they've just lost someone they love.

I can't do that with her. I just...can't.

Instead I run, past those double doors and through the waiting room and out into the bay. I find the edge of the sidewalk and then I collapse.

My father is dead.

How the fuck did this happen?

Crushing agony pierces my chest, making it impossible to suck in a deep breath. My hands wipe furiously at my tears that come and come and come.

I stare sightlessly into traffic until I feel someone slink down next to me on the edge of the sidewalk. I don't have to look over to know who it is. I smelled his cologne before he even sat down. Felt his presence like a force of a nature.

"Dr. Banner—"

"Finn," he corrects. "You can call me Finn."

I ignore that. First names are not helpful right now. "If you're here to offer me comfort, save it. I'm in no mood."

He edges himself closer to me until his white-coat-clad arm is practically touching my black gown. He doesn't say anything for so long, I eventually glance in his direction, insanely curious, because for the life of me I cannot figure out what the hell he's doing out here with me.

"I'm sorry," he says. "I know this—"

"Must be hard for you," I finish for him. "I thought I just told you to save it. I don't want platitudes. I don't want to hear that you guys did everything you could. I don't want to hear that he wasn't in any pain. I just don't want to hear it. And maybe that makes me a bitch, but I don't care. I'm all for being the bitch right now if it spares me the speech."

"Okay then," he states with the slightest of smirks, scooting just a bit closer to me. Now he's definitely touching me. No mistaking it. "No platitudes. No standard words of comfort." I nod. "How's this then? I lost my father the same way when I was twenty-two."

I examine his profile, his eyes fixed out into the street the way mine just were and I sort of feel like shit for dumping on him. "That sucks," I say instead of I'm sorry. Hearing I'm sorry only seems to make you feel worse.

"Yeah. It did. I won't even lie and say it made me stronger or a better man or that he's the reason I became a doctor because all of that would be a lie."

"Yeah?" I laugh, despite myself. "Don't sugarcoat it for me now."

He chuckles, peering in my direction and making it impossible for me to see anything else. "I had wanted to be a doctor since I was six. His death really had no impact on that. And I was already a much better man at twenty-two than he was at fifty-two so I can't say that either."

"Well, alright then." I swallow. Clear my throat, and brush off a few more tears that have subsequently slowed since he sat down. "Sounds like your father was a real prize."

"If that's sarcasm, then I'll say you get where I was going with that."

"It was sarcasm, so I guess I do."

He smiles the most beautiful of smiles at me, those eyes slaying my thoughts. His jaw is strong and absurdly sexy with just the right amount of stubble that says, I've been at this job for hours and haven't had time to shave. Even his freaking nose is perfect. It has the smallest bump on the bridge, making me wonder if it was broken long ago. It's just different enough to make him the most gorgeous man I've ever seen.

My father is dead and all I see is Dr. Banner. But it's so much easier to think about him than the fact that my father is gone. Than it is to think about how my father will never get to hear about the work I do. Or the fact that I'll never introduce him to the man I'll marry. He'll never know his grandchildren. *Fuck.*

I sigh, fighting the urge to succumb to the tears I'm desperate to shed. I hate today.

"My father was a doctor," I say. "Did my mother tell you that?" He shakes his head. "He was a cardiologist of all things so I think I'm drowning in irony." He rubs his arm against mine, but he doesn't laugh, which I appreciate it. "I come from five generations of doctors so when I–his only child–told him I wanted to be a nurse, he was surprisingly okay with it. He told me it was about time the family had someone who cared enough about humanity to try and fix it."

"Wow," Dr. Banner muses. "That's pretty incredible."

I nod. "Yeah, it really was. And when I told him I wanted to be a midwife, he offered to pay for graduate school. Said the future babies of the world needed a brilliant hand to lead them in."

"Shit," he mutters.

"Yeah," I agree. "Shit. Because today was my graduation and he's dead and I can't even tell him I got an award for being top in my class." I give him a self-deprecating smile. "I'm not bragging, I swear. I'm just pissed off."

And devastated. I don't know how anything will ever be right again.

"It's cool. I was top in my class too. So now we're both bragging." He smiles at me and despite the somber mood I'm drowning in, I feel that smile.

"Well, aren't you the big man on campus."

He laughs at my sarcasm and I find myself smiling despite my ache. "That's such a cliché. I prefer, most astute and talented man on campus."

"Noted. Whenever I think of you, it will be in those terms."

Dr. Banner tilts his head so he's catching all of my face, and my attention has nowhere else to go but to him. His eyes are piercing, his expression pointed. "This may be totally inappropriate, especially given the situation, but that's definitely not where I want your thoughts to go whenever you think of me." I swallow. Hard.

He opens his mouth to speak when one of the nurses comes out, calling my name. Dr. Banner's eyes shut, his face is lined with regret. Regret for what specifically, I cannot be sure.

I nudge him with my elbow and say, "See you around, Dr. Banner." And then I leave him, sitting on that curb, feeling him watch me walk away. Knowing I'll never forget him.

Chapter One

GIA

1 year later

"IT'S A FULL FREAKING MOON," Chloe states as she leans against the edge of the nurse's station, taking down her messy bun and redoing it into something a bit more structured. "Can anyone explain to me the medical reason women go into a labor at a higher rate than normal during the full freaking moon?"

I can't, but it's true all the same. Tonight has been rough. Ten women were admitted in labor. That might not seem like a lot, but in a six-hour period, it is. Add on to that, we're short two nurses and one of the doctors has been stuck in the OR dealing with an emergency hysterectomy, following a very complicated delivery.

"Are we caught up?" I ask instead of commenting on her non-question.

"Yeah. I think we are." Chloe sighs out, rubbing her blue eyes and twisting her head around her neck until it makes that sick popping sound. "What time are you off?"

"An hour ago," I say, massaging my own sore neck. "I had a patient whose labor stalled. I didn't want to leave her."

"Aww," she coos. "You're a good one, aren't you? I would have been out the door–" She pauses as Dr. Fernandez walks past us. "Damn, he's hot. Why are the new interns so hot?" She shakes her head. "Anyway, you should go home. We're caught up and your lady delivered her little bundle of joy."

I stand up, scrutinizing her. "What the hell made you become a midwife if you're all about the sarcasm?"

She shrugs with a smile I can't help but laugh at. "What can I say, I'm a sucker for vagina."

"The world would be a better place if everyone respected them the way you do."

"So true, my friend. So very true."

I laugh and so does Chloe and it somehow manages to release some of the night we just had. "Okay, I'm out of here. If you're sure you're set."

"I'm set. Go home and sleep."

Leaning forward, I give her a kiss on the cheek, sign out my last patient who is still in early labor to the next midwife coming on, and get the hell off the floor before I get sucked back into the vortex.

July in hospitals is a precarious time. New interns. New fellows. New medical students.

I've been working as a midwife for the last year and I finally feel like I'm hitting my stride with it. I got this job almost instantly after passing my boards. I do two days outpatient and two days inpatient and I'm loving it. The fact I get to work with Chloe is really only a minor incentive.

At this time of night, the main doors of the hospital are locked and the only way in or out is through the ED.

My father died fourteen months ago and even though it wasn't in this hospital, I hate the ED. Hate it. Every now and then, I get called down here to help a pregnant patient in labor who came in maybe just a bit too late. Or consult on a pregnant patient who came in for an entirely different reason.

But when I have to walk through here without any purpose, my gut sinks. It's a reflex more than anything else. I didn't spend a whole lot of time in the ED when he died. But it's still probably my least favorite place.

Taking the stairs in lieu of the busy elevator, I open the door which leads into the back hallway and am nearly knocked over by a gurney as a crowd of doctors and nurses rush some poor bastard back into the trauma room.

I don't watch them go. Instead I just continue in the direction of the waiting room which will ultimately lead me out into the street. I wave out a hello to a few other people I know, press in the large round metal button, and step into the waiting room. It's full. But most of the people here seem to be together. Like a big family or an intentional gathering. They're all dressed impeccably, lots of black tuxedos and gorgeous designer gowns.

And their expressions are distraught.

I wonder if I'll always feel that ache when I see something like that.

Probably, I decide. But I'm still in the phase where I'm okay with that. It doesn't annoy me. I like missing my father. I like that ache. It keeps me close to him. The day I stop feeling it scares me more than anything else.

My eyes linger on that group of people, hoping their worry winds up being for nothing.

The sliding doors make that mechanical sound as they part for me and I step out into the balmy, sticky night. I live close to the hospital now. I moved out of my four-story walk-up in Harlem and now I live in a nice one-bedroom, in a decent building with an elevator. Sure, it doesn't have a doorman, but I don't really need someone to open the door for me and collect the packages I never receive.

I was able to purchase it, instead of renting, because my father left me a substantial inheritance. I didn't want it. But my mother told me it would have made him happy to help me get the things I need and to live in a safe building. It still makes me uneasy. Profiting from the death of my father just feels wrong.

It's nearly midnight as I look up at the bright moon, shunning out any stars who would dare to shine against it. I'm exhausted. But the good news is I don't have to work tomorrow. Or the next day, now that I think about it. In fact, I don't have to be back in the hospital for anything until Monday morning when I have regular clinic hours.

That puts a smile on my face as I turn to head toward my apartment. My phone buzzes against my scrub pants and I can't stop my laugh as I see it's a picture from Chloe of Dr. Fernandez flirting with one of the nurses accompanied by an emoji of a sad face.

She really needs to let that one go.

Just as I'm sliding my phone back into its place, the edge of my clog catches the corner of a misaligned brick paver and my ankle rolls awkwardly. Losing my balance, I fall sideways, unable to right myself as I head directly for the street. A small startled scream passes my lips. A jolt of panic rushes through me, paralyzing me in terror as I catch sight of the bright headlights of an oncoming car, speeding in my direction. Their horn blares out as if it's capable of stopping my rapid descent into the street. Into their path.

My eyes clench shut in anticipation of the collision when I feel hands grasp onto my right biceps, yanking me back to the sidewalk. The quick shift in momentum has me screaming out again, blindly rushing toward the ground only to be captured by the hands which saved me.

A strong warm body cocoons me momentarily before my disoriented limbs are steadied, realigning my position until I'm standing upright, breathing hard and shaking like a leaf.

"Shit," my savior cusses, clearly as shaken as I am. "Are you okay?" I can't answer that one just yet. I don't think I've ever been so scared in my entire life. His fingers reach up, grasping my chin and raising my face to his and...*Oh. My. God. It's Dr. Banner.* He gasps, his bright-blue eyes wide, still rattled with the stress of pulling a woman away from certain death. We both stand there for a moment in the middle of the sidewalk just staring at the other, quietly stunned. "It's you."

"It's me," I say back and then mentally shake my head because, *really?* "You...um...," I shift slightly, needing to look away from him yet unable to do so, "you saved my life. Thank you. That really doesn't feel like enough, but I can't think clearly enough to effuse the proper gratitude."

Dr. Banner blows out a breath and then grins at me. "You're welcome. I'd say it was my pleasure, but that feels like the wrong sentiment in a moment like this. And considering the fact that you just used the word effuse, I think you're able to think pretty clearly."

I smile and laugh a little because–holy motherfucking hell–I almost died. And Dr. Finnigan Banner saved me. It makes me want to launch myself into his arms and hug him, but I think the moment for that has past and at this point, it would come across as slightly crazy.

"You work here now?" I push, instead, because he's wearing scrubs and he's standing outside my hospital, which is a different hospital from the one I met him in over a year ago.

He nods. That's it. And his response sort of pisses me off. I don't exactly know what I'm expecting from him, but given the situation, a nod feels a bit lackluster. "I take it you do too," he says, eyeing my scrubs.

"Yup. I've been here for about a year now. You?"

We're playing that game. The one where you bounce a version of the same question back and forth. It's unsatisfyingly awkward. Especially since my heart is still racing away in my chest. And if I had to attest to the cause, I'd say it's all related to the man standing in front of me and not the near miss with the car.

"Only a few weeks," he answers. "Probably why I haven't run into you before now."

He smirks at his play on words and I get locked on the way his lips look as they crookedly smile. The way his eyes appear to glow against the darkness of night. The way I catch a hint of his cologne when the breeze blows just right. The way my body comes alive, zapping with the electric current which swims between us.

"Probably," I laugh, smiling back at him.

I'd be lying if I said I haven't thought about him in the year since I first met him. In the beginning, sometimes I allowed thoughts of him to eclipse thoughts of my father. It was oddly comforting and warm to do so. Mostly because I imagined he was thinking about me too. And as I stand here, taking him in, I realize my memory of him didn't quite do him justice.

"I got called in tonight," he tells me. "I guess it's a good thing it's a full moon, otherwise who knows what would have happened to you."

"Yeah, no kidding." I shake my head, still a bit stunned. "Hey, can you explain that to me? I mean, why do women go into labor on the full moon and why is the ED always overrun?"

He looks down at me with those eyes of his which are now dancing with amusement. "Couldn't say? Gravitational pull of the tides maybe?"

I laugh. "I don't think that even makes sense, but sure, let's call it that."

He laughs too and I realize I really like the sound of his laugh. It's one of those deep sexy laughs you can't help but feel in the pit of your stomach. And other places as well. "Are you on your way out?"

I nod. "Yeah. I am. I should probably let you get to it then. I'm sure I'm not the only damsel in distress who needs you to save them tonight." I move to step around him, not wanting to say goodbye and definitely not knowing how to do it. "Have a good shift," I say, feeling myself frown like a small child would. "Thanks again for saving my life."

"I don't have to be on until midnight," Dr. Banner rushes, reaching out a hand and grasping my shoulder, stopping me before I can get too far. His hand drops instantly once I turn to him, my head tilted to the side, not fully understanding his meaning. "It's eleven forty. I have twenty minutes."

"Oh."

"Are you walking home?"

"I only live a few blocks away."

He turns in the direction I'm facing so he's now standing beside me, tall and impressive. "I'll walk you then. I don't like the idea of you walking alone without me to rescue you from the next fall."

I try my best not to smile. I really do, but it comes out anyway. "Okay. You can walk me home. You don't have to beg."

Dr. Banner laughs again, but it doesn't last long and I have nothing to follow up my cheesy comment with. But I don't think he cares about that, because he's watching me out of the corner of his eye. I catch him doing it since I'm doing the same thing. And suddenly, I'm filled with the incredible giddy urge to smile. Because, wow, I never expected this.

We're silent for about a half a block, watching the people come and go around the hospital. "Do you like what you do?" he asks once we're in the darker part of the sidewalk. He's walking with his hands tucked into his scrub pockets and I wonder if it's so he won't be tempted to touch me. I hope it's so he won't be tempted to touch me, because that means he's thinking about touching me, and I think that's exactly what I want him to be thinking about right now.

Definitely not, if I like my job.

But I answer him anyway because I find I want him to know about me. "Yes," I say in earnest. "I absolutely love what I do."

He gives me an appreciative smile for that. "I bet you're really good at your job."

I return his smile and neither of us can seem to stop smiling as we inch just a bit closer to each other. Because our smiles appear to have a gravitational pull to them. Sort of like the full moon. And the tides. And the full ED and the laboring women.

There is no reason for this type of compulsion with a complete stranger other than an inexplicable force of nature. Of chemistry.

But it's there. And it's strong. It's not even because he saved my life tonight, though admittedly, that's not hurting things.

"What about you? Are you still a resident?"

"No, I'm not a resident anymore. I completed my residency in June and am now an attending. I've been toying with the idea of doing a fellowship year in something specialized. Not sure what yet though."

"How old are you?" I ask and he laughs, nudging into my shoulder.

"How old do you think I am?"

I stop in the middle of the sidewalk and contemplate that as I gaze up at him. His face says he's probably a little older than me.

Maybe twenty-nine or even thirty. I mean, he has to be at least that since he just finished his residency. But there is something about him, something in his eyes or his mannerisms which make him appear so much older. It's actually why I asked him. I mean, how often do you ask someone their age?

"Thirty-eight."

His eyes bulge for a moment until he realizes I'm joking and then he reaches out and tickles my side. I'm not particularly ticklish, but he hit a sensitive spot and I jump with a yelp and a giggle.

It's the first time he's actually touched me, touched me. In an intimate way. More than just on my arm or any other area considered socially neutral. The near miss doesn't count. That was driven by instinct. So maybe I was right about the whole hands-in-the-pockets thing?

God, I hope so.

"I'm kidding," I laugh, swatting back at his hand that's trying to get at me again. "I bet you're thirty."

"Twenty-nine. I won't be the big three-o until October thirty-first."

"You're a Halloween baby?" My eyes widen as does my smile. For some reason, I like that. It makes no sense other than it's a holiday, but it seems to humanize him a bit. Lightens him up. "That must have always been a lot of fun."

He shrugs as we start to walk again. I realize time is ticking by and he's got to get back to the hospital so I quicken my pace, my building only another block up.

"I guess. I never really celebrated my birthday much, growing up, so it never felt like the big deal everyone else thinks it is."

I want to ask him why that was. Why he never celebrated his birthday much growing up. But it feels too personal. Maybe it was his expression when he said it. Or maybe it was the way his tone shut down. I don't know. But there is something about him which seems...dark. Sad. Lost.

"How old are you, since we're sharing ages."

"I'm twenty-seven." I glance up at him. "October baby as well, but my birthday is a few weeks before yours."

"Are you seeing anyone, Gia?" he asks so suddenly that I pause for a beat, only to start walking again as my mind begins to race. It's the first time he's said my name. To be honest, I wasn't sure if he remembered it or not. I wouldn't have blamed him if he didn't. After all, I only met him that one day. But he did and that fills me with so many butterflies I could take off flying around the city.

But my answer grounds me in a matter of seconds. "Sort of," I say, and hate that answer. It's true, but right now, I think I'm wishing my response was no. "This is my building," I tell him and I step off to the side of the glass front doors.

"Sort of?" he questions, his eyes bouncing back and forth between mine and the front of my building, taking it in while trying to observe my reaction.

"Yes. I've been dating someone for a few weeks, but we're not exclusive and we're definitely not serious." And normally, I wouldn't bother to mention that, but he asked directly and I don't want to lie to him. I've been seeing Colin pretty consistently, but it's not quite a relationship and not quite casual dating. It's at the in-between stage.

He nods his head, his posture turning strained and uncomfortable. His eyes flash away, back out into the street before his gaze turns back to me. I know he's about to say goodbye and I'll probably go another year without seeing him. The thought of that makes my stomach drop.

But I can't think of anything to say to him to make it better. To make him stay or ask me out.

"I should get going," he pushes out, sounding a bit breathless. "I have to be on soon." He steps into me, towering over me and making me crane my neck so I can see him better.

Shit. I blew it. A guy hasn't made me feel like this in a very long time. I want more of that. More of him.

"If I had the time, I'd walk you up," he says and I can't stop my smile. "But it's probably better that I don't." That smile that was just lighting up my face falls. That sentence just exterminated all the life from it. His blue eyes bounce around my face for a moment, like they're caught in indecision. "See you around, Gia."

Then he turns and briskly walks off, leaving me standing here on my doorstep stunned. He didn't even give me a chance to say thanks for saving my life or even for walking me home. Or that I'd rather be sort of dating him than Colin. Or that I'm so glad I ran into him again because it's like I got the silent wish I made that awful day outside that emergency department.

"Way to go, Gia," I mutter to myself as I unlock the front door of my building, and step inside. But then a soft smile latches onto my lips, tugging up the corners. We work in the same hospital. Who knows what can happen with that.

Chapter Two

GIA

Pulling the door open to the yoga studio, I let Chloe go in first. But only because she needs the prompting. "Explain to me why I need to get out of bed on a Sunday morning to stretch and breathe?"

"It's good for you."

She rolls her eyes at me. "But why do we have to do hot yoga? It's freaking ninety degrees and humid outside already and you're taking me into a room that is freaking 104 degrees and humid?"

I shrug, walking us into the back room and pushing her a little as we go. I get her point. It is hot as hell outside. Bikram yoga isn't my favorite either, but it's the only class they had available at this time on a Sunday. But now that I'm entering the room, I'm sort of regretting this.

"Oh, hell no," Chloe says, wrapping her arms around her waist and turning on me. "It's not even up to temperature yet and I'm already sweating. We're just standing here, Gia, and I'm sweating. It's freaking gross. I'm going to turn into a raisin and when I'm good and dehydrated, instead of getting breakfast and coffee, you'll need to start an IV."

I laugh, nudging past her and spreading my mat out on the floor. But to be honest, I don't really want to do this either. It is gross in here. "Come on, Chlo. Just stretch out with me. If you want to leave after that, we can."

Chloe growls something under her breath which sounds like a slew of curse words and then she's joining me on the floor. "Five minutes, Gia Bianchi. I'm giving you five minutes."

"Fine. Five minutes." Sitting on my mat, I stretch my legs out straight in front of me and then lower my body, wrapping my hands around feet and bring chin to my knees. "Did I tell you that I was almost killed on Friday night?"

"No. You forgot to mention that when you woke me up this morning and yanked me out of bed," she deadpans. "Were you mugged at gunpoint? Forced into an underground world of sex slavery? I know it's wrong, but that shit sort of turns me on. I mean, not in real life, obviously. That would be terrifying and fucked up. But in a book I read recently, it totally sounded hot."

Twisting my head, I look over at her with furrowed eyebrows. She's sitting on her mat and picking at her nail polish. "I don't have words for you Chloe Daniels." She shrugs and I sit up, watching the instructor talk to a few girls at the front of the room. "I was nearly hit by a car. There were no guns or people forcing me into a life of sexual servitude."

"For real?"

She looks a little startled as I move into a downward-facing dog. "Yeah, it was close. Like really freaking close."

"Damn. What happened? But before you answer that, you need to get a new sports bra, because the one you're wearing clearly isn't doing the job. You're about to suffocate in your cleavage."

I snicker.

"Shhhh," someone snaps at us from behind.

"Oh come on," Chloe says in an exasperated cadence. "The class hasn't even started yet."

"I'm trying to find my center and I can't do that with you two talking like that," the girl snaps, and now I'm trying really hard to stifle my laughter.

"Aaaand, I'm done here." Chloe stands up, popping a hip and waiting on me to right my body and join her. I do, because even from my upside-down position, I can see this girl means business and clearly, Chloe and I don't. I have no idea what a center is, let alone how to find it.

"Okay, let's go." I'm trying to appear putout, but I doubt I accomplish it.

Less than five minutes later, we're stepping back out into the hot Sunday morning.

"Good workout," I say, dropping my shades over my eyes. "I think we deserve a breakfast sandwich and a coffee."

"Now you're speaking my language." Chloe points across the street at the coffee place we like to go to. It's annoyingly close to the hospital, but the food and coffee are good so we ignore that small fact. "Tell me what happened with the car."

"Actually, I'm blaming you."

"Me?" she squeals.

"Yeah. You. Because you sent me that picture of Dr. Fernandez with that nurse and I was looking at it when I twisted my ankle on the sidewalk."

"I'm not taking the blame for your klutziness. This is not a new phenomenon. You topple over all the time. Especially in those fucking clogs you're so fond of wearing."

"Fine," I concede. "I'll give you the falling-a-lot-in-my-clogs thing. But, I was falling into the street this time and a car was literally bearing down on me."

"Ha," she laughs, opening the door to our coffee shop and walking inside. "Is that midwife humor? Bearing down?" I roll my eyes. "God, I love that smell." She breathes in a deep breath. "So you were falling in the street and a car was bearing down on you and then what happened? Obviously, you didn't die as you're standing next to me."

"Obviously," I say dryly. "But honestly, I don't think that would be the situation if I hadn't been pulled back at the last minute."

"Whoa." She stops, spinning around on me. "You're serious? You actually almost *died*?" I nod. "I thought you were just being dramatic."

"No. It was really close."

"Damn. Sorry, I was being a sarcastic bitch." Chloe gives me a hug. "I'm glad you're okay. Who saved you?"

"I'll have a large coffee and an egg and cheese on a bagel, please."

"Same for me, please," Chloe says and then she waits on me to answer. I was stalling. I won't even lie and say I wasn't. I don't know what to say about Dr. Banner. Not just to her, but to myself. I spent a lot of time thinking about him after he left me on my doorstep. Wondering if I misinterpreted the signs I thought I was reading clearly.

I came up empty.

I have no idea who Finn Banner is or what he's really like.

I only know how he makes me feel.

I can't even claim temporary insanity or PTSD following the near miss, because I felt all of that the first time I met him. Only now it's stronger. I wouldn't call it a crush yet, but we're certainly creeping up on that territory.

But I have no intention of telling Chloe that. Her big mouth will not be able to hold back.

"An ED doc."

"Was he cute?" she asks absentmindedly as we accept our coffees and go over to add cream and sweetener.

"Who said he was a he? Women can be doctors too."

Chloe gives me a look and I wish I had kept my mouth shut. "He *was* cute. Wasn't he?"

"Stop," I laugh, doing my best to play it off as I over-stir the cream into my coffee.

"Gia, you're a shit liar and you might in fact be blushing, so I'm going with gorgeous." I am blushing. I can feel it. I've never blushed so much in my life since I met this man.

And here's the thing about Dr. Banner. He was my father's doctor. So if by some miracle, he does ever ask me out and Chloe finds out he was not only the doctor who saved me, but also my father's doctor, she'll know I held out on her and get pissed. Women react like that. Chloe reacts like that.

"He was my dad's doctor, Chlo," I say and then leave her to

digest that for a moment as I snag our sandwiches off the counter and find us a table.

"Explain," she says with a somber expression.

Taking a bite of my food, I chew slowly as I ruminate on how I want to tell her. Swallowing, I take a sip of my coffee and then shift in my seat so I'm facing her better. "The day my dad had his MI?" She nods. "The doctor who saved me last night was his admitting doctor."

Her eyes bulge. "Holy meatballs and spaghetti. That's just... wow. That must have been rough."

I shrug, because it actually wasn't. That was the weird part. You'd think the sight of Dr. Banner would make me sad or angry or something. You'd think he'd be the last person I'd want to see. But he wasn't. In fact, I don't think I thought about my father once the entire time I was with him.

"So what? He just saved your life and the two of said holy shit this is a crazy coincidence and that was it?"

Another shrug. "Sort of."

"But you think he's hot." She says this like it's a statement. Like she knows it for a fact and that's one of the annoying things about trying to hide something from your best friend. It never works. They know everything anyway. "You should totally find him. Seek his gorgeous ass out and offer him something like a date or a blowjob as a thank you. Something memorable."

"Right," I deadpan with an eye roll so she believes I'm all attitude and not the least bit interested in doing either of those things with him. "I'll get right on that."

Chapter Three

FINN

It's been nearly two days since I saw Gia, but I still can't get that image of her falling toward that car out of my mind. I can't get *her* out of my mind. I walked her home and the entire walk back to the hospital, from her apartment, all I could think was *stupid*. Stupid for walking her home. Stupid for tickling her side. Stupid for asking her if she was seeing anyone. That last one most of all because the moment I asked it, I saw the look in her eyes.

That beautiful hopeful smile.

And when she said she was sort of seeing someone—but it wasn't exclusive or serious—I saw the window she was trying to leave open. I hated that I had to shut it all down. Hated the way her smile faded into a frown because I couldn't keep my fucking mouth shut in the first place. Yet at the same time, I was relieved. I don't know what I would have done or said if she wasn't sort of seeing someone.

Gia is the farthest thing from a backroom forgettable fuck I can imagine. But that's the only thing I'm interested in. She's far better served with her sort of, non-exclusive boy who will no doubt realize how inane that is with a woman like her, and in no time, they'll be serious, and I'll be forgotten.

Ignoring the irritating discomfort that thought provokes, I page cardiology to come and admit my patient after diagnosing their new onset atrial fibrillation.

This is what I love about doing emergency medicine.

The constant busy work. The required concentration. The challenge of a mystifying diagnosis, even if this one wasn't so obscure or complex. Of course, like anything else, you get your standard crap. Stuff that isn't emergent and would be better cared for in an outpatient setting. But I don't mind those cases the way many of my colleagues do.

Sure, the hours can suck. The work is taxing, but at least I don't have to remind someone to get their colonoscopy or mammogram. I don't have to manage someone's hypertension or diabetes. I get them in, fix them up and get them out.

There is nothing more gratifying that that.

"Hi, Finn," Felicia, one of the nurses says with that flirtatious intonation and smile. I glance briefly in her direction, but I don't respond. I don't fuck the women I work with. That formulates expectations I have no intention of filling, and generates gossip I have no desire to be a part of.

The night continues on, filled with patient after patient and when the night turns into dawn and the patients thin out and reinforcements arrive, I leave. My condo is only six blocks from here. An odd coincidence considering I purchased it long before I got this position.

A woman walks past me, heading into the ED panting for her life. She's nine months pregnant and looks like she's about to deliver any second. Typically, that's a sight that would make my chest clench, but right now, it makes me think of Gia.

Gia.

What is it about her that draws me in? I can't quite put my finger on it. It's more than her gorgeous face or alluring body. It's more than her long, thick raven hair or her magnificent blue-green eyes. It's more than her smile which makes my heart beat in a way it hasn't dared to before. It isn't her quick wit or sarcasm.

It's her, I realize. Just her. The entire death-of-me package.

I lied when I said I didn't know she worked in the hospital. On my very first day as an attending in this hospital, I saw her walking through the hospital cafeteria with some blonde girl. They were smiling and laughing and I found myself captivated.

She sat down at a table across the room from where I was and I spent the entire half an hour she was there just…watching her. It was impossible not to. She appeared happy and I felt satisfied that she had managed to rebound after the loss of her father. As I watched her, I instinctively knew that I should stay away from her. I would not engage her the way I did outside the ED that first time.

And I vowed that if I ever did run into her, I'd be polite but nothing more.

But the moment I pulled her away from that oncoming car and realized it was her whom I had just rescued, all rational thought and common sense immediate fled. All I could think about was she almost died in front of me, but *I* saved her. And out of that realization, an unfathomable need arose.

A need for her.

The door to my regular coffee shop chimes out with one of those annoying bells overhead and I walk up to the counter. "May I help you?" the woman says with a smile. I see her a lot. Every time I come in here, she seems to be working. I open my mouth to speak when she says, "Dark roast?"

"That would be perfect, but can you make it decaf?"

"Sure. Whatever you want Doctor…" she trails off, hoping I'll fill in the end of her sentence with my name.

"Banner," I say with a tone that shuts everything else down.

She takes my curt response for what it is, a brush-off, and then goes about making my coffee. When she hands it to me, I give her fifteen and tell her to keep the change. She grins at the tip and I feel just a little better about being a dick.

Stepping out into the warm July morning, I take a sip of my decaf just as my phone buzzes. Only my mother calls me this early and though I'm tempted to ignore her, I answer her on the third ring.

"Good morning, Mother." Yes, my mother is one of those mothers who insists on being called Mother. Probably because she was never a mom and quite the opposite of a mommy. Mommies love you. Mommies have your best interests at heart.

Mommies protect you from the boogeyman.

"Finnigan," she says and I inwardly groan at the use of my full name. My snooty, aristocratic mother should never have let my piece of shit, alcoholic father name me. Who gives a fuck if he was worth a half a billion dollars? What good was that money when he was beating us senseless? "How are you this morning?"

"Fine, thank you. How are you?"

"Very well." Our conversations always begin the same and I wonder what she would do if I ever told her that I'm not well. That things can be real shit sometimes. "I was talking to Olivia Prescot's mother last night at the club."

And here we go.

"Uh huh," I say only half listening, as I start my walk back uptown so I can get some rest before I have to do this all over again.

"She informed me that Olivia recently ended things with that man she had been seeing."

"Wonderful," I mock. I have no idea who Olivia Prescot is nor do I care.

"I'm glad you think so because I gave her mother your number."

"I hope you're kidding, Mother." I freeze in the middle of the sidewalk. Something about my mother just makes me goddamn furious.

"Finnigan," she starts slowly. "Olivia is a very smart, beautiful woman. She works as a marketing director for Precision Cosmetics." Right. Like that makes any sort of difference with me. You'd think she would know better by this point?

"Mother," I growl, because my patience with her seems to be evaporating faster than usual. "I am not interested in dating Olivia Prescot or any of the other daughters of the women at your club. I've asked you to stop giving out my number. The last woman you forced upon me, thinks I'm a dick for telling her I'm not interested. Pretty soon, your friends will start to shun you." Not that I care, but

I'm hoping my threat acts as a deterrent to my overly exploitive mother.

"Language, dear. And I doubt it. No one gets accepted to that club without me."

How this woman stayed with my father as long as she did is a mystery to me. She was completely different while he was alive. Silent and meek. Now she's a bigger bitch than I am an asshole, and that's saying something.

"How nice for you. I have to go."

I disconnect the call without waiting on her required pleasantry and then I head home to try and sleep for a few hours. But I'm restless. Unable to make sense of my thoughts. I just need...something. I don't even know what. Just a change from my ordinary.

Leaning my back against the rough exterior of the neighboring building, I take a sip of my coffee and shut my eyes. I'm probably just tired. Speaking with my mother certainly doesn't help with anything.

"Long night?" she asks and I inwardly sigh.

Gia Bianchi, how did you find me?

Will I ever be able to escape her now that I've seen her again? If I hadn't started this new job, I'd seriously consider leaving for something else.

"Something like that," I say, unable to look down upon her.

"But you get to go home and sleep, right? Why bother with coffee?"

"It's decaf. I'll still get to sleep. Why are you up so early?"

She doesn't answer right away and her silence is like a train wreck. I can't help but look, hoping to see something which will give me the sick thrill I love to pretend I don't feel. And when my eyes find hers, I realize that's exactly what she was waiting on.

"Early riser. Now I survive on caffeine and carbs. Very healthy."

My eyes scroll down her sensational body, taking in her exercise outfit and lingering on those tits I like so much and say, "Seems to do well by you." And this is why I can't be around this woman. Because I don't know how to shut the fuck up.

She grins. Maybe even blushes a little, though that's a bit more difficult to tell.

"Do you want to come with me? Let me buy you some breakfast? You know," she hedges, shifting her weight to the other foot, "to thank you for saving me from certain catastrophic and painful death."

Yes. "No," I answer instead and she nods, but it's the sort of nod that's more of an obligation than an affirmative. If she's hurt, she's hiding it well. "Sorry, I'm just really tired."

"Sure," she says with an easy shrug and I hate that shrug. I want her to be disappointed. I want her to want me to come have breakfast with her. "Of course. Another time, maybe."

Oh, Gia. If only.

She doesn't wait for me to say anything else, she just smiles at me, her perfect white teeth reflecting off the sun. "See you around, Dr. Banner."

Then she turns around and walks off, but not in the direction of the coffee shop I just vacated. No, she's headed home, I think. So it's not like she was going in there anyway.

Dr. Banner.

I cannot stand how she just did that. I should only be Finn to her. Never Dr. Banner. Dr. Banner is the man who told her that her father was dead. Finn is the man she should forever stay away from. We are very different and yet, that difference is everything.

Because even though I need Gia Bianchi to stay away from me, it's the last thing in the world I want.

Chapter Four

GIA

I get a text page twenty minutes before the end of my shift that I need to go down to the emergency department and evaluate a patient. This pisses me off for so many reasons. First, I hate the ED. I think I've already covered why. Second, the majority of doctors in the ED are completely incompetent when it comes to pregnant women. It's like these women have some rare and terrifying disease which makes doctors stupid, eliminating all logic and common sense with how to treat them.

I don't bother wasting time on trying to find someone else to go, I just suck it up and do it.

For one very specific reason.

The hopeful butterflies in my stomach aren't playing it cool at all. They're completely giving me away.

Opening the back door of the ED, I waltz over to the nurses' station because the page did not tell me who asked for the consult or in what room to find the patient. She directs me over to sutures area and tells me the request came from an intern and a medical student. The pretty young nurse laughs when I roll my eyes at that. Strolling down the long corridor, I can't help but scan the hallway and rooms–without trying to be obvious–for Dr. Banner. Yes, that is still what I call him in my mind.

Of course, he's not any where to be found and as I enter the sutures room, I want to sigh. A woman, probably seven or so months along is sitting on a gurney with her arm on a blue Chux pad, showcasing a two-inch laceration. And off to the side, standing as far away from her as the room will allow, are Larry and Curly.

"You called for an OB consult?" I ask them, stepping into the room and smiling at the poor patient who was unfortunate enough to have these two idiots providing her medical care.

"Yes," the one on the left with very blond hair says. "I'm Dr. Thomas and this is Andrew Thomas, no relation. He's a medical student."

"Hi," I say to both of them, in no mood for socializing. I want to get to the bottom of this and get out of here. It was a very long and exhausting shift and I don't want to be late in meeting Colin. I'm always late when we meet up and it annoys him. Can't exactly blame him for that. "What's the problem?"

"Well," Dr. Thomas says, his eyes flittering past me over to the gurney where the patient is seated, "she's pregnant."

I glance over at the woman who is shaking her head and rolling her eyes and I can't blame her for that either. I would be too. "I can see that."

"We can't stitch her up until you clear her," That's Andrew Thomas–no relation, now.

"What exactly do you need me to clear? She's pregnant." I raise my eyebrows at them. "What does that have to do with her arm lac?"

They both exchange nervous glances and now I sigh. "Okay, come with me and pay attention." I turn around and move across the room until I'm standing next to her. "Hello, I'm Gia Bianchi, one of the midwives here in the hospital. It's a pleasure to meet you."

"You too," she says with an air of frustration. "Look, all I did was cut my arm open after having to jump out of the way from a guy riding his bike on the sidewalk. I sliced it on one of those metal fences on the side of a building."

"Did you fall?" She shakes her head. "Did you bump your belly?" Another headshake. "Any abdominal pain or cramping?"

"Nope."

"What about back pain?"

"No more than usual. I'm seven months."

I knew it, I mentally high five myself. "Any blood or fluid from your vagina?"

"Definitely not."

I smile at her expression. "Are you feeling the baby move?"

"Yes," she sighs. "The baby is fine. I just want to get my stitches or whatever they have to do and go."

"I completely understand." I turn back to Larry and Curly and say, "She's cleared. I don't think we need to check a fetal heartbeat," I turn back to her, "unless you'd like me to."

The lady shrugs again. "Sure. Why not. I'm here and I can never get enough of that sound."

"I hear you on that." I pull out my pocket doppler and gel which I always carry with me for a consult, because if I'm not on the labor and delivery–L&D as we call it–floor, there is never any gel to be had. "You guys can start. But if you're using actual sutures instead of liquid, use regular lidocaine. No epi."

Both of their eyes widen and then Andrew Thomas–no relation–grabs the bottle of lidocaine that's on the table and goes to switch it for one which does not have epinephrine in it. In the small dose that's in the lidocaine, it's probably safe, but why risk it? Especially with these two.

Lifting up her shirt, I feel around for the baby's back, enjoying the way it moves beneath my hand. "Do you know what you're having?" I ask her.

"A girl. We're going to name her May. Like the month."

"Beautiful." I squirt some gel onto her abdomen and slide the diaphragm of the doppler around until I find the heartbeat and when I do, I check the rate. "Perfect. One thirty-five. Baby May sounds great."

"Thank you," she says. "Who knew there would be all this production for a cut."

I really have nothing to say to that, so I just smile, make my goodbyes to her and the two Thomas's and get the hell out of here. Typically, I would go back upstairs to chart, but I want to leave the hospital so I have time to shower and change before I meet Colin.

We've been dating for about six weeks now, but we're still far from serious or even exclusive. He made that last one clear when we were about four weeks in. And I probably should have sent him packing then, but I didn't. He's a nice guy, good looking, patient with my demanding and ever-changing schedule and decent in bed. So I don't exactly mind the fact we're not serious or exclusive. It actually fits my life pretty well.

I find an abandoned computer on a rolling cart, log in and start documenting on my consult. I'm just reading over my note when I feel someone behind me. Spinning around, I find myself peering directly into those blue eyes I was hoping to see.

"Did you change specialties?" he asks playfully.

I laugh, shaking my head. "No, I was summoned down here by an intern and a medical student who were terrified to suture a woman's arm because she has a baby growing inside her."

"Ah," he says with a knowing nod. "I wish I could say they're the only ones, but a lot of us are afraid of them."

I laugh because the thought of him calling me down for a consult like the one I just had doesn't bother me nearly as much as it did for the other two. "Are you one of those people, Dr. Banner?"

He steps into me a little, not a lot, but enough so I can feel his presence and smell his oh-so-enticing scent. Sandalwood and citrus, I think. My stomach swoops and the sensation makes me want to smile bigger. "Finn, Gia. Call me Finn."

"Finn," I repeat because I haven't allowed myself the pleasure of using his first name yet. He has forever lived as Dr. Banner in my thoughts. It somehow felt safer that way.

"Did you mouth off to my intern and medical student the way you did Michael Sanders?"

"What?" I laugh the word.

"That day in the ED when I first met you." He shifts so he's even closer. His arm is touching mine now. Just his stupid white coat, but it's deliberate. As deliberate as all the other times he's touched me. No other way to take it. "You told Dr. Sanders you weren't as clueless as the black gown would have him believe."

"I can't believe you remember that," I gasp, because that has my mind running circuits right now. He remembers what I said over a year ago? And he's touching more of my arm with his now. And his head is dipped purposefully close without being overly intrusive.

"It was impressive and definitely memorable. No one ever mouths off to Dr. Sanders. He's the epitome of a hard-ass with his staff."

"Jealous, were you?" I grin up at him, not even trying to hide the fact I'm flirting with him. I can't stop the cruel pleasure of it.

"Very. But now I get to be the hard-ass so it all works."

"Is that right? Should I mouth off to you too then?"

"I can think of better uses for your mouth," he says quietly, his head leaning in closer as he does, his blue eyes darkening as his pupils begin to dilate. My heart rate begins to spike and my breathing picks up. I can practically taste the mint on his breath.

I don't think I've found my voice yet. I swallow. Clear my throat. "Are you just starting your shift?"

He shakes his head. "No. Just finishing up. A bunch of us are going out if you'd like to join."

Shit. Why does this keep happening? "I would, but I can't tonight." I hope he can hear the regret in my voice. "Another time though?"

He gives me a short tight nod and then he does that thing where he looks away, up at nothing. He did it last time, after I told him about Colin. His eyes close slowly and when they reopen, his features are wooden. He takes an intentional step back, becoming distant and unapproachable.

I can't see past the blinders he has up. They obscure everything.

What the hell just happened?

"Probably better if we didn't," he says and I think those are my least favorite words put together. He goes from burning hot to

36

freezing cold in a matter of seconds and I don't know how to keep myself balanced with that. How to navigate through.

"See you around, Gia."

That's becoming our line. I don't want that to become our line. I want more of the line where we can think of better things to do with my mouth. I want him to show me in explicit detail just what those things are. But Dr. Finn Banner isn't going to do that with me. I can see it written all over him.

I sigh, feeling so very defeated with him. With myself. "You too, Finn."

He's already gone. Just like that night. But really, what the hell? I mean, all I said was I can't do it tonight. I didn't even tell him I have plans with another man. It's not like he asked me out on a date. He asked me to join a group of people.

So why the fuck does he get all sulky like that? It's aggravating. And infuriating. And every other synonym which works in this situation. I sort of want to scream, *I like you, Finn. I want you to ask me out on a real date.* I want to throw my hands up in the air and yell, *show me something real.*

But I don't know if there is a point to that. Maybe he's right. Maybe it is better this way. And really, why do I like him? Because he flirts with me? Because he's gorgeous?

Pathetic.

He's not even all that nice to me.

I leave the ED in a mood. Not a good mood either. I haven't seen Finn-fantastic, now he's Finn-in weeks and now he's all I can think about. Again. Last time it took me a solid two weeks until I wasn't totally consumed with thoughts of him. That really only gave me a week's reprieve, which isn't a lot.

I feel like he has a story. At least that's what I convinced myself of. He's movie star caliber hot. Smart. Funny. A doctor. Really good at the whole flirting thing. I mean, why is a guy like him single? And what's with the whole, *probably better if we didn't,* bullshit?

He's got to be hiding something, right? STDs? Yeah, that must be it.

Sadly, that thought doesn't put me off from him. Probably

because I know that's not the situation. Finn doesn't have STDs. But he doesn't exactly scream *player* either. If he was, he would have made his move already.

I need to let it go. I don't know him. I've only met him a few times and each of those encounters have been brief. Memorable, but brief.

I get home, shower off the day of birthing babies and slip on a black, low-cut V-neck dress with cutouts in the back. The color looks good against my hair which is nearly the same shade and I put on some shimmery eyeshadow and red lipstick because why not.

Colin likes a bar that's coincidentally only a couple of blocks from the hospital, but in the other direction from my apartment so it takes me almost fifteen minutes to walk over there in my four-inch heels which I really shouldn't be wearing, as my feet already ache from spending the whole day on them.

Stepping inside, I immediately spot Colin waiting for me at the bar, a new beer in his hand. I'm hoping that means I'm not all that late. "Hey," I say as I reach him, placing a small kiss on his cheek.

"You look nice," he says as he turns to face me, taking in my outfit. That's what he always says when he sees me. That I look nice. Is it considered nitpicky if I say I wish he'd use another adjective? Something like pretty or beautiful? It doesn't even have to be anything spectacular like gorgeous or stunning or exquisite. Dazzling might be a bit much. Especially from a straight male. But I certainly wouldn't object to it either.

"Thanks, you do too." That's my standard response to his standard compliment. That's what we've become. Standard. We go out and grab a drink or dinner, go home to his place or mine, have sex and then either leave or spend the night.

But we never spend the following day together.

One of us typically leaves before breakfast. It's not even a spoken thing. It just happens.

I'm aware this probably means I don't love being with him other than for those brief interludes. I don't get giddy or excited to see him. I don't get that rush of anticipation. Hell, I had more of that today at the prospect of seeing Finn than I've had for Colin in the entire six weeks we've been dating.

"What are you drinking tonight?" he asks and I can't tell if the fact I don't have a standard drink to go with our standard relationship bothers him or not. I like to mix up my drinks. Sue me.

"Hmmm. How about a margarita on the rocks with no salt?"

He shrugs like I was actually asking for his opinion on my drink choice instead of having him order it. Colin waves down the bartender and as he's ordering my drink, I glance around the bar, taking it in. It's pretty here. Kind of girly, with dark red and black furnishings, ornate crystal chandeliers and sconces, and candles on each tabletop. Very romantic.

It's fairly crowded despite the early–by New York standards–hour for Friday night drinking. Soft hypnotic music floats around, intermingling with the white-noise hum of people talking.

I feel Colin brush my exposed arm and just as I'm turning back to him, to catch what he's saying, I lock eyes with someone staring at me.

Chapter Five

GIA

It takes me a half second longer than it should to realize it's Finn staring at me. Probably because he's dressed in a dark-gray, button-down and jeans and I'm used to seeing him exclusively in scrubs. He looks so unbelievably handsome like this. I mean, he looks hot-as-sin in his scrubs, but this look? Damn. It's like fantasy hour.

His jaw is lined nicely with that thin layer of stubble which I like so much on him, but hadn't paid much attention to earlier. And his hair is styled instead of just all over the place. I can't pull my eyes away from him and he seems to be having the same difficulty with me. There are so many things swirling around those bright-blue eyes of his. Curiosity. Interest. Amusement. Anger. Desire. Yes, that last one is there too. Especially when his eyes dip down to my dress, caressing every inch of me.

Is it hot in here? Am I visibly panting? Holy hell, I'm a ball of lust and all he's doing is looking at me.

Colin hands me my drink and I take it reflexively, sipping at it while watching Finn watch me. When Colin reaches out and places his hand on the small of my back, on one of the cutouts, Finn's eyes darken. He looks like he wants to kill Colin and that possessive-jeal-ousy thing he has going on might just be my total undoing.

I want to shake my head. I want to tell him Colin is just a stand-in. But Finn's words from earlier come crashing back into me. *Probably better if we didn't.* That has me turning my attention back to Colin. Colin who is smiling at me. Colin who is talking to me about his day. Colin who does not excite me anywhere near as much as the man across the bar does.

It takes all of my concerted effort to keep my focus on Colin. I lose that battle with alarming frequency. And every time I sneak a peek over at Finn, he's looking at me. Even if he's talking to someone else. It's like he knows the exact minute I'm going to glance at him and does the same with me.

When my eyes aren't on his and his aren't on mine, I still feel him. Like a pulse. Finn is a constant steady rhythm. Something tangible and alive. Something that's making me dizzy and excited. It's addictive. This game we're playing right now.

Just as I'm finishing my second margarita, and Colin is finishing his third beer, he asks if I want to go somewhere and grab dinner. I don't. I don't want to do anything right now other than eye-flirt with Finn. But at the same time, I'm here with Colin and not Finn. And Finn said probably better if we didn't, so I say to him, "Sure, let's go grab something. Whatever you want," I finish with, because I feel just a touch guilty I'm openly feasting on another man in front of him.

Colin nods and as he's getting the bartender's attention to settle up, I feel someone brush my arm. My head twists around at the connection. The sensation of it so much more than just incidental contact by someone passing by. "Oh, sorry," Finn says with a sexy smirk, his eyes dancing over me to Colin before they return to mine. Colin isn't even paying attention.

"That's alright," I say, in a husky voice which cannot be helped.

Finn does it again. His fingers rake down the exposed skin of my arm, eliciting gooseflesh and an embarrassing shudder in his wake. When his hand reaches mine, he slips something into my palm, closing my fingers over it and giving me a squeeze. He looks intently into my eyes for a beat and then down at my hand which is still covered with his.

And then he walks away.

Provocative excitement blooms in my chest. Colin is signing the bill so I take the half second I'm afforded and check whatever it is Finn placed in my hand. It's a note written in neat, very undoctor-like handwriting, which says, "Meet me in the back where the bathrooms are."

"Ready?" Colin asks.

"I...um." God, I'm a horrible person. "I need to go use the restroom real quick. I'll meet you outside."

He nods and plants a small kiss on the corner of my mouth which I barely even register and then saunters off without another word. Moving through the overly congested bar to the back, where there is a long dark hallway which has the bathrooms and staff rooms off of it, I suck in a deep fortifying breath, doing my best to tamp down the seductive thrill threatening to consume me.

Sure enough, Finn is there, his back to me, but when he hears my heels clickety-clack against the hardwoods, he turns around to face me.

"Is he your sort-of?"

"Huh?" I smile, tilting my head at his choice of greeting.

"The guy you're sort-of dating. The guy you're not exclusive with?"

I nod up at him. "Yes."

"Are things still that way with him? Sort of and non-exclusive?"

"Yes."

He takes a step into me, his hand snaking around my waist until it finds that same spot where Colin's hand occupied earlier. His fingertips graze the exposed sensitive flesh of my lower back and I shudder again like the helpless fool I am.

That makes Finn smile.

"I don't like seeing you with him. In fact, I can't stand it." My breath catches at his unexpected admission. Lust sears through me. White hot and deliciously painful. "I know I said it's probably better if we didn't," he starts, breathing noticeably heavier, his warmth cascading over me, waking every pleasure sensor in my body. "And it would be better that way. For both of us. But I can't stop thinking about you, Gia."

I lean into him the way he's leaning into me. Holy shit do I want this man. I've never felt this sort of hunger before and all I want is for Finn to feed it. Cultivate it. Take possession over it and make me his in every possible way.

"Me either," I tell him, taking another step forward until our bodies are gently pressed together, my hand resting over his very muscular, manly chest.

Oh dear lord, his heart is pounding. Or is that my pulse pressing against him? His cologne cascades over me, becoming all that I can smell, adding to the hypnotic effect he has on me. I want him to kiss me. So goddamn bad, I hardly think of anything else but his lips on mine.

"Tell me how to make it stop. I need it to stop."

I shake my head. "I don't want it to stop."

"He's waiting on you, isn't he?"

"Yes. But—"

He shakes his head, cutting me off, his eyes growing impossibly grim. Hopeless even.

That desperate look freezes me. Pulls my hand from his chest and makes me take a baffled step back. He invited me back here. He was the one staring sexy stares at me all night.

But he's not backing down and he's not taking it back. *Take it back, Finn.*

I sigh, I'm getting really tired of his hot-and-cold-regret shit. Even now, I can see the conflict raging through him. Feel his indecision. "I want this," I tell him firmly, going for broke. He shuts me down with yet another a shake of his head, but the agitated fire which grows in his eyes at my words betrays the magnitude of his want. Of his desire.

Leaning down, his nose brushes the space between my neck and shoulder. I shudder again, my hands reaching up to grasp onto his shoulder, finding I suddenly need the support. My heart is racing out of my chest and I know he can feel it. I know he can.

"Finn," I breathe and he rumbles out a low growl which vibrates into me. My toes curl in my shoes. My eyes roll back in my head. Because his nose is skimming ever so lightly up the column of my neck until it reaches the space just below my ear.

He breathes in deeply, inhaling my fragrance. I moan. "Gia," he whispers against my heated skin. I grip onto his shoulders, tighter. His nose brushes directly behind my ear as he whispers, "Go back to your sort-of, non-exclusive guy." His words are stone. Rough and uncompromising. "He's waiting on you."

And then he walks away, leaving me alone in this dark hallway, trying to elucidate to myself everything that just happened.

I decide I can't. I decide there is no comprehending the enigma that is Dr. Finnigan Banner. I decide to take his words about being better if we did not do this, at face value. Even if it sucks and hurts way more than it should at this point.

I leave the bar and find Colin standing on the sidewalk texting something into his phone, a smirk pulling up the corner of his lips. I wonder if it's another woman, and I realize I don't care if it is. Which means I need to end this. Regardless of Finn and his mind-fucking ways.

The moment Colin sees me coming, he tucks his phone away in his pocket and smiles. It's a shame he's not more of a lot of things and less of others. There's potential, just no...spark. "Hey," he says. "Took you long enough."

Right. This is why I have to end it.

"Colin," I start and I think he can tell where this is headed just by my tone.

"You're ending this?"

I nod. "Yeah. It's just... I'm looking for more, you know? You're a great guy, but this isn't working for me anymore."

He sighs, running a hand through his light brown hair. "Is it because I said I don't want to be exclusive?"

I shake my head. "That's not it–"

"I guess I'd be willing to try if that's really what you want."

Way to sell it there, big guy. "No. I don't think I do. We're just not right for each other."

Colin looks at me long and hard and then he nods. He gets it. He's knows I'm right. When you've got something special with someone, being with them isn't a chore. Commitment just comes naturally.

"Okay. Yeah." He reaches out and gives me a hug and a small peck on my lips. "Thanks for being so cool about it."

"You too," I say. "Take care, Colin."

I don't wait for him to say anything else to me. I just walk away, back in the direction of my apartment. I'm out of sorts and none of it has to do with Colin. Part of me is tempted to track down Finn's number and tell him I no longer have a sort of non-exclusive guy. But I won't.

I know Finn is attracted to me. He's given every indication he is. Yet something is holding him back. Something is keeping him from moving forward and I instinctively appreciate Colin is not that reason.

Why chase after something which will only get me hurt?

So here I am, all dressed up and nowhere to go on a Friday night. I don't even have work tomorrow. I call Chloe and she picks up on the first ring like the phone was in her hand and she was waiting for my call. "Gia, my love," she yells into the phone because wherever she is, it's noisy as hell. "Where are you? You still out with Colin the douchetard?"

Yeah, Chloe never really liked Colin all that much.

"Nope. I ended it with him just now. Where are you? I need some food and girl chat."

She laughs loud and rancorous. I think Chloe might be a touch drunk already. "So glad you ditched that one. Come meet us. I'm at The Sevens with Monique."

"On my way." I hang up with her, hail down a cab and within ten minutes, I'm joining my grad school friends at one of the hottest restaurants in the city. Well, one of the hottest restaurants people like us can afford. They stand up when I arrive and we hug each other the way girls do.

I never mentioned Finn to Chloe again after that morning at breakfast. There was nothing much to say, really. And right now, I'm glad I had that foresight. Because as I listen to Monique tell me about the guy she's seeing, I realize the nothingness of Finn Banner will stay tightly locked away. I don't want people to ask about him. I don't want Chloe to do her Chloe thing and seek him out or nudge me every time we pass him in the hospital.

I think I want to hide him away and only pull him out for analysis when I'm feeling particularly masochistic and self-destructive.

We order food and more drinks and within fifteen minutes of being here with my girls, both Finn and Colin are forgotten. There are only the men in the restaurant. The ones who we're blatantly checking out for the sport of it.

"He's older than me," Monique says, leaning over in my direction so I can hear her over the vociferous background noise.

I laugh. This is not the first older guy she's dated. "How much older?"

She smiles and her white teeth practically gleam in contrast with her dark skin. "Eight years older. He's in his mid-thirties. But damn, is he a hot one."

"Mid-thirties isn't crazy. As long as he's not married."

She widens her eyes, shaking her head, her expression one of horror. She's already made that mistake once. She didn't know the guy was married until she did and then it ended in a very ugly way.

"What does he do?"

Monique rolls her eyes at me, as if the answer should be obvious. "He's a doctor of course. When the hell do I have time to meet anyone who doesn't work at the hospital?"

"Touché. What kind of doctor?"

"Emergency Medicine." I nearly spit out my margarita, but settle for choking on it instead. "You okay?" I nod, chugging down my water.

"What's his name?" I squeak out once I'm able to breathe again. I know it's not Finn. Finn is not in his mid-thirties, though I teased him that he was. But seriously? Why is it when you have a preoccupation with someone, every little bullshit insignificant thing reminds you of them?

"Michael Sanders." Now I really do choke. I might in fact be turning blue. "Jesus, slow down before we have to Heimlich your ass."

"Michael Sanders?" I gasp. "You're dating Michael Sanders?"

"Yes," she draws out the word hesitantly. "Do you know him?"

I nod. "Yes. He was my dad's doctor. The day of graduation."

Realization dawns on her face. "Oh sweetie, I'm so sorry. I didn't know."

"Stop it. It's fine. It was just a shock is all."

Monique reaches over and gives me a hug, but this night feels like it's going from bad to worse. That is until Chloe chimes in with, "We've got our own hot docs. Dr. Fernandez in OB is my personal favorite of the moment, but I heard one of the nurses saying there is a god of an attending working in our ED now." She winks at me and I'm officially in my own little version of hell.

"Yes," Monique exclaims excitedly. "Michael said his protégé, Finn something or another, went over to you guys. Michael said nurses, and patients practically bleed themselves for him, but he doesn't give any of them the time of day."

And because I can't help myself I say, "Why not?"

Monique shrugs. "Maybe he doesn't date people from the hospital? I don't know."

"Huh," Chloe says like this is a challenge she just accepted on my behalf because her eyes are glued to mine. Awesome. Little does she know it's never going to happen.

But I do.

Because that's basically what Finn told me. Or at least intimated.

"Well," Monique says. "I can't blame him for not dating people he works with. That shit can get messy. Workplace relationships are dicey."

"So says the chick dating someone she works with," I tease and we all laugh.

"Hell yeah," Chloe half yells. "The messier, the better," she says raising her glass for us all to toast to that.

We all laugh and morph into safer territory. At least safer for me. But I'm still stuck, fixated on the whole Finn not giving the time of day to the women he works with thing. Is that why it feels like it will never happen between us?

I have no idea and I hate that I care.

Chapter Six

FINN

7 years ago

SOMEHOW, I thought I'd feel different. Somehow, I thought I'd be relieved he's dead. But I'm not. And that bothers me because my father was a grade-A piece of shit. And now he's dead. A heart attack, which sort of makes me want to laugh because the malevolent son of a bitch didn't have a heart.

In fact, the only good thing he ever did for anyone in his entire life was to die and leave us his money.

"What can I get you?"

"Whiskey," I tell the bartender without even bothering to glance up at him.

"You don't strike me as a whiskey drinker," the man says. And really, what the fuck? The last thing I want right now is his commentary on my choice of alcohol.

"Well, I am," I say evenly, though it's a lie. Whiskey is what my father drank. The one I'm about to have will be my first ever. But if it was good enough for that asshole then it's good enough for me.

The guy doesn't say anything else. He doesn't ask for my ID. He

49

doesn't even ask what sort of whiskey I'd like, so I suppose that means I'm at his mercy there. At least he's not chatty, otherwise I'd have to get up and find another dive bar, instead of drowning my nonsensical sorrows here.

The harsh stink of whiskey permeates my nose as the small glass slides in front of me. My stomach rolls as I'm assaulted with a mélange of memories I'd just as soon forget. But in the most fucked up of masochistic ways, I'm making myself live them.

I raise my small shot glass and tip it back.

No toast. No self-pitying thoughts. Just blind drinking.

The wretched substance burns all the way down my throat, making me cough out and wince. I set the now-empty glass back down and point to it. "Another?" the old bartender chuckles, finding me comical in my quest for total blackout obliteration. "Didn't seem like you liked the first one all that much."

"I didn't. But keep 'em coming."

My eyes are fixed on the wood top in front of me. My hands gripping onto the edge of the bar. I'm beyond angry. Rage might actually be a closer description, but I can't decide who I'm pinning it on. Me or my father.

"Wanna talk about it?" a sweet melodic voice says as the chair next to me shifts and someone slides in it. A floral breeze brushes past me and as I turn, I'm greeted with a woman I never would have expected in a place like this.

She's blonde, petite and beautiful.

Long tanned legs cross at the knees as she leans forward, smiling at me in a way I don't feel I deserve. "You look like you could use a friend."

I take her in for a moment. She's older than me, but not by much. Maybe twenty-five, maybe older. Hard to tell. She's made up pretty heavily.

And she's dressed for a night of fun.

"Are you a prostitute?"

Instead of being wholly offended, which is what I anticipate, she's laughs. "Are you always this rude or should I excuse your nasty comment because you're having a bad day?"

I study her for a minute. "You didn't deny it."

She bends forward even more than she was a moment ago, alluring me with some of her small, but nice cleavage. "Would that make it easier for you? If I told you I wasn't a prostitute?"

"I don't care either way. It's more of a curiosity."

She smiles, her large doe-like brown eyes locked on mine as she says, "I'll have what he's having," to the bartender who is still waiting on her. "And in answer to your question, no, I'm not a prostitute. I'm just a girl who needed a drink to escape her first visit home in nearly five years. And you look like someone who is suffering as badly as I am, so I figured what the hell."

"I'm Finn," I say, my hand outstretched to shake hers.

"I'm Kelly. Nice to meet you, Finn."

"Likewise. Sorry about the prostitute thing."

She shrugs, clearly not bothered in the slightest. Her pretty smile shining just a bit brighter. She's not from the same neighborhood I'm from. I can tell that just by looking at her non-designer dress and cheap knock-off purse. But I don't care about this either.

In fact, I think I like this about Kelly.

"Cheers, Finn. To drowning your sorrows with complete strangers."

"I'll drink to that." And I do.

In fact, Kelly and I drink a lot together. She gets me. She understands that my father was an abusive asshole. She doesn't judge the fact I'm inexplicably torn up over his death. She loves that I'm in medical school. She even suggests we get together when we're both back in the city.

I like Kelly. She is pretty. And sweet. And smells really good.

Kelly has a beautiful body that I want to fuck so badly I can hardly contain myself.

So I don't.

I kiss Kelly and she kisses me back. Kelly kisses me back so much so that she climbs into my lap and whispers the name of a hotel not too far away.

Yeah. I think I like Kelly. I think I like Kelly a lot.

Chapter Seven

FINN

Present Day

THE HOSPITAL IS my go-to place. My safe zone. The one arena I'm in total control of.

And I like control. I thrive on it. I don't even give a shit if that makes me an asshole. Though I know I pretty much I am one. But the moment you let your guard down, the moment you relinquish some of that control, it all goes to shit. I'm not even being dramatic here.

It's Murphy's motherfucking Law.

And it always goes wrong for me. At least the things I don't have any control over do.

But not here. Here I'm meticulous. Methodical. Precise. Here I've got it all figured out.

That is until I saved her life on the sidewalk.

Work was my focus. But now I find myself wondering every time I go in or out of the hospital if I'll bump into her. Every time an OB consult is called for. Every time I go to the cafeteria. Every time I go to that goddamn bar with work people.

And when I don't bump into her, I tell myself I'm relieved.

Because I have to be.

"Yo, Banner," Max Slater says as he saunters up to me, slapping my back like we're best friends.

We're not.

I can't stand the guy and I'm sure he knows it because I do nothing to hide my general dislike of him. But he's after chief resident for next year and thinks that if he buddies up to me, I'll put in a good word for him. I won't. I don't work that way.

"Has anyone ever told you that you resemble your namesake?"

I give him my most irritated glare, not even caring if I'm proving his point. If he thinks he's the first person to ever liken me to Doctor Bruce Banner then he's an even bigger moron than I previously thought.

"Yes."

"Dude, you need to lighten up, man. The nurses, and every female doctor for that matter, are crawling over themselves for you, but if you continue to be…rough around the edges, then they'll give up."

I pause, taking a moment to observe him. Why do so many doctors have overinflated egos? Yes, we're educated and make decent money. But that's hardly a rarity in New York. Maybe it's the life and death stuff. But if anything, that should make us humble and not egotistical. If anything, we know just how precarious it really is.

"What do you want, Slater?"

"To help you out."

That almost makes me laugh. *Almost.* "I don't need your help and I definitely don't screw around with people I work with."

He shakes his head like I'm missing out and maybe I am, but I doubt it. And it doesn't matter anyway. None of these women are Gia Bianchi. And even if they were, I still wouldn't go there.

He laughs like I'm the fool here. "Whatever, man. More for me."

"Right. More for you. Now get back to work and leave me the fuck alone."

I walk off, leaving Max to sexually harass the nurses and doctors without involving me.

The ED is pleasantly busy. Perfectly so. But just as I finish up with one of my last patients of the day, all hell breaks loose. I get stat paged at the very second that a gurney comes rolling in through the ambulance-bay doors. A woman is screaming. Not just screaming, but shrieking at the very top of her lungs.

Which means she's breathing well on her own so that's an automatic plus. But then I see that she's pregnant. Very pregnant. And bleeding. In fact, blood is pouring out of the side of her chest as well as her right flank.

Fuck.

I run over, yanking my stethoscope off my neck and grasping it in my hand. "Thirty-two year old female," the paramedic wheeling her in starts. "Thirty-five weeks pregnant. G2P1 with stab wounds times two. One to the right flank and one to the right chest. Her vitals are surprisingly stable, but she lost a lot of blood at the scene. Patient is complaining of lower abdominal pressure. LR given en route and as you can hear, we did not need to intubate."

"Trauma three and someone page OB," I yell to the nurses as they come flocking over to help.

"Already done," someone says and the moment we get her into trauma three, the woman goes nuts.

"My baby," she screams. "You have to save my baby. Oh my god, he stabbed me. He stabbed me. My ex-boyfriend tried to kill me and my baby."

"What's your name?" I ask as I snap on gloves. The nurses are already cutting off her bloody clothes and covering her with a gown. She needs a central line. That much is clear, because she's absolutely going to need blood in addition to the fluids we're already giving her as well as medications. But I can't do a femoral one as she's pregnant so I go for her internal jugular, blindly inserting it by landmarks.

"Mariana," she sobs and the fact she's so vocal and alert despite her injuries is astounding. "Please, just save my baby."

"We'll do everything we can to save both of you."

I hate this. I can't stand it. Everything about this situation is twisting my gut into a knot. But I tamp everything down and focus on the patient because it's life or death time and neither she nor her baby are dying on my watch.

I turn to one of the nurses whose name I think is Jamie and bark, "Where the hell is OB?"

"On their way," she says with a nervous expression I know all too well. This woman is bleeding profusely from her side. It seems to have spared the abdomen, but still. She has a very pregnant abdomen. We have no idea the status of this baby or if that knife hit something vital.

Not even one minute later, as we're trying to examine her chest wound, OB comes in. Not an obstetrician, but goddamn Gia. Who is not a doctor. Who is not a surgeon. And who does not belong in my trauma room with this trauma.

"Where is OB?" I snap at her.

She looks up at me with those aqua-colored eyes of hers and I can't help the twinge of regret I have for the way I just spoke to her, but it doesn't change the facts. "They're tied up. You've got me."

"No," I bark. "We need a doctor. Not a midwife. Someone get OB on the phone now. This is not acceptable."

Gia gives me a murderous glare. "I'm just here to assess the patient, Dr. Banner. I'll take her up if the baby is at all compromised." And then she ignores me, going right up in between the patient's legs. She whispers something to one of the nurses who whispers something back to her and then she says, "Mariana, I'm Gia, one of the midwives here. Can you feel the baby move?"

"No," Mariana sobs. "I don't know. Maybe."

"Okay," Gia says far calmer than I would have thought. "I'm going to examine you and we're going to do everything we can for your baby." Gia sticks her gloved hand up inside of this woman and then quietly leans over to one of the nurses and says, "We need NICU and Peds here. Now."

"What's going on with the chest wound?" I yell out, bringing myself away from Gia and the baby and back into my job.

"Chest wound is superficial," Dr. Thomas says. "We can clean it and stitch it up."

"Then do it, Thomas," I bark and he flinches, but really? F̶ was just standing there waiting on instruction. He needs to ˊ how to swim. I will not be his life vest. "She's lost enough bk What about the flank wound?"

"Deeper," Dr. Slater says. "She's going to need some imaging and possibly the OR to repair any damage. I clamped the bleeders I could feel, but it's definitely not all of them."

"How are her vitals?" I ask.

"Stable," Corrine, one of the nurses says. "But she's tachycardic at one-thirty and her BP is holding steady with fluids and blood at ninety-two over fifty-four."

"Mariana," Gia says. "Your baby is ready to come out."

"No," Mariana screams. "It's too soon."

"I know, but we don't have a choice. You're having contractions, you're fully dilated and the baby is crowning. It's coming now."

"Oh, god!" Mariana cries.

"What are you having?" Gia asks with a smile which doesn't reach her eyes as one of the nurses puts a gown over her scrubs and protective gear over her face.

"A boy."

"Oh wonderful," she coos sweetly. "Do you have a name picked out?" she asks as she moves her hands inside the woman's body.

"Antonio," she sobs. "After his father."

"Oh, I love that name," Gia comments quickly, standing up and moving into position before she glances over to me. "Dr. Banner, we need pediatrics here this very moment, because Mariana is about to deliver Antonio. Right now." She emphasizes that last part, her eyes telling me just how dire this situation is.

I nod, but I don't have to do anything on that front as pediatrics and the NICU are rolling in.

"Where is OB?" I yell again, beyond frustrated that Gia is delivering this baby. But no one is paying me any attention. They're all too busy doing their jobs and I can't pull my eyes away from Gia and the baby she's trying to deliver.

"Can someone put an O2 mask on Mom?" Gia asks. "Okay, Mariana, you're having a contraction. I need you to push. Right now. I need a big push. I don't think it will take much, he's right here, but let's get Antonio out as quickly as you can. Do you understand me?"

Mariana nods and then she pushes, screaming through her mask. Gia encourages her the entire time, guiding her, helping her along. She's soothing and composed and does everything she's doing in a way which has Mariana calmer than she's been since she came in. It's impossible not to be impressed by her skill level. Especially since she's so new to the game.

Twenty seconds later, Gia removes the blue, non-crying baby from Mariana.

And I'm sick. I can't watch this baby die.

Pediatrics takes over from there and Gia is back to work, doing whatever she does with Mariana. The poor woman is sobbing, asking why her baby isn't crying. I need that baby to cry. I need it to cry right fucking now. I will not break that promise about neither of them dying on my watch.

I'm half-heartedly supervising as one of my interns cleans and sutures Marian's chest wound which is in fact, superficial, while surgery is assessing her flank wound. But my eyes are focused on the team working on that baby.

And just as I'm about to ask for the baby's status, he cries and everyone breathes out a collective sigh of relief. "Five-minute APGAR is a seven," one of the doctors announces with a smile, and Gia tells Mariana that Antonio looks good, but will be in a special nursery while they work on fixing her.

Mariana is crying, and thanking Gia profusely. But she's also starting to turn for the worse now that the baby is out and her adrenaline is ebbing.

OB comes bustling in. They examine Mariana quickly, congratulating Gia on a job well done before they leave. They don't even confer with me. Surgery takes a bleeding Mariana up to the OR. The NICU team follows the surgical team and the chaos is over, with only the remains of trauma left to be cleaned.

The nurses are cataloging everything that was used, documenting as needed. My intern is animatedly effusing about how that was the craziest trauma he's ever been in and the nurses are laughing because this is New York City and they've seen much worse than that.

Max Slater is bragging about how he had his hands inside the woman's side and I'm content because no one died in my trauma room.

Gia is silently scrubbing down at the sink. Once she's done with that, she grabs a dry blue cloth and wipes her hands off. "Dr. Banner," she says coolly with her back still to me. "May I have a word please." It's not a question. It's a demand. And then she stalks out of the room, leaving me with the smiles and snickers of the lingering crowd.

"You think I'm in trouble?" I tease because we're all in pretty good spirits after that one. Enjoying the positive high and endorphin rush.

"I heard Gia Bianchi is hardcore and doesn't take shit kindly," Corrine, one of the senior nurses says. The other nurses are nodding their heads in agreement.

"So that's a yes then," I deadpan and they laugh.

"You are the master of giving shit," Max Slater says and when I treat him to my most menacing glare, he tosses his hands up in surrender. "Just saying you might have met your match with that one." If only he knew. I throw a Corrine a wink and bow to the other nurses because they deserve it for all their hard work and then I leave.

Gia is out in the hall, waiting on me. Her cheeks are flushed and her skin is slightly tacky, and her hair is disheveled and her eyes are wild, and she's the sexiest fucking thing I've ever seen. *Goddamn.* I have the strongest urge to grab her small body and haul her off to a dark corner.

"Miss Bianchi," I greet her and she scowls at me.

"Dr. Banner, this way." Then she spins on the heels of her lavender clogs and marches off down the hall.

To be honest, if it were any other person, I wouldn't have let them get this far. I would have ended it in the trauma room or right here in the hall. But I'm enjoying this with her way too much. The fact that she's unbelievably hot when she's angry is only fueling me on.

Gia pushes open the door to one of the small exam rooms and storms in with authority. She spins back around, her arms crossed under her breasts and my eyes can't help but bounce down there for a moment. She doesn't speak. In fact, she's just glaring at me and while I'm liking the hell out of this little encounter, I really don't have the time.

"Well?" I prompt. "What can I do for you."

She lets out a torrent of air. "You were completely out of line back there when you made that comment about asking for a doctor instead of a midwife. You should have never done that in front of not only the patient but the other staff. You completely undermined me. That was a perilous situation and yeah, it should have been an OB instead of me. But obviously there wasn't a choice or I wouldn't have been sent down instead."

"Are you finished?" Her eyes flare, but she nods all the same. "You're right. I should have never challenged you like that in front of the patient or my staff. I apologize."

Her eyes widen and her mouth pops open a little and it's quite possibly the most adorable reaction. "Seriously? I'm right and you apologize?"

"That's what I said."

"Wow...um." Then she laughs, shaking her head. "I was totally gearing up for a fight."

"Nah. Not in the mood. They're both alive. We can fight about something else another time."

"Now I feel kinda foolish for making this whole scene."

I chuckle lightly, taking a few steps until I breach her personal space. I do this a lot with her. I can't seem to help myself. I'm oddly addicted to this. Oddly addicted to her.

For all her strength and bravado, she comes undone easily. Or maybe that's just with me because she swallows hard, taking a step back until her ass hits the empty gurney. Her eyes stay focused on mine as her breaths increase ever so slightly. Just enough for me to notice.

Just enough to make me want to push into her so she can feel exactly what she does to me. God, this woman drives me wild. Makes it nearly impossible to think clearly. To act rationally.

"I don't mind that you made a scene," I say oh-so softly, inclining my head in her direction. "You're very pretty when you're angry with me."

"Two steps forward and one step back," she replies.

"What does that mean, Gia?"

She laughs, pushing against me, but instead of creating more space between us, she leans into me on her tiptoes, her weight balanced against my chest. "It means, *Finn*," she emphasizes my name, "that I'm tired of the mind games. That I'm tired of the invasion of my personal space and your dirty, sexy flirting. It means stick to your fucking guns or don't. I'm done with the in-between." Gia places a kiss on my cheek, lowers herself away from me and then walks to the door. "See you around, Dr. Banner."

Met my match indeed. I don't think I've ever wanted a woman as much as I want Gia Bianchi in this minute. Certainly, no one has ever turned me on as much.

Which is exactly why I let her leave.

Chapter Eight

GIA

The hospital is crazy today. Absolutely nuts. It's filled with reporters and camera crews and people who showed up, hoping for a glimpse of Andrea Kent, the famous pop star. She broke her leg while performing onstage last night and needed emergency surgery for it. And though I feel bad for her, because that sucks, you can barely go anywhere without getting bumped into.

It's freaking annoying.

Like right now, I'm walking through the main part of the hospital, trying to get to the coffee shop before I leave for the day. But as my eyes catch the extensive line, I decide I don't need a coffee that badly. "This is ridiculous," someone says and I look over to see Lara Gould, one of the ED Nurse Practitioners scowling. "She sings and dances onstage in tiny outfits. And yeah, I get how that's appealing to some and I will concede that's she's pretty talented. But she's not wearing those outfits right now and she's not singing, so why the hell do hundreds of people have to crowd our hospital over her?"

"No idea," I agree with a shake of my head. "I'm thinking of skipping the coffee. That line isn't worth it."

"Yeah," she sighs, tucking a piece of her brown hair behind her ear. "But I'm just starting my shift and if I don't get my Diet Coke, no one will want to deal with me. Or be healed by me for that matter."

"Then I guess you better get going otherwise when I come back tomorrow morning, I'll find you still in line."

"I'll buy you a coffee, that way it will still be hot when you get back here."

We both laugh and I throw her a wave as I head for the exit instead of the coffee line. Just as I round the corner for the main drag which leads to the exit doors, a rush of people go sprinting down the hall, yelling and shouting, "She's coming. She's on her way down."

Oh hell no.

I'm about to spin around and find another way out when I'm suddenly bumped hard from behind by someone running to catch the action. I go flying forward, crashing into a bench and bashing my elbow on the metal arm. "Sorry," someone yells out, but they don't stop to make sure I'm okay.

Which I'm not. My elbow freaking kills.

"Asshole," I mutter, trying to pull myself up, being mindful of my smarting elbow.

"You called my name?" Looking over my shoulder, I find Finn standing there in his scrubs, a hard, pissed-off look on his face. "Here, let me help you up." Finn bends down, wrapping his arm around me just under my breasts and effortlessly lifts me up. "Are you okay?" he asks concerned, his eyes searching my face and body for obvious signs of injury.

"I think so. I just hit my elbow."

"At least there wasn't an oncoming car this time."

"No, just a stupid bench." I can't help but feel a little embarrassed. "Why do you always have to witness my worst moments?" I mean, seriously?

"Luck and good timing, I guess." His hand comes up, brushing a few strands of hair off my face and then lingers on my cheek as he stares into my eyes. "But seriously, are you okay? That was a pretty good fall."

"I banged my elbow," I say, glancing down and noticing how my white long-sleeve shirt is turning bright red. "Shit."

"Jesus," Finn says, taking my arm gently and examining it. "Can you lift this up?" he asks about my shirt, but it's one of those tight exercise sorts so it doesn't want to slide up very far and ends up getting stuck around my mid-forearm. "Come with me," he growls, not giving me the choice as he snakes his arm around me, tucks me into his side and then ushers me through a couple of back hallways to the patient area of the ED.

"It's not so bad, Finn. I can just clean it when I get home."

"No," he snaps. "You can't. Because your elbow is bleeding like crazy and you won't be able see what you're doing."

"Why are you angry with me?" I snap back. I didn't ask him to be my perpetual savior, especially if he's going to be a dick about it.

Finn gives me a sideways glance as he leads me into an exam room, sliding the door shut and pulling the curtain to give us privacy. I can't decide if I wish he had left it open or I'm glad he closed it.

That's the thing with Finn.

It's always a game of tug of war. Both with him and within myself.

On the one hand, I want him to want me. I want him to talk to me and touch me and yes, even help me when I fall. I want him to care. But on the other hand, he can be impossible to read, doesn't seek me out or even talk to me for weeks at a time and then when I do see him, he does that hot and cold routine.

It's like I can't win with him.

Time and distance seem to have no bearing on my reaction to him either, because even though it's been a couple of weeks since I've seen him last, I still feel the same draw. The same inexplicable pull which gives me butterflies and has my mind racing with stupid, teenage, girly thoughts. Thoughts I'm mortified to even admit to myself that I have.

Why do smart women allow men to turn us into a puddle of stupid?

"I'm not angry with *you*. I'm fucking furious at the piece-of-shit guy who tossed you aside without even a backward glance to make sure you were okay. I'm enraged you got hurt just so he could get a stupid picture of a stupid pop star leaving the hospital. It's ridiculous. They're not even allowed in the hospital and yet no one has done anything about it. And now you're hurt."

See what I mean? When he says things like that, it's impossible not to sigh dreamily at his whole over-protective alpha male thing. But I'm not the type of girl to do that. At least I wasn't before I met him.

"Take off your shirt," he says, washing his hands and grabbing some gauze and a clean chucks pad.

"Um…" My voice trails off, tilting my head at his back.

Finn rolls his head over his shoulder to smirk at me. "What? I need to look at your elbow and I can't get access to it with your shirt on." I just stare at him. "It's not like I haven't seen it before."

"Not mine," I say, trying for resolute and maybe a touch indignant since he lumped mine into a category with everyone else's. But really, I want to take my shirt off for him. I want to take my shirt off and watch his expression as I do. But like I said, I'm not that type of girl.

"Gia," he pushes out like I'm trying his patience, but I don't think I am. I think he enjoys this as much as I do. "The sleeve of your shirt is saturated in blood. Take it off so I can examine you."

"Give me a gown or a drape." He huffs out, but opens a drawer and tosses me a paper drape. I don't even get a jonnie. "Turn around, Dr. Banner. This show isn't free."

He smiles, "How about I just close my eyes."

"You'll cheat." He nods, those eyes smoldering and playful. As playful as he's ever been with me. I'm really liking this Finn and that's not a good thing. "Turn." I move my index finger around in the air in a circular motion.

"You're no fun," he says and I laugh as I do my best to remove my scrub top followed by my shirt. The shirt doesn't come off so well. In fact, I have to twist and wiggle around because it's tight and clingy and my elbow hurts a lot, so moving it around isn't all that fun.

Finally, when I realize it's a losing battle, I sigh, because I'm going to need his help getting undressed and that just feels like a win for him. "Finn?"

He turns around and when he sees me, he laughs. "Do I get the pleasure of removing your shirt?" I nod, swallowing hard because while he might be joking, I feel very vulnerable suddenly. "Hey," Finn says tenderly, noting my changing expression. He walks over to me, and kisses the side of my head, before he cups my face in his hands and dips down until we're eye to eye. "I'll take care of you, Gia. I won't cross the line. You're hurt. All I want to do is fix it."

I want to ask him not to say things like that to me. I want to tell him he's easier to tolerate when he's a domineering jerk and not like he is right now. Because this Finn slays me. He's such a contradiction from the other one. Like two different men. Light and dark. Smooth and rough.

I don't mind the rough side of him. It keeps me on my toes. Makes me tingle and feel just the smallest bit dangerous. Like playing with fire. Sexy and alluring.

But smooth Finn is something else entirely. Smooth Finn is the sort you imagine. Not fantasize about, necessarily. Imagine. Smooth Finn makes you want, in a completely different way, than rough Finn does.

And right now, I need this side of him. I was pushed to the ground and my elbow hurts and is bleeding. So a delicate touch is just the thing. I just wish it didn't make me ache so much.

"I'm going to lift up your shirt. I promise to be gentle when I get to your elbow. Here," he says, handing me the drape. "Cover yourself up so I won't get distracted." He winks at me and I giggle, my uneasiness melting away.

And yes, he's trying to be professional, but he's also not. His eyes are on mine and his pupils are dilated just enough to let me know his thoughts aren't entirely on my injury. His knuckles skim up the sides of my stomach as he pulls my shirt, tickling my skin and making me shudder. Finn blows out a heavy breath at that as he manages to get the shirt up and over my head and I cover my chest and stomach with the paper drape.

"I'm going to pull it down your arm now," he says hoarsely, before he clears his throat. I don't even attempt to speak, instead I go for the very safe nod that seems to serve me well where he's concerned.

But when he gets to my elbow, I wince because Jesus shit, that fucking stings. "Ah," I whimper, dropping my forehead to his chest as he slides it the rest of the way down my arm.

"You okay?" he asks softly, running one hand down my hair and over my exposed back. His other hand is covering my wound with gauze, applying some pressure to it.

"Yes," I breathe, my eyes closing. "You smell good," I say and he chuckles, the sound rumbling into me.

"Happy to be a distraction for you, babe, because this is going to need stitches."

I sigh. "Can't you just use Dermabond?"

"No," he says, still running that hand down my hair to sooth me. It's working. "It's a jagged wound and the edges won't approximate well. I'm afraid it will open up again and not heal right if I glue it."

"Then go for it. I just want get this done and am actually looking forward to the lidocaine."

"Hurts, huh?" I nod, reluctantly pulling myself away from him to sit up straight. "The guy is lucky I didn't see who he was. Otherwise he'd be in Trauma One right now."

"Tough guy," I smirk.

"Protective. You make me feel very protective." Then he turns away from me and heads over to the supply cabinet.

"How many stitches are we talking about, Doctor?" I ask, because if I don't focus on my elbow, I'll focus on Finn and I really don't want to focus on Finn. I can already feel how hurt I'll get.

"Three, maybe four."

"Have I mentioned that I hate needles?"

"What?" he laughs the word, returning with a few sterile packages filled with various instruments. "How is that even possible? You're a midwife."

"I can put them in other people no problem, but in me is a different story."

"Are you going to pass out on me? As much as I'm in favor of you swooning, I'd rather you not do it now."

"No. I just don't want to look and I might ask you to distract me if you're capable of multitasking."

Finn rolls his eyes at me with that smirk I like so much. "Gia, I can throw in a couple of stitches in my sleep. I'm happy to distract you, but I'll have to do it with my mouth as my hands will be occupied." He winks and I wish I could reach out and smack him, but one arm is hurt and the other is holding the pathetic paper gown against my chest.

"Pervert."

"I prefer distractor. Pervert gets me brought up on charges. You're a fellow hospital employee." Finn drops into a rolling stool as he snaps on fresh gloves and goes about cleaning my elbow. "What's your favorite movie?"

"*Hannah and Her Sisters*," I say automatically. "I have an odd thing for Woody Allen movies."

"Didn't he marry his daughter?"

I shrug. "No one's perfect."

He chuckles, and then the door slides open and the curtain is drawn back. "Dr. Banner?" a guy walks in, his eyes raking in my bare back and side and I hate that he just did that. I feel so exposed right now. Especially since I've seen him around the hospital before.

Finn's head spins around, his expression lethal as he stands up to block the guy's view of my body. "What do you think you're doing walking in here without knocking? I'm with a patient, Slater and I'm technically off. So out. Now." The guy blanches, his cheeks reddening before he turns around and scurries out without another word, closing the curtain and door behind him. Finn growls out something unintelligible. He's fuming. It's way too sexy for me to even think about.

Protective indeed.

"Sorry about that," he says in a calmer tone, though I can tell it's eating at him. "I wish he hadn't seen you like this."

"I'll live."

Finn lets out a deep breath as he continues tending to my arm. "Favorite band?"

"It changes frequently. Maybe *Strumbellas* or *Kodaline*." My eyes close as he squirts the wound with sterile water and then rubs it down with betadine.

"How's your sort-of, non-exclusive boyfriend?"

"Hasn't been my sort-of, non-exclusive for a while now," I manage.

Finn pauses for a beat before continuing. "Oh. You're together then? Small burn," he warns.

I shake my head, wanting to smile at his tone, but am too uncomfortable to accomplish it. "No," I hiss through my teeth as he sticks the needle into my arm, injecting me with the lidocaine. "I ended it."

"How come?"

Because he wasn't you, I don't say. "Not what I wanted," I go for instead.

"Okay, so no men," he says and I can't figure out how he feels about that. "I'm glad you got rid of that guy. He looked like an asshole."

I smile now that I'm all numbed up and feel like I can actually relax a little. "So, said the asshole."

"Yeah, but I'm different. I not only saved your life, I stitched up your arm. To perfection, I might add. And I properly distracted you." I don't move and he laughs a little. "Open your pretty eyes, Gia. I'm done."

"Wow," I marvel, looking down at my now bandaged arm. "You're fast."

"Only with stitches. With everything else, I like to take my time." He gives me a look which floods me with heat. "But now I'm discharging you."

"Oh. That's sort of anticlimactic."

Finn helps me put on my scrub top before he takes my face back in his hands. "That would never happen with us." He leans down and brushes his nose against mine, our eyes locked. My breath hitches at both our proximity and the not so subtle meaning behind his words. Then he draws back and his expression switches to apathetic in the blink of an eye. "But now I need you to go home. Come back to me in seven to ten days and I'll remove the stitches."

Shaking my head, I want to scream so many accusations at him. Why does he constantly do this? I don't get it. *You want me, Finn.* He does. But there is something holding him hostage. Something keeping him from taking this to the place we both want it to go. I just don't have the balls to ask him what that something is.

I knew this was going to happen. It's why I won't bother saying all of the things which are driving me crazy about him right now. Instead, I push him back and hop off the bed. "Thanks for stitching me up and coming to my rescue yet again. I'll have a friend remove them, so you're off the hook with me. See you around, Dr. Banner."

And then I walk out. I don't wait for him to say anything back. I don't even check out his expression. I'm done where he's concerned. I'm done.

Chapter Nine

GIA

"There was nothing you could have done," Chloe says to me, her hand on my shoulder, her blue eyes filled with sympathy. I can't say anything. I can only nod because if I speak, I will absolutely break down. "These things happen. They're horrible and gut you, but it's part of the job." Another nod. "Go home, Gia. You're done for the day anyway. I'll come by later."

I shake my head. "You don't have to come. I'm just going to go home, have a soak in the tub and then go to bed."

Chloe stares at me for a moment, trying to decipher my bullshit level, before blowing some of her long blonde bangs out of her face. "I'm so sorry. I really am. It sucks the big suck. Are you sure there isn't anything I can do?"

"No," I sniffle. "I'll be fine."

I think that might be a lie. I don't think I'll ever be fine again.

"Come here." Chloe pulls me into her arms and hugs me snugly against her.

I push her back, wiping away at my hot tears. If that hug continues, I'll cry more and I don't want to do that. Especially here in the breakroom at work.

"I'll call you tomorrow. Get some sleep, okay. And don't torture yourself the way I know you're apt to do."

More nodding. "Goodnight."

I throw her a weak wave, before tossing the strap of my bag over my head and leave the breakroom. I ignore the way the nurses are talking behind the nurse's station. I ignore their pitying looks. I ignore the other patients in labor who are walking the halls with their smiling faces and the pained deliberate masks of concentration.

I ignore all of it.

Because today was the worst day of my life.

Even worse than my father dying, I think. I don't know. It's certainly up there.

Stepping out into the cool September evening, I stand in front of the hospital not knowing what to do next. I can't go home. I know I told Chloe that's what I was going to do, but there is no way I can be alone in my apartment with my thoughts. I can't stand them right now and I'm practically still at the hospital. They'll be a million times worse at home.

My phone buzzes in my scrub pants and for a second, I debate whether or not I should check it. But I do, because it could be my boss or something else important. I already spoke with her about what happened and everything was documented, but still.

It's not my boss and it's not Chloe or Monique even.

It's the guy I went on a date with the other night. I sigh. He was cute, but it just wasn't there for me. I hate to be a bitch and not text him back or worse, tell him over text that it's not him, it's me, but I believe that's what I'm about to do. Number one, I decide, because I really don't want to have a meaningless text conversation with a meaningless guy at the moment.

The electronic doors open and shut behind me and I hear people coming and going. I need to get away from this place. My feet take off without premeditated intention. I'm just walking because people say that's a good thing to do when you need to think. Or is it to clear your head?

Shit, I can't remember which it is.

Walking for either purpose has never really been my thing.

It's still not, which is why after I make it only a couple of blocks, I'm done. I need to sit and drown myself in copious amounts of alcohol. That's never really been my thing either, but after you lose a patient, that's the thing to do, right?

I walk into the first bar I see and find myself laughing out loud like a crazy person when I realize it's the bar I had drinks in with Colin the night Finn was eye-flirting with me.

Whatever. I don't care.

That ship has long since sailed. I haven't even seen Finn in like a month, other than in passing, and I never speak to him and he never speaks to me. How lame is it that that's now our thing?

Sliding onto the barstool, I grab a laminated menu off the counter and peruse it, searching for the strongest thing they have. I am not a shots person. They tend to make me sick. Even the sweet girly ones. Especially the sweet girly ones.

But I do want to get very drunk and I want to do it quickly so maybe those shots are the way to go? Who the hell knows. All I know right now is that a new mother is dead and her baby is up in the NICU with possible brain damage from asphyxia.

Oh, and the father is a fucking mess. How could he not be? I could barely look at him and that made me feel so much worse because he deserved my eye contact. He deserved the respect of me looking him squarely in the eyes when I told him that his wife didn't make it and his baby was fighting for its life.

"What are we having?" the pretty young bartender asks and I wonder if her job is as cool as it looks. Maybe I'm in the wrong profession. I highly doubt that people die on her watch. And you get to wear whatever the hell you want without getting blood on it.

"What do you recommend for the shittiest day in the history of shittiest days?"

She crosses her colorful tattooed arms over her black low-cut blouse. "What sort of shittiest day we talkin' about?" She notes my scrubs. "Patient die?"

I nod.

"Your fault?"

I sigh, because it wasn't my fault but that doesn't make me feel better. "No."

"You good with rum?"

"Sure. Why not."

"Okay, I'm going to make you a drink with Bacardi 151 which is over seventy-five percent alcohol. I'm not going to make it too sweet otherwise you'll be puking your guts out with the worst headache of your life tomorrow. So don't ask what I'm putting in it. Just drink the drink."

"I think I might love you," I tell her and she laughs.

Leaning back in my seat, I scrub my hands up and down my face. I don't think I've ever felt like this before. So completely helpless and ruined. So tormented.

"You going to tell me what happened or just leave me here in suspense," the bartender asks and for some reason, the thought of talking to a perfect stranger is so much more appealing than talking to my best friends or anyone else I know.

"I was the midwife for a very healthy thirty-one year old lady. It's her second baby and she had no complications or issues with the first one."

"Okay, I'm following. Go on."

Leaning forward, I prop my elbows on the counter and take a sip of the pale-green concoction she slides in front of me. "Wow, that's really good."

"I know," she smiles, mirroring my position against the bar. I realize it's dead in here and I'm extremely grateful for that as she's giving me her undivided attention. "I'm an awesome bartender. It's my one great."

"You're one great?"

"Yes, the one thing I'm great at. Everyone has one, whether they know what it is or not."

"Huh," I say, swirling that thought around my brain for a moment before I take another sip of my oh-so-yummy drink. It's not sweet. It's not sour. It's not fruity. It's like the perfect combination of all three. "So yeah, she was rocking along at seven centimeters and then all of a sudden–literally out of nowhere–she said her head hurt and then ten seconds later, she was gone. Her vitals tanked, and even though I hit the code button that second, and we did everything we could for her, it was too late. A burst aneurism, we think or possibly a stroke. We'll know more after the autopsy."

"Shit," the bartender mutters, and I point my finger at her because shit just about covers it.

"Yeah. Shit. And if that wasn't fucking tragic enough, her poor baby was without oxygen for far too long by the time we finally got him out. He's in the NICU now and it's not looking all that great."

"I'm Ophelia."

I tilt my head. "Like from Hamlet?"

"Yeah. My mother did it to me, don't ask."

"I'm Gia. My father did that one."

"Well Gia, I agree that your day was beyond shitty. This first one is on me. And after you're completely plastered to the point you're aiming for, let me know, and I'll get you an Uber or call someone to take you home."

"Ophelia, I think you just became my favorite person ever."

"Wow," she muses. "Not only did you already profess your love, but now I'm your favorite person? Your day might be shit, but mine's looking up."

I laugh. Well, it's really more of a cackle, because I think this Bacardi 151 stuff is already starting to get to me. Admittedly, I'm a bit of a lightweight and I haven't had anything to eat in several hours.

But I do not care.

In fact, it's already working. I'm feeling better albeit chemically induced, but whatever. I'll take what I can get right now because things were going so well. So goddamn well.

My job was awesome.

I was rocking it.

And now? Now I feel like all my confidence is gone. Not just gone, but shattered.

Yes, it wasn't my fault that this mom had an undiagnosed aneurism or threw a clot. And yes, those things have been known to happen at any minute, and given the strain of childbirth, it's not a surprise that it picked that moment. But still. It's a life lost. A baby who might never recover. A father who lost his wife. A four-year-old daughter who lost her mother.

It's just not fair.

And I get that sounds childish, but you come to expect certain things to be fair. You don't expect really horrendous things to happen to good people. To new moms and tiny babies. You don't expect lives to be totally and completely annihilated in under five minutes. Now that father has to go home to his daughter and tell her that not only is mommy never coming home, but that her brother might not make it either.

And if by some miracle he does survive, what sort of shape will he be in?

"No crying," Ophelia says, handing me a bar napkin.

"Sorry," I sniffle through my tears. "It just doesn't make sense, you know?"

"It's not meant to. It's life."

"Yeah, that's not all that reassuring."

Ophelia laughs, taking my empty glass and mixing me another drink. "I already told you what my one great is. If you're looking for brilliant words to make you feel better, you're drinking at the wrong bar."

"Noted," I say, picking up my newly delivered cocktail and taking a big pull of it through the straw. "But I think your one great is exactly the great I need right now. Ophelia, here is my address." I pull a pen out of my bag and write it down on the napkin. "And here is money. Don't let me have more than four of these no matter what I say to you, and at that point, call me a cab and hand the driver this."

"You got it. I'll make sure you get home safe. Even if I have to take you home myself."

Chapter Ten

FINN

Today is an absolute anomaly. I have no explanation for it either, other than being a fucking awesome doctor and efficient as hell. Today represents the first day I actually leave work on time since I became an attending. At exactly nine p.m., the doors of the ED close behind me and I'm stepping out into the crisp air.

The trees lining the streets are covered with a medley of colors. Golds and cranberry reds and burnt oranges. Even in the dark of night, with only the light from the street lamps and the glow of the storefronts to illuminate them, they're beautiful. Fall in New York is one of my favorite times of year, even if it does lead into the holiday season.

I'm not slated to meet up with Mike for another hour, and though I could text him and ask him to meet me sooner, I won't. I'm actually looking forward to the quiet drink after the long day before he shows up. Since starting in the hospital, this bar has quickly become one of my favorites. It's low-key with good drinks, comfortable seating and pretty women who are occasionally eager for my particular brand of one-night stand, without being a hookup bar.

That said, I haven't gone home with a woman since my second week here and I refuse to think too deeply on the reason behind that. Maybe tonight is the night for that. The night to bring myself a little pleasure for once.

Pulling open the heavy glass door, I'm instantly assaulted with the warmth and din which only a neighborhood bar can provide. My eyes flitter around, taking in the selection of eligible women, as well as trying to find a good place to park myself so I can continue my observations. But then something stops me in my tracks.

Not something. *Someone.*

Gia. Of course, it's Gia.

I've successfully avoided her since I stitched up her elbow. That was what? Seventeen days ago. As tempted as I am to turn around and walk out, I can't help but watch her. She's leaning against the bar, her head resting heavily against her hand with some lime-colored drink in front of her. The finger of her free hand glides up and down in the condensation. A frown mars her beautiful, full red lips. But the feature that stands out to me the most? Her eyes are partially closed and even from my vantage point, half the bar away, I can tell they're glassy.

She's drunk. And that bothers the fuck out of me.

Is she asking to be taken advantage of? Doesn't she know how vulnerable she is right now?

My body ignites with the ferocity and determination of a brush fire. Red-hot heat consumes me. Has me marching across the smallish bar until I'm standing next to her. She must hear me or sense my presence, because Gia's head spins around like something out of *The Exorcist*, her eyes wide before a slow lazy smile spreads across her beautiful face, and her eyes go back to half-mast. She looks sexy as hell and I'd be turned on if I wasn't so pissed off.

"Oh Finn," she slurs. "Have you come to rescue me from myself again?" Her petite body sways on her stool, before she slurps down more of her cocktail through her straw.

"How much have you had to drink tonight?"

She rolls her eyes at me. "None of your business, Doctor. I am none of your business."

A deep growl climbs its way out of the back of my throat. No one drives me crazy like this woman.

I should turn around and leave. She's right. She's none of my business. But even as I think that, I know I'm not going anywhere. I may not do a lot of things right where Gia Bianchi is concerned, but leaving her in this state would be reprehensible. "Gia?" I ask in a softer tone, because clearly barking directives aren't getting me anywhere with her. "How drunk are you?"

"Scale of one to ten?" she asks and I nod. "Probably somewhere close to a seven or eight. But this is my last one." She points to her glass, nearly knocking it over when her hand misses its target. "I made Ophelia promise me. Though if we're making comparisons here, Ophelia is way better than the chaste vessel of morality she's named after. I mean, she sells alcohol, right? And she's freaking awesome. I never liked Ophelia in Hamlet."

I have no idea what she just said. It's like she's speaking in goddamn riddles. "Who's Ophelia?"

"I'm Ophelia," the pretty bartender with colorful ink adorning her arms, says. I've seen her working here several times over. I just never knew her name. "And she's right. She's done. She's hit her four-drink max."

"Great," I snap. "And you didn't think four drinks was three too many?"

Gia giggles, like what I just said was the funniest thing ever. She giggles so hard, she practically falls off her damn chair. "Finn, stop being my dad. He's dead, remember? You were there for that. He's dead. Just like my patient." And then she breaks down into tears.

What the hell is going on here?

I eye the bartender expectantly. She gives me a conciliatory half grin, pointing to the stool next to Gia, for me to sit. I do sit, but not because she silently asked me to. I do it because when Gia cries, my goddamn lifeless heart breaks. Gia wipes away at her eyes with a deep heavy sigh, a small ring of black mascara stubbornly clings to the top of her lower lid.

"She lost a patient tonight," Ophelia supplies, with more sympathy than I would have expected. "I was letting her drink while keeping an eye on her. She said four drinks, so that's what I served her, but the last two were on the weaker side."

"Hey," Gia snaps indignantly.

Ophelia shrugs unapologetically. "You're a lightweight, honeypie," she says with a hint of softness as her eyes linger on a still-sniffling Gia. "I was going to walk her home when my shift ends in an hour. But now you're here," she finishes with a big smile.

"See," Gia points to Ophelia while looking at me, "I told you she was awesome. It's a shame I'm not a lesbian," Gia says with so much sincerity that a laugh sputters out of me. "No, I'm being serious. Ophelia here is not only a beautiful bisexual, but she's smart and funny and I like her. She doesn't fuck with my head," she turns to me, takes me in for a moment, her expression growing accusatory as she ends with, "the way you do."

I can't for the life of me think of something to say back to that.

I do fuck with her head. It's not intentional. It's not something I methodically plot out or particularly get off on. It's just my reaction to her. It's the fact that I react to her in the first place, that has me fucking with her head.

"Yet here you are again," she continues on, unaware of my silent contemplation. "Right when I need someone, you're there. It's aggravating in so many ways." She pivots back to face Ophelia who seems to be enjoying the hell out of the verbal lashing Gia is giving me. "He always finds me at just the right moment." Every ounce of sarcasm drips away, leaving her bare and raw. "My perpetual hero. He saved my life, you know? Pulled me out of the way of an oncoming car. I would have gone splat." She slams her palm against the wood of the bar with a loud smack.

"Hero, indeed," Ophelia grins. "How about a beer then, hero?"

I can only nod. Gia has a way of cutting me to the quick. It's impossible not to feel conflicted where she's concerned. On the one hand, she just said I fuck with her mind. That sucks. I'm not typically that guy. I'm usually very upfront with my endeavors. But Gia is not one of my endeavors.

On the other, she called me her hero. Not just rescuer, but *hero*. And yeah, I realize those two terms are closely related. Nearly the same thing. But for some inexplicable reason, they feel different.

Terrifying and exhilarating. That's how this feels.

Gia turns to me with watery, bloodshot eyes. "My patient died today, Finn." There is so much heartbreak in her voice. The tears she just shed were not her first. This is eating her up.

I can't stand her hurting.

Without conscious thought, I reach out and cup her face. She sighs, tilting her head and leaning further into my touch, yet she doesn't know what to make of the gesture. More mind fuck, I realize.

She's so beautiful. So sweet and pure and innocent. She's also strong, forthright and tough as nails. I like all of this about her. It keeps me on my game. Keeps me up at night thinking about her. But it's this incredible childlike vulnerability she emanates which leads me to want to wrap her up and keep her safely tucked away from anything that could potentially consider hurting her.

I don't think. I don't second guess. I just act.

I text Mike and tell him we'll meet up another night. Then I slide my phone back into the pocket of my scrubs, take a sip of my newly delivered Stella and turn back to her when I think I've got some modicum of control over my emotions. "Tell me about your patient."

She blinks at me, her eyes welling up once again with those big tears she cries. "It's so awful." A tear cascades down her cheek and I reach out to swipe it away. "I think she threw a clot or an aneurism burst. But she died, Finn. She died. And her baby…" she trails off, shaking her head, unable to finish her thought as she swallows down audibly.

"I'm sorry about your patient," I say, taking her into my arms as she cries a little harder. My lips press into the top of her head as I hold her close to me. "It sucks. I know. But it wasn't your fault, Gia. And if this is the first patient you've lost in the year plus you've been practicing, then you're doing something right. I've seen you in action, sweetheart. You're incredible at your job. Sometimes no matter how perfect we are, shit goes wrong anyway."

"Thank you," she mumbles against me. Squeezes me back a little to let me know she means it. "I don't want to cry anymore. I was drinking so I would stop." She sniffles, pulling back and wiping her fingertips under her eyes, removing any remaining moisture. "Holy cheeseballs, I hate this crap." She blows out a hot puff of air and then gives me a forced smile. "So," she laughs lightly. "What brings you into my new favorite bar?"

"I was meeting a friend."

"And now?"

I shrug. "Now I'm with you."

"Because you're protective over me." It's not a question, but I find myself nodding all the same. I am protective over her. She really has no idea the lengths I would go to. "I wish I didn't like you, Finn," she laughs. "You're sort of an asshole. A hot asshole, but still."

"I knew you thought I was hot."

She rolls her eyes at me, but she can't stop her broadening smile. Those tears drying up with her amusement, which was my intent. "Seriously? That's what you took from everything I just said?" Gia sways slightly, reminding me just how shitfaced she actually is.

No. Actually all I can think about is the fact she just admitted she likes me. It's like I'm fifteen all over again. It's that good. "Do you know what I do when I lose a patient?"

"What? Tell me, Finn. I'm all ears. Because this alcohol stuff isn't all it's cracked up to be. All it seems to do is make me have to pee. It also makes my head spin and my thoughts a little fuzzy. My inhibitions are probably out the window right now. But it hasn't taken away the ache."

God, what would I give to be able to take away that ache for her?

"I usually run, but that's not going to help us now."

"Nope. Try again." She sinks against the side of the bar, her eyes growing soft and heavy. Then she yawns and I'm suddenly relieved. I was thinking about places I could take her. Things I could do with her to lift her spirits.

That's the problem with Gia. She has me scheming.

"I was going to say Skee-Ball, but I think you're too tired for the arcade." That's not really what I do when I lose a patient. I was serious about the running. But it just so happens the last time someone died unexpectedly, a group of people went to an arcade and I tagged along. It did help so why not say it? And because I know it will amuse her. It will take her mind off of her patient and that's all I can ask for.

"Skee-Ball," she smiles so big, showcasing all of her white teeth. "You play Skee-Ball when you lose a patient?"

I shift until I'm sitting closer to her. Until our knees are touching. Until she looks down and stares at them. Then I take her hand and lace our fingers together. She looks at those too and I know what I'm doing. I know this is more of my mind fuck. But I don't know how to stop.

That's another problem with Gia. I don't know how to stop.

"Skee-Ball is the ultimate tension releaser," I tell her as I lean in just enough to catch a hint of her perfume which I like so much. "Think about it. You get to toss a decently weighted ball for points and then you get tickets that earn you prizes. It's genius."

"Skee-Ball," she says, testing the word on her tongue. "I'm in, let's go."

I shake my head. "Not tonight. It's late and you're drunk and tired." She frowns and it's an adorable response. "Did you know there is this game which has a disclaimer, warning against increased seizure risk."

She laughs, the clouds parting as her eyes brighten. "Which game?"

"Space Invaders. And if you ever stop to watch the game, you'll understand why. That's another reason not to go to the arcade tonight. I believe alcohol lowers seizure threshold."

She rolls her eyes at me again. "I believe it does, Doctor. Fine. Not tonight. But another night. Honestly, I think I should go home. The room is starting to spin a little."

"Then let me walk you."

Her eyes bore into mine and then she glances down at our hands which are still linked. "Okay," she whispers. "You can walk me home."

Chapter Eleven

GIA

My eyes slowly peel back only to be assaulted with the ferocious light of day streaming through my open window. I guess I forgot to close that last night when I got home. Home. That is where I am, right? Yes, that's my window and those are my curtains and that's my phone ringing on my bedside table.

My hand reaches out, slapping at the offending phone, screaming out the worst noise in the history of noises. It takes me two tries to pick it up, but once I do, I realize it's my mother. "Crap," I mutter. "Hi Mom," I say after I accept the call. Oh god, my voice sounds like I swallowed gravel and my mouth tastes like I drank dishwater and then washed it all down with cotton.

"Gia, what time are you coming today, because I still haven't gone out to the store and I have nothing in the house."

My eyebrows furrow in confusion, but that doesn't feel all that great so I stop and go with inwardly confused instead. It takes my foggy, alcohol-saturated brain exactly five full seconds to remember I did, in fact, promise my mother I would come out to visit her today and we'd have lunch. "What time is it?"

My mother sighs, clearly not all that impressed with me right now. "It's seven-thirty, Gia. I wouldn't have called this early, but you're usually awake by now."

She's right. I'm typically an early riser. But that's not the case after I spend a night drinking the way I did last night. Last night. Wow, I really can't remember all that much.

"I'll be there by noon. Is that okay?"

"Yes. That's fine. I was going to make that salad you like. You know, the one with figs and goat cheese."

My stomach rolls and I'm unable to stop my groan of nausea. My eyes close and I take two deep breaths which help to suppress the urge to vomit all over my area rug. "That's fine. I have to go. I'll see you later."

I hit the end button and then set my phone back down. All I really want to do is curl back under the covers and close my eyes, but I have to pee and that seems to be winning right now. Stupid alcohol. This is why I don't typically have more than two, three drinks max. But judging the level of hangover I'm sporting right now, I went way beyond that limit.

Not more than four though. Ophelia promised and she stuck to that.

Sitting up, I twist, planting my feet on the floor. I need a minute to sit here before I can move or even stand up. Looking down I realize I'm in a t-shirt and my panties. Nicely done, me. And there is even a glass of water on my nightstand. It's full, which means I passed out before I drank any of it. That probably explains why I feel like I want to die about now.

Standing up on unsteady legs, I allow my body to sway, before trying to right myself.

Jesus, I really did a– "Morning beautiful."

"Ahhhh!" I scream, spinning around far too quickly as it takes my brain another couple of seconds to stop. And when my brain does stop spinning, I see Finn Banner in my bed, pulling himself up into a sitting position, leaning against the fabric of my headboard, naked. At least he appears naked because the sheet is covering him from the waist down and he's not wearing anything on top.

Which means his chest is exposed to the overabundance of daylight streaming in my window.

Holy mother of sin, his chest and arms are something else. Strong and smooth and muscular with just the perfect amount of light hair. His abs are another matter altogether. I'm going to confess that I've never actually seen a six-pack in the flesh. At least none of the other men I've ever been with have had one.

But Finnigan Banner most definitely does.

I realize I've been standing here staring at him, most likely drooling, for longer than I should have, because once my eyes manage to find their way back up to his face, he's laughing at me.

"What are you doing here?" I'm so confused. I remember leaving the bar with him, but...

Now he just looks even more amused and that's sort of pissing me off.

"You don't remember?"

I shake my head. "Oh my god, we didn't..." I trail off, unable to finish the end of that very obvious question.

"I'm hurt, Gia. Really hurt that you don't remember our wild night together." *I'm going to be sick.* And worse, I can't tell if he's messing with me or not.

"Finn?" I say his name very slowly and very clearly and with the distinct intonation of a question at the end of it.

"No. We did not have sex." He scratches his lightly stubbled jaw line and the motion is very distracting. In fact, everything about him right now is distracting. "The only thing we did last night was talk while you drank yourself into oblivion and then I brought you home."

"I remember some of that. I mean, I remember you showing up and us talking a little. I remember leaving the bar with you. But I don't remember you staying."

"That's because you were pretty much asleep by the time we got back here. I had to practically carry you up. I only stayed because I was afraid you were going to vomit on your back in your sleep."

I look down. "Did you do this?" I ask, waving my hand in front of my short t-shirt. I think my panties are showing. I'm almost positive they are and I can't remember if I'm wearing plain cotton or something pretty and sexy. Please let it be the latter. I don't think I've ever been so grateful for getting waxed two days ago as I am right now.

He gives me an impish grin and shrugs. "I couldn't let you sleep in your bed in your scrubs. That would have been nasty. Think of all the microbes I just saved your sheets from. But don't worry, I was as much of a gentleman as I'm capable of being. I barely looked. Promise."

"Barely?" I raise an eyebrow at that.

He returns my raised eyebrow, only his is accompanied by that damn sexy grin of his. And then he shrugs, not willing to clarify further.

Why don't I care if he looked? I should care that he stripped me down and put me in only a t-shirt while I was wasted. But I don't. What is wrong with me when it comes to this man? I'm no longer the girl who knows better. I'm the brainless schoolgirl who shamelessly throws herself at the boy she likes, hoping he'll come around.

And he does. So freaking often. Maybe that's why this is so difficult. Finn likes me. I know he does. Because I'm not that brainless schoolgirl. I know when a man is attracted to me. And Finn is more than attracted to me. Finn wants me just as much as I want him.

"How are you feeling?"

"That depends on what you're referring to. Are you asking about how I feel after my night of too much alcohol or are you asking how I feel about waking up to find you in my bed?"

"Both," Finn chuckles. "Though I think I know how you feel about the second one since you told me you liked having me in your bed last night."

Oh shit.

"Anything else regretful I should be aware of?"

"Probably, but those are for me to hold onto and for you to torture yourself over."

"God." I shake my head and immediately wish I hadn't. "You really are an asshole."

"Yup." He grins even bigger now. "You said that last night too, but you called me a hot asshole, amongst other things, so I'll keep the compliments."

"I remember that one. And I'm sure I was being ironic when I said I liked having you in my bed. I mean, you basically invited yourself there." He's not at all bothered by my accusation. Plus, I think he knows I'm lying. How could he not? Alcohol is like my own version of truth serum. I don't tend to hold back. It's why I don't usually drink that much.

And right now, with the way he's looking at me, I wish I had kept my big mouth shut. Because I told him I liked him. I told him he was hot. I told him he was fucking with my head. And now that I focus on it, as the memories slowly trickle in, I vaguely remember remarking on how good he smelled before I fell asleep. Snuggling into him!

I am never drinking again. I realize everyone says that after a night of too much alcohol and bad decisions, but I absolutely mean it right now.

"I am going to pee and vomit and brush my teeth and when I come out, hopefully you'll be dressed. And then after you're dressed, you're going to promise me that you'll never ever tell anyone about anything that happened last night. Ever."

"Does this mean I'm no longer your hero?" He gives me a cocky smirk. *Asshole!* Now he's just messing with me. And enjoying the hell out of it. And he looks unbelievably hot and sexy in my bed. I can't believe I called him my hero to his face. Jesus Christ. Could I have said anything cheesier to him? I hate everything right now.

"Jerk," I mutter, walking around the bed and straight for my bathroom.

I slam the door behind me because I feel like that's what I'm supposed to do, but the sound has me wincing. Once the throbbing subsides, I smile because Finn tried to make me feel better when I was sad and then stayed with me so I wouldn't aspirate on my own vomit. *You like me, Finn. I know you do. One day you'll have to get over yourself and admit it.*

Five minutes later, my face is washed and my teeth are brushed and I'm feeling a little better for it. When I exit the bathroom, Finn is indeed dressed in his scrubs and is now sitting on the edge of my made bed, doing something on his phone.

He made my bed.

"Hi," I say, just a bit–or maybe a lot–embarrassed. I spent that whole five minutes in the bathroom trying to remember everything I said last night. I think I've gotten most of it. I hope I've gotten most of it.

Finn puts his phone down and peers up at me. "Feeling better?"

"A little." I shift my weight. "I, uh, I just wanted you to know I don't typically get drunk like that. It was just a really awful day."

He nods his head. "I know. You told me that too. I'm really am sorry about your patient. I wish I could tell you it gets easier, but it doesn't. It always sucks."

"Thanks," I say, sitting down next to him, but making sure there is enough space between us. I'm in shorts now. I pulled a slightly dirty pair out of my hamper, but desperate times and all. At least my panties were of the sexy variety. "Have you ever had that? A patient die on you like that? So unexpected?"

"Yes. I have. I work in the ED, remember? Your dad was one of those people."

"Really?" I say, my eyebrows raised.

"Yeah. He came in and was in such rough shape, but we managed to get him back and off to the cath lab. I was really hopeful. Especially after I saw you come in." He shifts his position, angling himself so he's facing more of me. His bright-blue eyes dance all around my face. "You looked so distraught and I knew by your black gown, it was graduation day for you. All I could think of when I saw you was, not her. I didn't want you to lose your father like that on a day that's supposed to be one of the best of your life."

I don't know what to say to that. I'm overwhelmed by it. By him.

I just know I need to kiss him.

My eyes lock with his and I lean in ever so slightly. Just enough to let him know exactly what my intention is. Finn blinks, his eyes dropping down to my lips and then back up to mine. My stomach coils with anticipation. With want. He leans in too, tilting his head, and even smiling a little. Just as our lips are about to meet in what I know will be the best kiss of my life, his phone rings in his lap.

But instead of silencing it or chucking it across the room and devouring my mouth, he pulls back and checks it. And then after he does that, he answers it with, "Dr. Banner."

This is what I meant when I said to him two steps forward and one step back. When I forced myself to believe I was done.

Every time we get somewhere, he puts the brakes on. Every time I think, yes, this is the moment—it's not. I'm so very tired of it. I don't do well with in-between. I think I told him that. Indecision and I have never been friends.

And we're certainly not about to become them now. I don't care how good he looks with his shirt off. Or the fact that he comforted me, brought me home and kept me safe. Or that he saved my life and stitched up my arm. Or even the fact he made my fucking bed.

I do not care.

I've had enough.

I. Am. Not. That. Brainless. Girl!

Finn continues his conversation which really isn't all that important. I can hear what they're saying. They're asking if he can come in a little early for his shift and he's saying yes. That's it. That's what broke up our potential first kiss. An inconsequential phone call. Something that could have been managed over a text.

But in the back of my mind, I know he did it on purpose.

I realize he didn't have someone call him at that precise moment, but I bet he was relieved it came. Finn has been pushing me off this thing between us since the very start. We're talking months here, if I don't count our initial meeting.

It's time I take the goddamn hint.

I get up off my bed and move away from him. I stand over by my bedroom door and I wait for him to finish his call. It doesn't take long. As I said, it wasn't all that important.

"That was work," he says after he ends it, like I needed him to actually tell me that. "I need to get going."

I nod. I'm pissed off. Completely exasperated. "Sounds like it."

Finn rises, watching me like he's not sure what to do with me now. I solve his dilemma for him. Spinning around, I march out of my bedroom and over to my front door, fully expecting him to follow me. He does, but it takes him a second or two.

"Have a good shift," I say as he approaches. "Thanks again for last night."

I open the door, but he stops in front of me, peering down at me in silence. He's conflicted. Like he's waging some sort of inner battle with himself. Only I don't think there are any winners in this case. I think no matter what, I lose. Because if he kisses me, he'll regret it. And if he doesn't…well, then he doesn't, and I end up feeling the same way I feel whenever he's blown through me like the tornado he is.

But his eyes right now. God, I don't know what to do with them. I'm desperate to look away or shift or something because he's intimidating me with their intensity. But I don't do any of that. I hold that stare, daring him to do…something. *Do something, Finn.*

But all he does is sigh and shake his head, once again finding his resolve as he says, "See you around, Gia."

And then he leaves. He doesn't even turn around or look back. I know because I watch him until he disappears around the corner on my floor. I wait to shut the door until I hear the ding of the elevator.

"Goodbye Finn," I say to myself as I lock the door. I flip the deadbolt and latch the chain because I'm just that angry.

I've never met a more frustrating man. Every guy I've ever gone out with, other than in high school or middle school where they're just too immature to get out of their own way, has been direct. Either they want you or they don't. Either they kiss you or they make it clear they're not feeling it.

And sure, they might do the whole, I don't want a relationship thing. They might say they only want something casual. Like Colin. He did that and I was cool with it because I knew where we stood and I was in the same mindset.

But I want Finn Banner.

And I know Finn Banner wants me.

So just what the absolute fuck is his problem?

Chapter Twelve

FINN

Six years ago

I WALK OUT of my genetics final with a huge smile on my face. I aced it. I know I did. And that was probably the hardest test I've ever taken. No lie. I start my internship with the pharmaceutical company in a week, which means I have exactly seven days with absolutely no responsibility and nothing to do other than live inside Kelly.

In two weeks, we'll have officially been together for a year and it's been without a doubt the best year of my life. All of the pain and guilt surrounding my father's death is gone. My mother is doing really well and is actually seeing someone who is good to her.

And I have Kelly.

Kelly who is running across the quad in my direction this very moment. A broad beaming smile spreads across my face as I see her long blonde hair whip behind her. Those gorgeous brown eyes sparkling against the sun. Her thin, petite frame, moving like a gazelle until she reaches me, launching herself up into my arms.

I catch her automatically and plant my lips on hers. I kiss the hell out of her because even though it's only been eight hours since I saw her last, I missed her. Damn, I am such a pussy-whipped, lovesick fool. I don't even care. Not one bit. In fact, it makes me blissfully happy.

Just like Kelly.

She's the first and only thing to ever make me happy. To ever make me feel loved and I will do everything I can to keep her. To make her happy in return. To fucking worship her.

She pulls back with a breathless laugh. "How'd it go?"

"Aced it," I say and she smiles even bigger.

"I knew it." She gives me another kiss and then jumps out of my arms, taking my hand and leading me away from campus. "And because I knew you'd ace your final, I'm taking you out for dinner to celebrate."

"Oh baby," I kiss the side of her head. "You don't have to do that."

She shakes her head. "It's fine. I've got it. No complaints."

Kelly does not have a lot of money. In fact, the first time my mother met her, she referred to her as a gold-digging whore. Not to her face, of course. That conversation came later. But Kelly is no gold-digging whore. She works hard as an administrative assistant for a medium-sized law firm. She makes okay money, but in New York, okay money is basically nothing.

She shares an apartment with two other girls and the apartment is a tiny two-bedroom. I offered for her to move in with me, but she said she didn't want us to take that step based on financial convenience. See, not a gold digger.

No, Kelly is perfect.

Which is why I'm going to ask her again to move in with me tonight.

The entire time we're at dinner, I'm debating how to do it. Do I just come out and ask her? Should I make some big romantic gesture with it like having a special key made for her? I don't know. I'm new at this. I never wanted to live with anyone before Kelly.

I decide not to do it at dinner. Instead, I bring her home with me and the moment we step over the threshold of my apartment, I kiss her. She giggles into my lips, because I didn't even wait until I shut and locked the door behind us. She's giggling because Kelly loves it when I do this sort of thing.

"Move in with me," I say against her lips.

She pauses and pulls back, her doe-like eyes blinking at me. "Really?"

I nod. "Yes. I've never been so sure about anything. I want us to live together."

The most breathtaking smile lights up her face and then she kisses me. "Yes! Hell yes!"

She giggles into my mouth again and I don't think I've ever been this happy before. "I love you," I say.

"I love you too, Finn."

I make love to Kelly in our bed, because it's no longer just my bed. We also do it in the shower and the kitchen because those are both ours now too. But after the kitchen sex, she ends up throwing up in our sink.

"Jesus, baby. You okay?"

"Oh god," she moans. "I don't know. Can you get food poisoning from chicken this fast?"

"No," I say, rubbing my hand in small circles on her back. "We ate only three hours ago. What else did you have?"

She shakes her head, holding up a finger which tells me to wait a minute as she dry heaves into the sink again. And even though I love Kelly and I'm going to be a doctor, this is sort of nasty. I mean, it's the sink. We wash dishes in there and we don't have a disposal or anything.

"Nothing. I haven't eaten anything all day before dinner. My stomach felt a little off. Maybe I'm getting the stomach flu."

"Maybe you're pregnant." I laugh, but Kelly doesn't laugh with me. Instead she turns to face me, her cheeks flushed and a small amount of drool is clinging to her chin. She just stares at me with wide, unblinking eyes. "Are you?"

She shakes her head, but it's not the sort of headshake which says no. It's the sort of headshake that says, *oh shit*. "I missed two pills earlier last month."

"Okay," I draw out the word.

"But I tripled up. I called my GYN's office and they said that would be fine."

"When was your last period?"

"I haven't had one in years, Finn. I'm on the pill that you don't get one with."

"Should we get a test?"

Kelly looks like she's going to be sick again, but I don't think it has anything to do with her stomach.

Me? I'm not sick at all.

In fact, I think I might just be a touch excited by the prospect. Sure, the timing isn't all that great. I just finished up my third year of medical school, but money isn't an issue for me and it's not like we're teenagers. I'm twenty-four and she's twenty-seven and we're in love.

"I'm scared to."

"Oh baby, come here." I take her into my arms even though she smells like vomit. We're both standing naked in the kitchen because we just finished with our kitchen sex and now we're talking about the possibility of being pregnant. "It's going to be okay. Better than okay. We can handle this. Whatever this is, we can do it. I love you."

Kelly pulls back and looks at me. Then she smiles. "Okay, Finn. Let's get a test. I love you and we're going to be fine. Everything will be fine."

Chapter Thirteen

FINN

Present Day

"YOU'RE COMING UPSTAIRS WITH ME," Mike says as he stands there, staring down at me. He's getting more annoyed by the second, but I never invited him over and I certainly never said I was going to go to that stupid party with him.

I don't respond as I lean back on my sofa, sipping on my imported beer and watching the Red Sox play the Indians in the first game of the ALCS. Even though neither of them are my team, I'd much rather watch this then go up to the penthouse of my building and deal with people I used to work with.

"Come on, Finn," he whines. What sort of grown man whines? "I want you to meet my girlfriend."

Oh right. I remember this now. Vaguely. I was going into work this morning, talking to him on the phone, when he mentioned his newish girlfriend was going to be at the party. I haven't met her yet. I've been pushing it off, if I'm being honest. I'm happy for Mike and all that good shit, but the last thing I want to be around is a happy couple.

I just so happen to live in a building where the trauma surgeons occupy the penthouse. I was here first, which makes me sound like a child, but I don't care, because it's true. Those fuckers moved in a year after I did.

I bought this apartment three years ago after my life fell apart and I've been here ever since. The trauma surgeons, three of them in total, bought the penthouse together. It's like a frat house up there and I hate it. I'm just happy I don't live directly beneath them. They're not my favorite group of guys either so it's not like spending an evening shooting the shit with them is an incentive.

"Bring her down here," I say without bothering to move my eyes away from the television.

Mike sighs, propping his hands on his lean hips. "She's bringing friends. Friends who I'm sure are every bit as gorgeous as she is. Friends who I'm sure would love to meet a guy such as yourself."

"Not interested."

"Jesus fucking Christ," Mike snaps and it's not like him to get to this point. He's typically more in control of his temper, so this has me sitting a up a little straighter to meet his eyes. "I'm so sick of your perpetual fucking negativity. How long are you going to live like this?"

"Don't," I warn.

"It's been three years, man. You haven't dated a woman in three years. You need to live your life."

"Mike," I say firmly. "I get you're trying to be a good friend to me and all, but you need to shut the hell up and get out of here now."

Another sigh, this time his chin drops to his chest. "Just come upstairs with me. Just meet my girl and then you can go back to your sulking in the form of beer and baseball. Ten minutes. That's all I'm asking for."

I deliberate this for a few moments.

I inwardly sigh. "Fine," I stand up and bring my now empty beer into the kitchen, placing it by the sink so I can recycle it later. If it were anyone else, I wouldn't. But Mike has been there for me. He's unbelievably patient with my bullshit. I owe him.

"You're going to change, right?"

I look down. I'm wearing a t-shirt, very old worn jeans and no shoes. And as much as I really am in the mood to be a dick right now, Mike doesn't deserve that. "Give me five minutes. Or better yet," I say with a smile, "go on up and I'll meet you there."

He laughs. "No, I think I'll wait."

I shrug, leaving Mike in my living room while I walk down the long hall into my bedroom. This may not be the penthouse, but it's still a very nice apartment. In fact, it's my favorite place where I've ever lived, if for no other reason than the view of the East River and the wraparound balcony which faces it. And I'm high enough up that I don't have to deal with the noise or view of the FDR or other buildings.

Eight minutes later, I'm ready. Mike is smiling at his phone before his eyes do a sweep of me, taking in my black button up, dark jeans and black shoes. I even brushed my hair. "Better?" I ask.

"Much. Let's go. She's already there."

"Don't want to keep her waiting."

Mike rolls his eyes at me. "She's great. You'll love her." I nod, not really caring either way. "Did I mention that she brought friends with her?"

"Once or twice." He laughs at me, slapping my back as we step into the elevator to go up the two flights to the penthouse. The doors open not even thirty seconds later and we step into the apartment. It's relatively crowded here and I already recognize a lot of faces.

Mike leads me over to the bar that's taking up the entire island in the kitchen. "Sup, man," Liam says to me, reaching out to shake my hand. "Glad you could make it."

"Wouldn't miss it," I deadpan, swiping a beer out of the bucket of ice. Liam laughs. He knows as well as I do I'm full of shit.

"The place is stacked tonight," he goes on. "Whatever your pleasure, we've got it. But I already called dibs on your girlfriend's friend," he says to Mike, holding up his beer bottle like he's saluting him. "You weren't lying when you said her friends are hot."

This is why I can't stand the trauma surgeons.

"As long as it's not my girlfriend, I don't care," Mike says. "Speaking of which," he claps a hand on my back, "let's go find her."

I take that as my cue and give Liam the requisite nod. I have nothing to say to this guy. Liam nods his head back at me while mixing up some crazy alcohol concoction.

"What an ass," Mike says once we're out of earshot, which isn't exactly far considering how loud it is in here. Music is blasting and people seem to be doing their best to talk over it so they can be heard. "I might have to warn Monique's friend about him."

"Probably should," I agree.

We move through the crowd, stopping here and there to say hello as we pass people we know, which is pretty much everyone since most people here work at the hospital I previously had. Finally, Mike points his finger over toward the back of the living room. I nod, following him, while I sip my very expensive beer, the showoffs felt the need to buy.

"Hey," Mike says, tapping a very pretty black woman on the shoulder. She spins around—and the moment she sees who's interrupting her conversation—gleams at him.

"You made it," she says. "I was starting to wonder." She leans in and gives him a sweet kiss on the lips and Mike puts his arms around her. I've never seen Mike like this with a woman. Typically, they don't last all that long with him.

"Monique, this is my friend, Finn. Finn, this is my girlfriend, Monique."

She smiles brightly at me, reaching out to shake my hand. "Hi," she greets me. "I've heard a lot about you."

I tense a little at that, but she isn't saying it in a particularly knowing way. More of a you're Mike's best friend way. "You too." I really know nothing about this woman other than her name and the fact she's Mike's girlfriend. I'm sure he's told me more, but I don't think I listened all that well.

"I thought you said you were bringing friends," Mike says and Monique laughs.

"She did," a voice chirps behind me and I turn to see a familiar-looking woman with shoulder-length blonde hair, heavy bangs and blue eyes. "I'm Chloe," she introduces. "I work at the hospital with you."

"Oh," I reply feeling a little bad that I can't place her other than vaguely recognizing her face. "What do you do?"

She laughs, shaking her head. "Same thing as Mo here." That doesn't help me and when she realizes I don't know what Mike's girlfriend does, she laughs even harder. So does Monique, so I guess she's not put off by that. "We're midwives, Dr. Banner. You know, the people who deliver cute little bundles of joy into the world."

Great. Mike's girlfriend is a midwife. And so is this chick. And she works at my hospital which means she knows Gia. Now that I think about it, that's why I recognize her. I've seen the two of them together before.

Just. Fucking. Perfect.

I've successfully avoided Gia for weeks following that encounter in her apartment. I pissed her off when I answered my phone instead of kissing her, and that was it.

It was for the best. That's what I've continued to tell myself. Because wanting Gia the way I do is a problem. I don't just want her for a night or a week or even a couple of months. She's the type of woman I could want for the long term and I won't go down that road again.

I won't.

But every time I run into her, she chips away at my resolve a little more. Each time, I end up just a step closer to crossing that irreversible line with her. It was nearly impossible not to that night I slept in her bed with her. I held her all night, even if she doesn't remember that part of it. I allowed myself to have that, knowing it would never happen again.

I just didn't expect it to feel so…perfect. So right. I didn't expect to sit up half the night just so I could watch her sleep. So I could bury my nose in her hair and breathe in her unique fragrance.

The night at the bar, when I found her completely drunk out of her mind, all I could think about was wanting to be the one to make it all better for her. Her hero, she called me. I can't shake that one.

I may be the broken one, but she's the one who always needs saving.

That's really why I stayed the night, even if I did give her a half-hearted excuse for it.

"So how do you know each other then," I ask Chloe in reference to Monique. "You work at different hospitals."

"We went to graduate school together," Chloe says like it should be obvious, which I guess it probably should be, but I'm thrown off right now.

"Actually," Mike interjects, "do you remember that girl who came in on her graduation day? Her father ended up dying from a STEMI?" I can only nod. "She's actually Monique's friend."

"Gia," I say because I have to say her name.

He nods, his expression a mixture of sympathy for Gia and surprise for me. "You remember."

"She works at the hospital with me. I've run into her a time or two." I leave it at that and then turn back to her friends to see if anything else registers. Nothing does and I don't know if it bothers me or not that Gia hasn't mentioned anything else about me to her friends.

Chloe steps into me, her blue eyes sparkling up at me. "Come buy me a free drink, Dr. Banner. I think our friends would like to be alone."

I have no interest in buying Chloe one of the free drinks here. "I believe Liam already called dibs on you," I say with a wry smile.

Chloe laughs, shaking her head. "Oh no. That wasn't me. That was Gia. He zeroed in on her like Mark Walberg from that movie about the stalker."

"*Fear*," Monique supplies with a roll of her eyes. "And it wasn't that dramatic."

The two of them go back and forth for a minute, but I can't focus on anything other than the fact that dipshit Liam called dibs on Gia. That Gia is here somewhere with that asshole who is no doubt trying to fuck her at this very moment. *My* Gia.

That thought is eating me alive.

And since Chloe here started with the movie clichés, my brain is running with that line from *The Godfather III*. Not my favorite of them, but the line still works in this situation. *Just when I thought I was out, they pull me back in.* Only it's not them, it's Gia.

Gia. Gia. Gia. It's always Gia.

Or at least it has been since I set eyes on her a year and a half ago.

"Where is she?" I ask. I don't even care how I sound right now or what they think of the desperate tone in my question. I need to get her away from Liam. He cannot have her.

"Outside on the terrace," Chloe responds with a smirk. "And I do believe our friend Liam is still at his makeshift bar."

"Sorry, Chloe," I say to her with a smile, because I may actually like this girl. "I think you might have to find someone else buy you that drink."

Chloe lets out a dramatic sigh. "I figured as much. You're lucky this place is like a meat market, otherwise I wouldn't let you off the hook so easily."

I grin at her. "You're mixing metaphors."

"Part of her charm," Monique says with a wink.

"Catch you later," I nod at Mike who might just be smiling bigger than Monique and Chloe combined. I ignore that. Because even though I'm being a selfish prick and trying to cockblock Liam, that doesn't mean anything is going to happen with Gia and me. It just means I don't want her to end up as another notch in his bedpost. And for the record, I know he does that. He bragged about it all through residency, only he's smart enough to put the notches on the bottom of his bed where women can't see them.

Which makes him the official asshole and not me.

Mike gives me a pat on the back and I wave bye to his girlfriend who seems nice enough and her friend Chloe and I go straight for those glass doors which lead out onto the balcony.

Gia Bianchi will not end up with anyone tonight but me.

Chapter Fourteen

FINN

Opening the doors to the penthouse terrace, I'm instantly assaulted with a rush of cold wind across my face which temporarily steals my breath. It's fairly empty out here. Just a few people sipping at drinks and talking. It's a cool night and most of the women here are not dressed for these conditions, which is why I think it's far more crowded inside than it is out here, despite the view.

Gia is easy to spot, even in the dark. She's wearing red, so maybe that's why. Her long silky black hair is twisted into some kind of updo, revealing her upper back and neck. She's leaning forward, her forearms propped up on the railing and from here, it looks like she's staring down at the street.

She's alone and I sigh.

What are you doing? I don't have an answer for that.

But right now, I'm not driven by rational thought. I'm driven by fucking jealousy. And that shit's as necrotic as it comes. It makes perfectly levelheaded men, like myself, do really stupid illogical shit.

Like go after a woman they're crazy about, but should stay away from.

"Miss Bianchi," I whisper up against her neck, because I like making a big entrance where she's concerned. I like catching her off guard.

Her head whips in my direction, those blue-green eyes of hers wide as saucers. Her lips are red. And I really wish they weren't because, *damn*. Then there's that dress she's wearing. It's strapless. That part I already knew, but I didn't realize the front of the dress dipped into a V and that her full tits would be pressed together into that V.

Is she trying to kill me? Thank god, it's dark out here, otherwise the tent in my jeans would be not only be obvious, but a touch awkward. She's sexy as sin and I don't think I've ever seen a more stunningly gorgeous woman in my life.

She doesn't smile. In fact, she might be scowling a bit though it's tough to tell out here.

"Aren't you cold?" I ask her because the wind off the river is whipping in our direction and it's not all that pleasant. I wish I had the foresight to wear a jacket so I could put it on her.

She shakes her head. "No. I like the cold."

That's all she gives me and I realize I have a lot of ground to make up where she's concerned.

"What are you watching?" I ask, jutting my chin in the direction of her phone which seems to be playing something.

She grins now, like I just busted her. "Watching the Red Sox," she says. "They're up, two to one."

And I'm in love. Because Gia is outside watching baseball on her phone instead of inside mingling with assholes.

But wait… "You're a Red Sox fan?"

She laughs, nodding her head. "Yes. I'm originally from Boston. Or didn't you know?"

"I didn't know. But now that I do, I don't think we can be friends."

"I didn't realize we were friends."

Ouch. Point one, Gia Bianchi.

"I guess we're not."

"Then you don't have to linger. Besides, I was expecting

someone to bring me a drink. A male someone in case you were curious. I know your philosophy on sharing."

I smile because I can't help myself. "I have drinks," I say, moving in next to her as close as I can so our arms are touching on the railing. She doesn't pull away and I take that as a sign to proceed. "I have lots of drinks actually. I just didn't think you'd ever drink again. Isn't that what you said?"

"Did I?" she smirks. "I don't recall."

"That doesn't surprise me," I lean my shoulder into her, nudging her just enough for it to be flirtatious.

"What do you want, Finn?"

I hate that question. Mostly because I don't know how to answer it. *Everything*, I think, but will never say.

"For you to come and have a drink with me. I thought I already offered that up."

She purses those full red lips at me. God, she's stunning.

"Besides, Liam isn't your type."

She smirks at me again, twisting her body so she's facing me. Her damn cleavage is like a shining beacon in the dark. I couldn't look away if I tried. And for the record, I am trying.

"How did you know it was Liam who was bringing me a drink?"

I lean into her, our faces inches apart. My stomach coils and my cock thickens again and my lips tingle and my hands twitch and I'm beyond desperate for her. "Because I know everything. Haven't you figured that out yet?"

"Except women."

Doesn't she have my number pegged. "Except them," I agree. "But that doesn't mean I'm wrong about Liam."

"Okay, Dr. Banner—" *I hate it when she does that*, "—I'll bite. Who's my type then?"

My face comes so close that our noses are practically touching. That our lips are practically tasting. Our breaths are definitely mingling in the cool air. She lets me do this and I don't think at this point, I need to answer her.

I'm her type. Me. No one else.

"Come have a drink with me," I say, my eyes staring into hers.

And while I can't stand how attracted I am to her, I also won't tolerate her doing anything else tonight.

"No," she says and I can't stop the bubble of laughter as it flies out of my chest.

"No?"

"Was I unclear?"

My eyes train away from hers, out into the dark Manhattan night, but I make sure I can see her out of my peripheral vision. "Is it because I'm an asshole?"

She doesn't laugh, but she does nod.

"Well then, I guess I have a lot to make up for."

"Or not," she shrugs and that pisses me off.

"No. I think I do." I turn on her, standing up to my full height and pushing my size into her. "Come with me."

"I really don't want another drink."

"Something to eat?" She shakes her head. "Cappuccino, Miss Bianchi?"

She laughs, her sweet breath brushing against me. "È troppo tardi per il cappuccino."

Oh hell. "You speak Italian?" Another head nod and an arrogant smirk. "Come with me," I say again.

I don't give her the option to protest this time. And she allows me to drag her. I'm not exactly knocking her out and tossing her over my shoulder–caveman style. I'm more leading her and she's letting me, so I take that as an affirmative.

The room is warm and the crowd is dense, but she holds on firmly to my hand as I escort her through it until we reach the elevators.

"There you are," Liam says, catching up just as I press the down button. "I was looking for you, Gia."

She glances over at him and then down at our linked hands.

"Goodnight, Liam," I tell him, catching the hint of a smile from Gia as the elevator doors open and we step on. Liam watches us go, a scowl on his face as the doors close.

"I think he's mad at you."

"Couldn't care less."

She shrugs and twenty seconds later, the elevator doors open onto my floor and Gia laughs. "You're kidding me. I thought you were taking me out for coffee."

I smile now. "I live in the same building. And I am taking you out for *cappuccino*," I emphasize. "I just need to grab my wallet, keys and a coat for both of us."

She shakes her head and steps out, waiting for me to direct her. I never locked my door when I left so I just twist the nob and we're in.

"God, you're irritating, Banner."

"Finn," I correct. I should only be Finn to her.

"No," she says with a headshake, turning to me and then walking backward, away. "Banner. It allows me to keep my distance."

"And that's a necessity."

It's not a question, but she answers me all the same. "You bet."

I don't bother responding. She's with me and that's all I care about.

Grabbing my phone, wallet and keys, I shove them into my pockets and then snag my coat from the front closet as well a blazer for Gia that's a bit too small for me. Walking back across the room, I pause, watching her. She's making herself at home, in my home, taking my remote off the coffee table and flipping on the television.

Then she laughs, shaking her head because the Red Sox and the Indians are still on.

She peeks over at me with a smile which lights up those cyan-colored eyes.

"You're really a Yankee's fan, aren't you?" she asks incredulously.

"Yeah. I guess that means we're officially incompatible."

"Officially."

"Except you're here, aren't you?"

"Looks that way. Doesn't change the fact I'm a Boston fan and you're a New York fan and a total asshole, to boot."

I laugh, wrapping my arms around her and placing my extra jacket over her shoulders. She looks good wrapped up in my things.

"How's this then? I'll work on not being an asshole if you work on giving me another chance?"

Gia steps back, her eyes focus on mine.

"Okay, Finn. You've got yourself a deal."

"Perfect." I take her hand in mine and lead us to the door, because I can't have her in my apartment without throwing her down on my sofa and lifting up that dress of hers. Or yanking it down. Or both. "Let's go."

Locking up my apartment, I direct her back to the elevator and down into the cool New York evening. "Does this mean you're a Giants fan?" she asks as we amble down the street. There is a really good coffee shop near here and they stay open until one a.m. "I should warn you, if you tell me you're a Jets fan, this night is over."

I laugh, tugging her into my side and kiss her head.

I don't know what I'm doing with her.

I know what I'm risking. I know my gut is telling me to run every time I get closer. But right now, all I can think about is the way Liam looked at her. The thoughts swirling through his mind which he didn't bother to hide in his expression. Yes, I'm a dick for not wanting her with anyone else.

But at least I'm a self-aware dick.

"No. Not a Jets fan, so I think the night is safe. I'd say I'm a Giants fan, but I'm more into baseball than football."

Gia shakes her head. "I guess that's better than you being a diehard fan for the enemy."

I laugh again and I realize I haven't laughed this much in more than three years. "This is us," I say, opening the door for her. It's decently busy in here, but I spot a vacant two-person table in the back. "Come on."

Pulling out the chair for her, Gia sits down with a nod of appreciation. "Thank you."

"Do you want a cappuccino? I know I said that's what we were getting, but they have a lot of really good drinks here."

"Hot chocolate, please."

"Hot chocolate?" She nods and I can't stop my spreading grin. "God, you're cute." I lean down and kiss the corner of her lips before I can stop myself. She smiles. She likes that I just kissed her without actually kissing her. And that I called her cute, I think. And even though I like making her smile, I'm a fucking idiot for it. "Do you want whipped cream?"

"Of course. That's the only way to drink it."

"Anything to eat?" She shakes her head. "Okay, Miss Bianchi, sit tight and I'll be right back with your hot chocolate and whipped cream."

"Thank you so much, Dr. Banner. You're quite the gentleman when you want to be."

If only she knew.

Turning away, I rub my fist against the tight spot in my chest.

What the hell am I doing?

Chapter Fifteen

GIA

I don't know what I'm doing here. Every single time I tell myself I'm over Finn Banner, he finds me. Every single time I tell myself I'm done with Finn Banner, he manages to get me to follow after him like a mindless fool.

And I am not a mindless fool. I'm not. I like to believe I am strong and in control.

But I'm not when it comes to Finn. I don't even know what it is about him which has me relinquishing that control so readily. I meant it when I said he's an asshole. Because he is. I meant it when I told him no, out on that balcony. Because I did.

It just didn't last. He stood there, staring into my eyes and I found my resolve to stay away from him soften. It didn't just soften, it completely melted. Liquified. I wasn't strong or firm or solid.

I hate that I like him as much as I do.

It's only going to lead to more confusion, frustration and hurt. I know it will. I can see it coming. But I'm still sitting here, in this café, at eleven thirty on a Friday night, waiting while he goes up and gets me my hot chocolate with whipped cream.

I pivot in my chair so that I can watch him instead of playing with my phone the way everyone else does.

But I can't seem to help it right now. He's a conundrum. Something I don't comprehend and I have a feeling if I pried, I wouldn't be afforded the luxury of an interpretation. Because Finn holds everything back. Yet it only makes me want him more.

Goddamn the challenge is just as enticing as the man.

Finn glances in my direction as he finishes speaking with the lady behind the counter and when he catches my observing eye, he smiles. I can't find it in me to return it. His smile slips as his body twists, facing me fully. He stares back—and for a moment—that's all we do. We stare. And the longer this moment lasts, the more I accept that my heart is in trouble.

The woman behind the counter gets his attention, handing him two ceramic mugs, one topped with a healthy dose of whipped cream. Finn thanks her and saunters back over to me.

I follow the entire thing.

"One hot chocolate with whipped cream."

He sets it down in front of me and then takes his seat. "Thank you." I swipe my finger across the fluffy white cream and pop it in my mouth, savoring its sweetness. Finn watches that. We're all about watching the other tonight. Like, the longer we do it, the easier it will be to figure the other out.

But I don't think he has to try very hard with me. I'm about as transparent as it gets.

"What did you get?" I ask, sitting up a little straighter and leaning across the table to catch a glimpse inside his mug.

"Decaf cappuccino."

"Any good?"

"The best. Want a sip?"

I nod, reaching out for his mug, our fingers brushing as he hands it to me. "You can have some of mine if you'd like. I share just as well as you do."

"I don't think I've had hot chocolate since I was eight." He chuckles, reaching over and taking a small sip out of the side of my mug. I take a sip of his too and it is very good.

"You're missing out, my friend. One is never too old for hot chocolate."

He grins, taking his mug from my hands as I slide it back across the stone table to him. "I thought you already established we're not friends."

I laugh despite myself. "Yes, you're right. I did. So if we're not friends, then why did you bring me out here?"

He considers me for a moment. Takes a sip of his coffee. Wipes away an errant streak of foam and then shrugs. "Because I didn't want you to end up in Liam's bed tonight."

"Jesus," I cough, choking a little on the sip of my drink I was in the process of swallowing. I was not expecting that answer. Or his bluntness. "You're such a jerk. Were you always like this?"

He shrugs again, but something in his eyes tells me that he wasn't. Tells me that at one point, he was a lot more than this cold, seemingly apathetic man. That the sweet, smooth Finn is possibly the real him, just well hidden.

Or maybe that's just my personal observations, because I've seen him be more. Like that time on the stoop outside the hospital after my father died. And that night he saved my life and walked me home. Definitely the time I fell and he sewed me up. Without a doubt the night he took care of me when I was drunk.

"So you don't want me for yourself, but no one else can have me?"

"Something like that."

I hate he just confirmed that. I was hoping for a contradiction there. I don't know what to do with that. What to say. I should get up and walk out on him. That's what the smart girl inside of me is saying. *Run, Gia. Run as fast as you can.* Because Finnigan Banner is damaged goods.

What happened to you, Finn?

"Does that bother you?"

"Yes," I say through a sardonic laugh. "It does."

"Which part?" he asks as he bends forward, his bright blue eyes sparkling, his hands still holding onto his mug like he's enjoying the warmth it provides.

I shrug because I can be evasive too and I don't think I want him to know the answer, though I'm sure he must know both parts bother me. The first part definitely more than the second. I had no intention of ending up in Liam's bed. Honestly, he was a bit too... Liam for me. He sort of screamed, *I fuck women and then blog all about it on the Internet because I'm the type of douchebag who likes to brag.*

Finn grins at me in a way which says I was right. I don't have to answer him. He already knows every inner thought I've ever had about him.

"If you're from Boston, what made you come to New York," he asks, changing the subject entirely. It makes me smile for some reason. Another battle, I realize. Another round of the fight. Finn is the strong silent type. He's the man who watches and takes everything in and only comments when necessary.

But he talks to me. He asks me questions. He interacts.

And he does this because he can't help himself. Even if he tries to fight it. I know all of this. I see all of this. It's part of the reason I come back time and time again.

"Nursing school," I tell him, crossing my legs and leaning back in my seat. His coat is still draped over my shoulders and even though it's warm in here and I'm not the least bit cold, I keep it on. It smells like him. That's just how pathetic I am when it comes to this man. "I came here for undergraduate and stayed. Then I went to graduate school and was offered a job. Besides, I like New York."

"More than Boston?"

"No. They're just different. Did you go to medical school here?"

Finn nods his head. "Yes. I went to Dartmouth for undergraduate and Columbia for medical school."

"Like me. That's where I went."

"Like you." He picks up his coffee and takes a sip, his eyes haven't left mine the entire time since he sat back down. "Are you dating anyone?"

I shake my head. "No. Not exclusively, anyway," I smirk. He doesn't. In fact, his eyes grow dark and so does his expression. He hates that answer and I love that he hates it so much.

"Do you do that a lot?"

"What?"

"Date men non-exclusively?"

"God, Finn, are we really having a conversation here? I mean, just come out and ask me what you want to know. I'll either tell you or I won't."

"I already asked you what I want to know."

I huff out a breath because it's late and I'm tired and my hot chocolate is getting cold from the pound of whipped cream they put on top and I just don't have it in me to dance around the ring with Finn Banner anymore.

So I cross my arms and narrow my eyes and go for broke. "No. I don't. I go on dates with men on a fairly regular basis. I'm a single woman living in New York. But most of them don't turn into a second date and if they do, they rarely get past the fifth. Colin, that guy you saw me with that night at the bar, was the last guy I sort of dated with any consistency and that's been over for months. Does that satisfy your curiosity?"

"Yes. Doesn't mean I like the answer though."

"Which part?" I ask, throwing his own words back at him.

"All of it, Gia. All of it." He runs a hand down his face and his cocky exterior crumbles. "I have a problem."

"What's that?" I glare, leaning forward over the table the same way he is. His eyes dip to my chest for a half a beat, and I wish I didn't enjoy that as much as I do.

"I'm very attracted to you. I think you know that already. I don't do the best job of hiding it and every time I'm around, it just seems to come out. It's why I've been avoiding you all this time." Jesus, I cannot believe he just said that. I can practically feel my eyes widening and my jaw dropping. "But the more time I spend with you, the more I realize how much I enjoy it. That I want to do more of it. That I like you just as much as I know you like me."

"And that's a problem?"

"Yes. It's a big problem. Because I don't want any other man to take you on dates. To have you, even if it's in a sort of, non-exclusive way. The thought of it makes me fucking insane. Obviously it does otherwise you wouldn't be sitting here across from me now. Otherwise I wouldn't have gone out on the balcony and said whatever I could to get you to leave with me."

"But?" I whisper because my voice is weak with his confession.

"But I don't want to hurt you. I don't want you to be angry with me. I don't want to fuck with your head." His eyes close for the briefest of moments before they reopen. Blue fire. The hottest part of the flame. "I don't know how to do this," he admits, his finger waving back and forth between us. "I don't *want* to do this. So I'm going to order you an Uber and you're going to go home alone and I'm going to go back to avoiding you."

I have absolutely no words.

I watch him as he takes his phone out and does in fact order me an Uber home. I watch as he slides his phone back into his pocket when he's done. I watch as he stands up and reaches for my hand to help me up.

I watch him the entire time he walks me outside, still holding my hand with his jacket over my shoulders. And when I'm tucked safely inside the Uber he ordered and paid for, and I'm alone, I cry for him.

What happened to you, Finn?

Chapter Sixteen

FINN

Six years ago

"YOUR MOTHER HATES ME," Kelly says to me, her eyes focused down on the engagement ring and wedding band which are now prominently displayed on her left hand. "She's going to be even more pissed she didn't get to see her only son get married."

"She doesn't hate you," I reassure her, my hand reaching over to Kelly who's sitting in the passenger seat of our car. I squeeze her hand and then rub her beautiful swollen belly. Everything about Kelly is beautiful. My ring on her finger. My baby in her belly. My last name at the end of her first name. "Besides, it's Christmas and we're giving her a grandchild."

"I don't think that matters, Finn. She told me she was too young to be a grandmother."

I laugh, shaking my head. For a woman who had the shit repeatedly kicked out of her for her entire married life, she's certainly come into her own since my father died. It's like that giant filter she had clamped over her mouth while he was alive has evaporated.

"Too late now, baby. In sixteen weeks give or take, she'll be a grandmother. At least your parents are excited."

Kelly throws me an agitated look. She does not like her family. To be honest, I don't believe they're that bad. I think what Kelly really objects to is the fact that they don't have a lot of money. White trash, is how she refers to them, which I don't agree with. Her father is a working-class guy who's done what he can for his family. Kelly's mother is a bit…overbearing, but very sweet. I like them a lot actually.

Night and day from my family and I mean that in the best possible way.

"My mom wants to throw me a baby shower."

I smile at that. Kelly doesn't have a lot of girlfriends, and the few that she does have, haven't offered to do that for her. "That's great. When was she thinking?"

"I don't know," she huffs, folding her hands over her belly. "Maybe the end of February. A little closer to the due date."

"Sounds–" *Bang!* Out of nowhere, we're hit from behind with a loud grating crunch.

The car spins clockwise on the slippery road, my hands flying around the wheel, trying desperately to get us in control, but to no avail. My foot pressing down on the brake doesn't do anything either, it just makes the tires screech and burn. Kelly is screaming as she stares in petrified horror at something out her window. The cement barrier we're headed straight for.

My eyes fly over as I reach across her, trying to shield her from the impact. I can't get to her. My seatbelt has no give to it. "Kelly!" I yell just as we slam into the barrier.

Our airbags deploy on impact. Kelly's head bounces off the side-impact one of hers, and mine bounces off the one which comes out of the steering wheel, breaking my nose instantly with a sickening crunch. My knee slams into something with so much force that I holler out at the pain.

Blood squirts out of my nose and down my face, some of it pooling in the back of my throat, making me cough and choke. It takes me half a second to come back around and when I do, I look over at Kelly who is staring down at her hands which are covered in blood.

"Baby?" She turns to me. "Are you okay?"

Her eyes are wide and her forehead is bleeding a lot and she just stares at me, like she has no idea what just happened or if she's okay.

"Kelly," I command. "Talk to me."

She blinks and nods. "Yes, I'm okay. I'm okay."

"Does your belly hurt? Can you feel the baby at all?" I ask, unbuckling my seatbelt and trying to move over to her. The entire passenger side of the car is crushed in, pressing against her.

"I don't know, Finn," she begins to sob. "I don't know."

"Okay, baby. Calm down." Her eyes close and they don't open again. "Kelly, look at me, baby. Keep your eyes open and on me. Stay awake."

She opens her eyes and focuses on me.

Someone is knocking outside my window, they're yelling, asking if we're okay. I tell him we need an ambulance. He tells me they've already been called and are on their way.

I don't think I've ever been so grateful for anything in my life.

"Kelly, I'm going to reach between your legs."

"What?" she shrieks. "Why?"

"I'm just going to check and make sure everything is okay."

"No, Finn. Just wait for the ambulance."

I nod at her. She's panicked. I'm panicked. I've never been this terrified before in my entire life. "Kelly, do you feel like you're bleeding down there?"

"No. And I feel the baby, I think."

"Does anything else hurt?"

"I'm okay, Finn."

I breathe out a sigh of relief at that and another one when I hear sirens approaching. Ambulances and fire trucks descend on us. They're shouting about how they can't get Kelly's car door open as they refuse to let her come out my side because they're afraid of a head and spinal cord injury. So instead they use the jaws of life to get Kelly out. They won't let me stay in the car with her either despite my yelling and fighting.

As I watch my pregnant wife being carefully extracted from our crushed car, I let the paramedic work on my nose and check out my knee. I don't give a shit. All I care about is Kelly and our baby. I cannot stand sitting here while they're in there and I can't do anything to help them.

The fire department finally manages to extract Kelly from the car. She's crying. Sobbing. Fuck, I can't take this. My heart is beating out of my chest. Adrenaline is coursing through my veins. I need to get to my family. They're all I've got. Racing out of the ambulance I was sitting in, I reach her side. I take her hand and stare into her eyes as the paramedics strap her to a backboard and put a brace on her neck, before bringing her to the ambulance.

I follow her into the rig and the guy has the audacity to throw me a look. "I'm going with her," I tell him and the look in my eyes has him keeping his mouth shut about it. *Don't even try it*, that looks says.

"Turn her on her left side," I yell at the paramedic as we race down the highway towards the hospital. Kelly's blood pressure is not good, but it improves when he does that. "She's pregnant," I snap at him like that's not blatantly obvious. "When she's on her back she's putting pressure on her vena cava."

He just nods at me and continues to take care of Kelly. Putting pressure on her head laceration and making sure her vitals are stable and that she's getting enough fluids and oxygen. I want to be the one taking care of Kelly. I want to hear my baby's heartbeat and know they're okay in there.

But I can't do any of that.

All I can do is hold her hand as we ride to the hospital with our shared fear swimming between us. "It's going to be okay," I tell her even though I don't know if it is, because the paramedics won't check the baby. Ten minutes later they're wheeling Kelly in. The baby's heartbeat is ninety-eight. Not great, but at least there is one.

"Kelly, do you feel any pressure? Any contractions?" the doctor asks.

"No. I don't think so. My back and side hurt as does my shoulder and head. But my stomach feels okay." Kelly looks to me, like she's asking more than telling and I nod at her. I kiss her head. I reassure her that everything she's doing and saying is the right thing. But my hands tremble against hers and I know she can feel it.

"Good," the doctor says with a relieved smile. "Okay, we're going to get an ultrasound. The baby's heartrate is a little low, but we're going to monitor that very closely. Do you know how far along you are?"

"Twenty-four weeks today."

The doctor nods, that relieved smile slipping. It's obvious she wishes Kelly had said that she was farther along. I'm wishing that too.

"Finn?" Kelly sniffles, doing everything she can to hold herself together, despite the tears rolling down her cheeks. I don't know what to do. How to fix this. She looks to me when I don't respond. "Finn?"

"I'm here, baby. It's going to be okay." That's my mantra. That's what I keep telling her, because if I tell her that enough, it will come true. It has to.

Kelly nods. Kelly believes me even if I'm not sure I'm telling her the truth yet. The alternative is too much to fathom.

Just as they're wheeling us to ultrasound, Kelly lets out a loud scream, arches her back and then there is a gush of blood. All hell breaks loose.

The doctor is between her legs and they're running with Kelly on the gurney who is still screaming, down the hall and into the elevator and down another hall until we're in the OR.

"You need to gown up," one of the nurses says to me and she pulls me away while I watch them place a mesh cap over Kelly's hair and an oxygen mask over her face and cover her with blue sterile drapes. "Here," she says, throwing me a bunch of things which I catch reflexively and put on.

Dread is pooling deep in my gut, twisting and stabbing at me like a thousand knives. I'm shaking and my heart is pounding and I can't stand this lack of control. I can't stand that Kelly is on that table and my very premature baby is about to be born. I can't stop this. I can't make them okay.

"Dear God," I pray aloud. "Let them be okay." And then I walk back into that OR and sit up by Kelly's head, resting my face next to hers as we cry together. I tell her I love her. That's all I know for sure in this moment. We cry until the nurse tells us that our son has been born. We cry while I stand up and watch as the neonatologists work furiously on my son to get him intubated and his heart to beat.

Because he's not breathing on his own and his heart isn't beating.

My hand grips Kelly's, who cannot see him. "He's tiny," I say, more to myself than to her, but she hears me and she sobs. My words are hurting her, so I keeping my mouth shut. His skin doesn't look real yet. And his eyes are fused shut. And he's blue. And he still isn't breathing or beating.

But he's without a doubt the most beautiful thing I've ever seen and even though I haven't touched him, I love him more than my own life.

"Is he alive?" I manage, but they ignore me. They're pumping him full of drugs through a catheter in his umbilical cord and they're breathing for him and pushing on his chest and I don't know what to do. I turn back to Kelly, but her eyes are closed as she helplessly weeps, while the doctors close her up.

I had no idea love could hurt this much. Could be this terrifying.

After another three minutes, they stop working because there is nothing more they can do for my son. I can't breathe. Everything inside of me hurts. The pain is unreal. Like nothing I've ever experienced before and I am no stranger to pain. I collapse back onto the stool, my legs no longer capable of supporting my weight. Holding Kelly's head in my arms, we cry out our anguish, wishing we could die with him.

Chapter Seventeen

GIA

"That's the weirdest shit I've ever heard," Chloe says to me. She came over for breakfast which I was not in the mood for, but Chloe doesn't take kindly to the word no. So now we're sitting in the diner on the corner from my apartment, waiting on eggs which I have no interest in eating. "I mean, when I told him Liam was hot for your bod, he went all caveman and stormed off after you. I thought for sure when I saw you leave with him, I'd have to drag you out of his bed for this breakfast."

"Nope. And I think at this point, I can safely say that will never happen with him."

"There has to be something really wrong with him, right? Like crazy STDs or erectile dysfunction or something else."

"You know it's funny you say that. I recall thinking something very similar after one of the times he rejected me."

"Maybe he's gay?"

I shake my head. "I don't think so, but you never know."

Our massive plates arrive and I woefully stare down at the omelet which could easily feed a small country and sigh. "You have to eat. You can't let that dick take your appetite. Then it's like he wins."

"Fight the power."

"Exactly," she says through a mouthful of food. I take a bite of my eggs because I don't want to listen to her bitch at me the entire time about my not eating.

I didn't tell Chloe everything. Just most of everything. She's my best friend and I love her, but she also has a big mouth. So I told her Finn is not interested in me. That he took me out for coffee and told me nothing was ever going to happen between us.

All of that is true.

I just left out the part where he talked about how he wanted more with me and how attracted he was to me and how the thought of me with another man makes him insane.

"Did you tell him it was your birthday?"

"No," I laugh. "Why would I have done that?"

"I don't know. It just doesn't make sense to me. It wouldn't bother me so much if he wasn't fucking hot."

"Then you go for him," I say and then scowl. Damn, I can't even help that.

Chloe laughs, clearly reading my reaction. "I tried. I asked him to buy me a free drink, which everyone knows is code for let's hook up. I could have told him I'm a championship blowjob giver and I'm willing to do anal on the first date. It wouldn't have mattered. He wasn't interested in me at all. He didn't even look twice in my direction until I mentioned your name."

"Is that true? I mean, about the blowjobs and anal?" Chloe sighs at me, evidently not amused. "What?"

"Nothing."

I point my fork at her. "Just tell me."

"You just haven't liked a guy in a while."

I swallow down the piece of potato which is threatening to choke me. "I date."

"I know you date. Hell, you date more than me. That's not what I'm saying here. I just want you to be happy is all."

"God, Chloe," I throw my head back in frustration. "You sound like my mother. I am happy. I don't need a man to give me that."

"I know," she shrugs, playing with an impaled potato, running it in a pattern through her ketchup. "I'm just wondering if it has to do with Aiden."

"No," I say emphatically. "It doesn't. I'm well past that now."

Aiden was my boyfriend of about a year, but in my second month of graduate school, he got a job opportunity in San Francisco. He half-heartedly asked if I wanted to move with him and when I said I couldn't because I had just started school, that was it. It hurt. I shed a lot of tears over that one. But that was years ago and now I don't even think about him.

"Okay then. I'm done talking about this."

"Freaking finally," I laugh. "What time does your shift start?"

"Ten, so eat up because I want to buy you a cupcake at that really amazing bakery which we always walk by but never go in to because we're afraid just stepping inside will make us fat."

"Because it will," I tell her. "I don't think you can go in there without sampling one of everything."

Chloe shrugs, her blonde hair on top of her head in a very high ponytail that only she can get away with. "Fine by me. It's your birthday and calories don't count on your birthday."

"You said that to me when we were in grad school and I was stress eating."

She points a finger at me. "I stand by that philosophy. Our brains were burning like a million calories with all the crap we were trying to learn."

"Probably true. Eat up and let's go. I suddenly have the desire to consume a lot of sugar and then go shopping."

I leave Chloe a block from the hospital with a hug. I could walk her to work, but I don't. I know it's unlikely I'd bump into Finn. He and I go weeks without seeing each other, but I'm still ruminating over everything that happened last night.

I'm raw with it.

I was surprised that his words affected me the way they did.

Maybe it's because I agreed with him. Every time I'm near him, I want more of him. I'm insanely attracted to him and I know for a fact we wouldn't be a sort-of, non-exclusive thing because any time

I'm with him or I think about him, I get that happy-bubbly sensation in my stomach.

Even when he's being an asshole and I'm mad at him.

And I'm only mad at him because I like him. Otherwise I wouldn't care about the crap he pulls with me. He's held residence in me in one way or another for such a long time now, I don't remember what it feels like to think about another man. I don't even know how to turn it off.

But I do my best as I spend my afternoon shopping for clothes.

Every year on my birthday, my father would take me out shopping for whatever I wanted, within reason of course. The year I asked for a pony, he said no. And the year I asked for a Cadillac Escalade so that I could drive all my friends around, he said no to that too. But everything else he got me.

Being an only child with a wealthy doting father, pretty much gets you that.

My parents tried to have other children after me, but after a few miscarriages, gave up. When I went off to college, they traveled a lot and did that for a while, which I thought was awesome. But my mom didn't continue it after my father died. Instead she left Boston and moved to Westchester to be closer to me. She's taking me out for dinner tonight, but I know she's going to have a tough time because my dad won't be with us.

I end up getting a very pretty cream-colored sweater dress, tan suede booties and a new pair of jeans.

Just as I open the door to my building, my phone rings. I have to juggle the bags in my hands in order to reach into my purse to retrieve it, but once I do, I groan because the bags with the shoes in it just fell out of my hand.

"Hi, mom," I answer, the phone tucked between my shoulder and ear as I pick up my bag and unlock the front door. Okay, maybe a doorman would be helpful in a situation like this.

"What time are you coming?" she asks. I don't know why she does this every time we make plans. We typically set up a time that I'm coming and I'm pretty good at being on time.

"Six-ten," I say as I tuck my keys into my pocket and readjust the shopping bags so I can hold the phone with one of my hands. "I just got home so I'm going to shower and then I'm grabbing the train from Grand Central."

"Okay, because I need to talk to you about something so I don't want you to be late."

The way she says this has my gut twisting and me leaning back against the elevator wall. "What?"

"We'll talk about it when you get here."

I shake my head. "You can't say something like that to me over the phone and then not tell me."

My mother sighs into the phone and then goes silent. The elevator doors open and I step out onto my floor. "I met someone," she says quietly. "A man." Yeah, I got that part. I didn't need her to say it aloud. "I'd like you to meet him tonight. I invited him to dinner with us."

She invited a strange man I've never met before to my *birthday* dinner? Seriously? "Um…" I trail off because I can't think of anything to say to that. On the one hand, I should be happy for my mother that she met someone and isn't alone. And on some level, I am. But why did she have to pick today of all days to tell me about it?

"His name is George Santiago and he's–" My mother continues to tell me about George Santiago but I stopped listening the moment I turned the corner for my apartment. Because Finn is standing in front of my door, his head positioned down and his back is to me, but there is no mistaking it's him. He's not knocking on my door and it doesn't even appear like he's waiting for me to open.

He seems like he's caught in a moment of indecision and I have to wonder how long he's been standing there like that because someone had to let him into the building and it sure as hell wasn't me.

"Mom," I interject and at the sound of my voice, Finn turns around with wide eyes which say he did not want me to catch him here. "I have to go. I'll see you when I get there." I disconnect the call and walk down the hall toward him, pulling my keys out of my pocket.

He silently watches me approach and part of me is tempted to go into my apartment and slam the door on him. Maybe I would if it weren't for the expression on his face and the wrapped package in his hands. He looks really freaking good and I wish he looked like shit because it would be so much easier not to feel all of the things I'm feeling right now. He's wearing a blue sweater which hugs his muscular chest, accentuating the bright blue of his eyes. His chestnut hair is styled in a way which draws it off his face, making him appear almost boyish.

"What are you doing here?" Giving him my back, I unlock my door, open it so I can set my bags down inside and close it again before I turn back to face him. I'm not inviting him in. I'm not.

"I...uh," and then he chuckles, running a hand through his hair and ruining that boyish style I was just enjoying. "I've been standing here for far too long, debating if I should leave this here or not."

I peer down at the wrapped package in his hand. The wrapping is lavender, with a deep purple bow tied into a perfect knot. "What have you come up with?"

He smiles and I decide I hate his smile. It's misleading. It's the sort of smile which says you're all I think about and a lot of those thoughts are deliciously dirty. It's the sort of smile you can't help but feel in the pit of your stomach as well as a few other key places. I want to tell him his demeanor is false advertising, but I keep my mouth shut and focus my attention on the package in his hand because it's easier to stare at than that smile.

"Well, since you caught me, I don't think I can leave without giving this to you."

I shrug. "You could, but it would be a real dick move." I manage to raise my eyes to his. "How did you know?"

"I looked you up," he says and those words shouldn't have the impact on me that they do. "Shortly after we met. You were on my mind one night and I went online and found your Facebook profile. It had your birthday on there," he adds like I didn't know.

He looked me up. I was on his mind. God, I don't know what to do with that. How to feel when he makes admissions like that.

"So can I have it? My present?"

Finn considers the box in his hands and then slowly extends it out to me. "Happy birthday, Gia."

"Thank you, Finn." Damn, this makes me so sad and so happy.

He leans forward and plants the sweetest of kisses on my cheek and then starts to walk off.

"Wait," I call out and he freezes. "I have your jacket."

He turns around, patiently waiting while I frantically open my door, put the pretty purple box with the perfect purple ribbon on the floor. Opening my coat closet, I yank his jacket off the hanger.

"I was going to have it dry-cleaned and leave it at the hospital for you."

He shakes his head, taking the lumped up material from my hands. "This is fine. Thanks."

Finn turns away from me, but I don't miss it when he brings the collar of the jacket up to his nose, inhaling a deep breath. He's checking to see if it smells like me and suddenly I'm so glad I didn't get it dry-cleaned. I wish I had slept in it last night, so I could be sure it does.

"Wait," I call out again, because I cannot stand this. Not another fucking second. None of this makes sense. None of it. And I'm just...well, I'm done with the drama. He twists back around, albeit reluctantly. *Come on, Finn. Give me an inch.* "Would you do a favor for me if I asked you?"

He measures me for a moment, weighs his response, and then smirks. "That depends on the favor."

I try not to smile. I really freaking do. But the way he says that?

"Today's my birthday. You already know that since you just said it," I laugh. Shit, why am I so freaking nervous right now? "Anyway," I continue with a mental headshake. "I'm supposed to go to my mom's house in Westchester for dinner in a couple of hours and she just told me—like right now—she has a new boyfriend. She called him her man friend, Finn." I shake my head, letting him know how serious this situation is. "I cannot go and meet my mother's new *man friend* on my birthday without backup."

"Gia," he sighs, his hands going to his hips.

"Please, Finn." I hold up my hands in supplication. Clearly, I'm not above begging right now. I don't even know why I asked him other than I just...I want more time with him. I need to figure this man out or he'll always be a question mark. Something left unanswered. "Please don't make me face this alone."

"I'm the doctor who admitted your father. She's going to see me and think of that. It'll be beyond awkward."

Yeah, I thought of that. But I don't really care. Maybe that makes me a bitch, but screw it, it's my birthday. "The whole night is going to be awkward, why not add more to it? Come on, Finn. Pretty please. With a cherry on top?"

He chuckles lightly, shifting his weight and glancing down at the floor. He sighs again, but I think it's the resigned sort because I can see him grinning despite his best efforts. "Okay," he says on a long drawn-out breath. "I'll go with you. I can't seem to say no to you." Another sigh but that one is for himself because he's also giving me an indulgent smile. I'm so happy, I could squeal like a teenage fangirl. "Let me go home and shower. I'll meet you at Grand Central."

"Ah, you're a lifesaver." Then I laugh out, throwing him a wink. "Literally."

He shakes his head at me, but he's amused. I can tell. I amuse him and he can't say no to me. I can be such a child sometimes, but a win is a win. "I'm taking the 5:10 train. Thank you. Really."

"I'll see you soon."

He walks off with heavy, possibly aggravated steps, leaving me standing in the hallway with a big beaming smile on my face. But then I think about my present and my smile slips.

The second he rounds the corner, I scurry inside my apartment, shut the door and sink down to the floor. I drag his present to me and stare at it for far too long. I have too many things swirling through me right now and this present might just ruin me for good.

But I can't not open it, so I pull off that perfect ribbon and take off that beautiful paper, making sure I don't so much as tear a corner of it. And then I open the box.

A bubble of a laugh climbs its way up, but gets lodged in the back of my throat where a significant lump now resides. Inside the box is a lavender rose, the same shade as the paper, a container of expensive hot chocolate and a purple mug which says, *If you speak to me before I finish this then I'll stab you,* and it has a picture of a syringe next to the writing. But the best part, are the two tickets to a Jets versus Patriot's football game in November.

Everything in here he had to have purchased today because he wouldn't have known about any of this before last night.

I don't bother to wipe away the tears falling down my cheeks as I open the card.

My one regret in life is that I am not someone else. Happy birthday, Gia.

He quoted Woody Allen. I told him that Woody Allen was my favorite writer/director in passing, months ago. And he remembered. I set everything back into the box and just stare at it, trying to figure out how to make myself not fall in love with Finnigan Banner.

Chapter Eighteen

GIA

I'm late. By the time I get to Grand Central, our train is about to leave the station and Finn isn't all that pleased with me. I couldn't help it. It took me forever to pry myself up and off my floor. Even longer to stop my tears.

I think I might be falling for Finn Banner.

It's a cruel reality to face. Especially since I know he doesn't feel the same way back.

Finn doesn't comment beyond his bruising scowl. And he spends the entire train ride up to Westchester, on his phone silently ignoring me. No sideways glances. No surreptitious looks. Nothing. I might as well be a stranger and I'm starting to think his comment about things being awkward was dead on. I don't even have the courage to thank him for the present because I might get choked up again and that's the last thing I want.

But the moment we pull into the station and the train lurches to a stop, he stands up and takes my hand. Like he knows I need the comfort. The support. I do. I didn't realize how much the idea of my mother having a man friend would bother me. Or maybe it's just the day she's presenting him on? I don't know. It just sucks.

We step off the train and my eyes don't have to go far to find my mother standing next to her Mercedes SUV. And next to her is…George Santiago. What the fuck? What happened to talking about this? I assumed she was going to tell me more about him, we'd talk, and then he'd meet us at the restaurant. But at the goddamn train?

"I know you're…something with me," I say to Finn, staring straight at my mother. "But thank you for coming with me. In this moment, you really are my hero."

Finn squeezes my hand. "I'm definitely something with you, Gia. But I'm happy to be here for you if that's what you need. Hero or not."

If I had it in me, his comment would make me smile. But I don't. "Let's get this over with."

We step off the platform and head to the parking lot. "Gia," my mother coos. "Happy birthday, baby girl." Her arms are outstretched like she hasn't seen me in a decade. She gives me a two-cheek kiss—which she's never done before—and then stops when she looks past my shoulder and spots Finn. "Dr. Banner?"

My mother can't quite figure this out. But really, was I supposed to tell her about him before now? No. No I wasn't. There was nothing to tell. And there probably still isn't. Other than the fact he's physically present with me. "Mrs. Bianchi," he says, extending his hand to shake hers. "It's a pleasure to see you again. Especially under better circumstances."

My mother shakes his hand, but her eyes are on me with a look which questions my basic sanity. "He works with me, Mom. At the hospital. He's my…" Crap balls. What are we? Nothing. How sad is that? I can't even call him my friend. I probably should have thought this through more than I did.

"Finn," Finn supplies. *Was he just saying his name or was he finishing my sentence?*

My mother's eyes widen and mine do as well and we both stare over at him. Then she smiles the smile of an elated mother who thinks he's my new special someone. I frown because he not. He freaking sent me home in a cab last night because he didn't want to be my Finn so that makes him a liar. Not a liar to me, I suspect, but

131

a liar to my mother. Or maybe I'm reading way more into this than I should.

My mother finally manages to blink, though I still haven't found that semi-automatic response yet. "Finn," she asserts in that motherly intonation. "I'm so pleased you could join us." She takes a step back and then reaches out for George who steps forward and takes her hand. Then he kisses it tenderly. In front of me. Finn is still holding my hand I realize, because he gives me another squeeze. "This is my man friend, George."

I cannot believe she actually used the term man friend in front of him. I thought that was like a joke or a placeholder or something. Not actual descriptive words.

George envelopes me in a hug. He doesn't even give me the option for anything less. He's average height with a small round pot belly, and a full head of thick silver hair. He smells like he bathed in cologne. Expensive cologne at that. He's wearing a bright-blue polo shirt, which seems to correlate with Finn's eyes more than George's dark furry arms and brown pants. Who wears brown pants? They're not even khaki.

"Happy birthday, Gia" he booms and holy Jesus is his voice loud. Like a sports-announcer-with-a-megaphone loud. I wince. It's not a voluntary reaction. It just happens. "It's so great to meet you," he yells. And I'm deaf. Like officially. My ears are ringing. Full-on tinnitus. But he has a warm smile and soft brown eyes and my mother is beaming.

Shit. I can't hate him.

Finn releases my hand and takes my arm, pulling me back and tucking me into his side. I have no idea who this Finn is. All of this is very confusing. On so many levels in so many ways.

"Your mother talks about you constantly." More yelling before he turns on Finn. "Finn, is it?" He reaches out his hand and they shake. "These women are a handful," he laughs loudly, patting his belly. I'm not laughing. But my mother is. No, she's *giggling*. "Glad I'm not the only male presence tonight."

What the hell does that even mean?

I look to Finn. He's smirking. He's trying not to laugh, which means he's absolutely no help.

"Let's get to the restaurant. I thought we would go to that steak place you like," My mother says, her attention focused on me, but she can't possibly be talking to me. I don't eat steak. I've never eaten steak. Hamburgers are the extent of my red meat. She's my mother, which means she knows this already.

So there is no steak place which I like.

My mother is all girlish flutters as George kisses her hand again. I have no words. I don't know what to say. I just watch as he helps her into the passenger side of her car and shuts the door behind her. He throws us a wink as he moves around and gets into the driver's side.

"Is it too late to make a run for it?" I whisper. I still haven't moved. I'm standing, tucked into Finn's side as my mother and her new man friend sit patiently in her car waiting on us. It's like I've stepped into an episode of *The Twilight Zone*. Nothing is as it's supposed to be.

"Are you kidding me?" Finn chuckles, dragging me over to the side of the car. "We're going to that steak place you like."

"I hate steak, Finn."

"Hmmm…well, I have nothing for that. Let's just get through this meal and I'll buy you a drink or a cupcake or something after."

My eyes move on their own volition. My feet stop moving without conscious thought. I just stare up at him. I don't know if I should thank him again or ask him what he was intimating at when he finished my sentence earlier. I don't know if I should kiss him or slap him. I just don't know with him.

He stares back at me and for a moment, that's all there is.

I'm still trapped in my indecision as he blinks, opens my car door for me and helps me slip inside.

The heat is blasting to an audible degree. Finn takes my hand quietly in the dark, but his attention is trained out the window at the passing landscape. Not even five minutes later, we pull up in front of a chain steak restaurant and a valet eagerly rushes over to open our doors. Finn steps out, waits for me and extends his hand to take as he helps me out of the car.

"Thank you for my present," I say to him as we follow my mom and George inside the restaurant. "I love it." Understatement of the century.

"It was my pleasure, Gia."

That's the last thing Finn says to me the entire night we're with my mom and George. He doesn't look over at me. He barely acknowledges me. Except for his hand. His hand absolutely acknowledges me.

Finn finishes his steak, sets down his fork and knife. Wipes his mouth with his napkin before setting that down too. He's listening to something George is saying–because George hasn't stopped talking– and suddenly, I feel his hand on the cushioned booth between us, his thumb absently brushing my leg.

Then, ever so slowly, with obvious methodical intention, his hand skims across my exposed thigh, pushes my crossed leg away so that my legs are side by side and partially open. And then his hand engulfs my right thigh. My dress is relatively short. Not obscene by any means, but well, I knew Finn was coming to dinner. So I wore something a little on the sexy side. Now he's taking full advantage of the length I chose.

But that's it. His hand doesn't move. It just rests comfortably and much like everything else with him, I can't figure out what he's doing. Except for that thumb. Jesus shit. That thumb is gliding up and down and if I weren't chatting with my mother, I'd moan. Loud. It's as exciting as it is frustrating. It's also consuming. It becomes all I can think about while George tells us the details of a cruise he wants to take my mother on.

It continues like this until George asks, "So what's the dating scene like out there for you kids these days?" The sip of wine I was in the midst of swallowing gets sucked into my trachea instead of my esophagus as I breath in and choke. Finn pats my back twice before moving his hand back to my leg as I gulp down water, sputtering into it as I go. "Your mother mentioned that Colin boy you had been dating," he continues, ignoring the way I'm gasping for air, "But I see you got rid of him." He wink–actually freaking winks–at Finn.

"Yes," my mother chimes in with a big nod of her head. "I have to admit, I wasn't disappointed you ended it with him. He sounded like a real…" she pauses, tilting her head at me, "What was the term Chloe had for him?" I close my eyes, willing this night to be over. "Douchetard? That was it, right?" Both my mother and George start cackling rather loudly at my expense and I can feel my cheeks turning an exuberant shade of red.

I don't think I expected the word *douchetard* to come out of my mother's mouth. It would be funny if this situation wasn't so fucked up.

Finn's hand squeezes my upper thigh, his goddamn thumb is practically brushing the thin fabric covering my pussy, but his expression is placid. He's not giving anything away.

"Mom, can we not go there?"

"Oh right," she laughs again, nudging George in his side. "Not in front of Finn." She winks at me like we have an inside joke going. "I get it." And I want to die.

"Can we get the check?" I might be begging.

"No dessert? It's your birthday." My mother looks hurt and now I feel bad.

"You have to get dessert, Gia," George says, taking my mother's hand. "Your mother wants them to sing to you."

"Yes, Gia," Finn concurs with that satisfied smirk as he continues to torture me with his thumb. "They have to sing to you."

Asshole!

And that's what happens. My mother orders Tiramisu because it's my favorite dessert and even though she brought me to a steak place, my mother loves me and knows what I like. After they sing to me and George graciously picks up the bill, despite Finn's objections, they take us to the train station just in time to catch the 9:10 back to Grand Central.

Finn still hasn't said one word to me since that one time at dessert and even though he had his hand on my thigh for the better

135

part of an hour, I can't help but feel like I made an epic mistake bringing him with me.

In fact, it's making me morose. I asked him to come in a moment of weakness without thinking it through. Finn doesn't want to date me. Finn doesn't want my mother thinking that we're dating. He was trying to be a nice guy by saying yes to my begging. That's all this was.

We get on the train and it's pretty much empty. We have the whole car to ourselves save for a few college-aged kids at the front who are laughing as they pass their phones back and forth. I sit down heavily, crossing my arms and legs, my eyes immediately going to the window. To my surprise, Finn sits next to me.

"I'm sorry," I say to the glass, though I'm actually watching his reflection in it. "I shouldn't have asked you along. I wasn't thinking and I'm sorry you got sucked into all that."

He doesn't say anything for so long that I eventually close my eyes so that I won't obsess over him in the glass. But then I feel his hand on my thigh again, where it meets the edge of my long coat. My head finally falls against his shoulder and that's how we spend the hour or so it takes to get back into the city.

Chapter Nineteen

GIA

Finn orders an Uber once we reach the station and by the time we exit one of my favorite buildings in New York, it's waiting on us. I expected him to say goodnight here. To put me in the car the way he did last night and send me home. But he doesn't. He gets in with me and my heart starts to beat just a bit faster.

The sweet tortuous tension is building between us, egged on by our silence as we fly up the dark city streets. The car stops at a stoplight, two blocks from my building. I don't want this night to end with him. At least not in this way. Where I feel like everything I did was wrong. I close my eyes and suck in a deep breath.

"I'm glad I came with you," he says so quietly that his words are almost lost against the soft purr of the car engine. I open my eyes and pivot my face up to his. He's staring straight ahead. Seemingly at nothing. He's lost in something. "It's been so long since I've seen what a normal loving family looks like. I realize this wasn't your ideal. I know you miss your father and wish it had been him there instead of George." He blinks once and then angles his face to mine. "But I'm glad I came with you," he says again and I can't help but smile.

His eyes drop to my lips and that familiar conflicted demeanor crosses his features.

I want him to kiss me so bad that my lips are practically vibrating with the thought. My hand reaches up, gliding along the crest of his stubbled jaw, up his cheek and into his soft thick hair. His eyes shut briefly before they reopen, dark and filled with heat. "Gia," he breathes. "I can't do this with you. Despite how badly I want to. It's why I sent you home last night. I'm just not that guy anymore. I don't want intimacy. I don't want love or a relationship. And that's what you deserve."

I shake my head. It is what I deserve. It's also what I want. I know Finn has something dark about him. Something which makes him scary and damaged. I don't know what it is, but I've been at this game long enough to recognize the signs.

But I still want him. Even if just for tonight.

Maybe that's naïve of me. Maybe that's beyond pathetic and juvenile. And maybe I'm hoping that after one night he'll realize that more with me isn't so bad. But even if he doesn't…

The car glides through the now green light and less than a minute later, we're pulling up in front of my building. I can't say anything to him. My pride is telling me to shut up. It's telling me I shouldn't have to throw myself at a man for them to want me. It's telling me Finn only leads to heartbreak.

But when he steps out of the car behind me, I don't object. I don't tell him no. But I don't allow myself to hope either. I assume he's just making sure I get into my building safely, but as I twist the key in the lock, the Uber pulls away and that hope I was just tamping down turns into a million excited bubbles. Finn tugs open the door once I get it unlocked. He lets me enter first and then he's directly behind me, his hand wrapped around my waist as he guides me to the elevator.

"I'm just walking you up," he explains, but his voice his thick with want and his hand is pressing me against him in a way which lets me know those words were meant more for him than for me. I don't say anything. There really is nothing I can say back. Stepping onto the elevator, he draws me to the very back, leaning me against him, my back to his chest. His fingers glide across my neck, moving my hair away from my shoulder and then his face drops into it with a deep sigh like there is no other place in the world he'd rather be. My eyes close and I take in a deep silent breath.

The elevator chimes and the doors open. This is going to quickly. I'd give anything to have the power to alter time right now. To make it slow instead of fast. To turn these seconds with him into hours. He releases me, taking my hand and leading me down the hall to my door. My heart is pounding. My breaths short and ragged.

Finn removes the keys from my hand, unlocking my door and opening it. Then he pauses, my keys encapsulated in his large hand. I stare at it for a moment, trying to force my eyes up to his. It's not easy feat. I've been rejected by him a time or two already. Indecision. That's what the look on his face says.

He wants to leave, but he can't make himself do it.

He wants to stay, but he knows he shouldn't.

Finn is a very black and white person, I realize. He exists within the realm of all or nothing. A lot of doctors are like that. They like their facts. They have an empiric way of viewing the world. Clinical. But ironically, he isn't there with me. He's very much in-between. Stuck there, might be a better way to phrase it.

Because it's not at all where he wants to be.

And as is common with him, I find myself growing tired.

So I move to step away from his lingering form, just about ready to go inside and shut the door in his face when he latches onto me. I don't even see him coming, but suddenly I'm glued up against the wall of my hallway and his large warm body is pressed to mine. His hands cup my face, tilting it until I'm forced to meet his steely gaze.

"This is wrong," he says and I can't stand that he led with that. "It is. I want you like I've never wanted another woman, but it won't go beyond tonight. It won't," he says fervently and I despise that he's so adamant with this and yet, I respect his honesty. I appreciate he cares enough about me to make sure I know exactly where we stand and exactly what this is. He doesn't want me to get hurt with unfulfilled emotional expectations and the irony of that is not lost on me.

"And even though I'll hate myself tomorrow for the position I'm putting you in tonight, I can't leave unless you tell me to." His head dips and his nose brushes mine once, twice, before his forehead drops to mine and he holds my gaze captive from mere inches away. "Tell me to go," he pleads.

"I can't," I admit, hating myself a little for it. "I want this too. Even if just for tonight."

He examines me closely. Trying to determine if I'm full of shit or not. I am and I'm also not, but I doubt he can tell.

His eyes close and a shuttered breath passes his lips. And then his mouth finds mine in what is easily the most desperate and passionate kiss I've ever experienced. I detonate. A thousand grenades going off simultaneously. Stars dance behind my eyes and I realize it's because I'm not taking in enough oxygen. I'm trying so hard to capture every one of his sounds, every pant he lets go of.

A loud rush of air sucks its way into my chest and he pushes me deeper into the wall. I hold onto him. Beyond unsteady. My knees weak. Our lips move against each other, our tongues dancing sensually, fighting for control. He wins. I want him to win. One hand is threaded through my hair, holding and adjusting my head however he wants it. The other is opening the buttons of my coat, desperate to get at what's beneath.

My neighbor's door clicks, making the telltale sounds of locks unlatching before it begins to open. Finn jars back abruptly. He smiles down on me and I feel that smile in the darkest recesses of my heart. The parts I'm trying to turn off in order to allow this. "Inside?"

I nod. I wish he would stop trying to give me the out my brain is begging me to take. The rationalizations are much easier to listen to when he stops questioning my motives.

He opens my door, allows me to pass him, shuts and locks it behind him. His eyes flitter around my apartment, going from space to space before they land on the purple present he gave me earlier. They change then. Growing more of one thing and less of something else. And when they find me again, his smile shows me everything. Everything he keeps hidden. It only lasts for a moment. The briefest of seconds. He quickly tucks it away, but I saw it and that's what I cling to as I step into him, reaching up on the tiptoes of my high heels and kiss him with everything I've got.

If it is really only one night, I want everything. And if I can change his mind on that position, well, I'm going to give it my all. Pathetic or not. Right or wrong. None of those things matter in this moment. That's the thing about lust. It blinds. It covers up rational thought with its own brand of logic. It obscures true feelings until they turn into something else entirely.

Finn growls into my mouth, sighs out my name and then rips my coat from my body. He slams it to the floor, followed by his own. He lifts me, wrapping my legs around his waist, hiking the hem of my short dress up until our bodies are aligned at the most perfect point. I moan, throwing my head back and he takes full advantage of my exposed neck, kissing, nipping and sucking as he goes.

"Gia," he breathes against me, making my body erupt in chills as a shiver runs down my spine. He walks us across the dark expanse of my apartment until he reaches the door to my bedroom. But he doesn't go in. He pauses here and just…stares at me.

And then something hits me. It hits me so hard and with so much force that I actually feel my eyes welling up and my chest clenching with a tightness which has me gasping for air.

I can't do this.

Finn told me point blank that he doesn't want intimacy. He doesn't want a relationship.

He doesn't want love.

And I think I might be falling for him.

If I sleep with him, where will that leave me?

"I can't do this," I utter before I chicken out and give into something that has the potential to ruin me. Finn nods like he knew it all along. Like he actually agrees with me. I don't think he can do it either and for some reason, that makes me feel a little better. It makes me feel like maybe I'm not the only one hurting here.

"I'm so sorry," he says with so much pain in his voice that some of that wetness which had been pooling in my eyes leaks out. "It's not you, Gia. It's not. This is all on me."

"I know," I say because I do. I know it's not me. I know it's him. He kisses me on the lips again, this time it's slow and sweet and filled with so much sorrow it makes me want to wrap my arms around him and hold him close.

So I do. But I lower my body to the ground, tug the skirt of my dress back down my thighs and then I hug him. And when he's done kissing me, when the sadness begins to turn back into lust, he draws back, pressing his forehead to mine once more. His anguish in his crystalline eyes cuts me to the quick.

"My one regret in life is that I am not someone else," he says quoting Woody Allen and the card he gave me earlier tonight. "At least that's the case with you. Because if it were ever going to be someone, it would be you."

I smother the sob climbing up the back of my throat.

He presses his lips to mine once more, but this time it's a goodbye.

"See you around, Gia."

I smile, but it's not real. He knows that's it not real so I don't know why I'm faking it. He's not even bothering with pretenses. I can see his pain. Feel his heartache.

"See you around, Finn."

He releases me, turns and walks out of my apartment, shutting the door behind him. And as the door makes that clicking sound, and I know it's good and closed, I collapse to the floor. I acknowledge it was the right thing to do. So does he.

So why does it hurt so much?

Why do I feel worse instead of better? Empty instead of gratified? The answer is not something I want to contemplate too closely, so I don't. It won't solve anything to come to realizations in this moment. Epiphanies have no place here.

Tonight should have never happened.

Because now I have to find a way to get over him.

Chapter Twenty

GIA

The bar is perfectly loud and jam-packed to the nines. The walls are embellished with creepy orange lights, not-scary-at-all masks, cotton cobwebs and plastic skeletons. Halloween is not even for another two weeks, but it's the official start of the season and everything around us is illuminated in a holiday festive glow.

And the worst part about that? It reminds me of Finn because Halloween is his birthday.

"So your mom actually had this new guy there? Like, waiting to meet you and shit?" Ophelia asks me as she pours me a very safe glass of red wine. Ever since my night of drunken debauchery, Ophelia and I have become friends. I don't know if it's the bartender in her, but she likes to ask questions and she's a sensational listener. I haven't told her yet, but I think that's one of her greats in addition to concocting the perfect cocktail.

"Yeah," I say, taking a sip of my wine. "She totally ambushed me with him. There was no talk. No, how do you feel about this. She was all, Gia meet my 'man friend,' George Santiago." I put air quotes around the word. I haven't mentioned Finn came with me or anything that happened–or didn't happen–after. I'm not ready to share that yet and it's already been a week since my birthday.

Chloe lets out a derisive snort. "She actually used the term, man friend?"

"Yup," I scoff, vacillating back and forth between them. "Because that's what happens when you're over fifty. You no longer have boyfriends, you have man friends."

"Is he nice at least?"

I shrug, running my finger along the stem of my glass. "I guess so. He seemed to make her happy and that's all that really matters. He's a retired hedge funder so he's got plenty of money. They were talking about going on a cruise together over Christmas."

"Wow, that's something," Chloe says, astonished, and all I can do is nod.

"What did I miss?" Monique asks, dropping down into the seat next to me.

"Gia was just telling us about her mom's new man friend," Ophelia offers with a shrug.

"Can I have a glass of whatever she's drinking, please" Monique points to my wine. "And what the hell is a man friend?"

"What it sounds like. A boyfriend for cougars."

I glare at Chloe. "My mother is *not* a cougar."

"She's not," Monique agrees. "A cougar is a woman who wants sex with a younger man. Not someone her own age. This new man friend is her own age, right?"

"Yes, and holy hell I cannot believe I'm actually having a conversation about my mother's sex life. That's the sort of shit that puts people in therapy."

"Should I get a tattoo?" Chloe asks out of nowhere, her eyes focused on Ophelia's colorful arms.

"That depends on what you would get," I hedge.

"I don't know. I've never really thought about it."

Ophelia snickers. "Then I wouldn't have something permanently inked on your body until you do. I'll be right back, I gotta go help those people out down there."

Ophelia saunters off and the three of us watch her go for a second. "Is it weird that we have a non-medically related friend?" Chloe asks.

"No," Monique says. "I think it's healthy. All we ever talk about is women's vaginas and babies. And men. It's like we have nothing else going on in our lives."

"Because we don't. We work and we go out with men. What the hell else is there?"

Monique and I both examine Chloe as we consider this. Is that what our lives have become? Work and men. "We need a hobby," I say with a scowl.

"No time for one," Monique yawns.

"Says the girl having regular sex with the hot ED doc."

Monique smiles, her dark eyes twinkling. "Speaking of hot ED docs…" she trails off and I know what's coming next so I put up my hand, stopping her before she can go there.

"Nothing's happening and it never will."

"He told her he wasn't interested even though he clearly is," Chloe adds unhelpfully. "But they also haven't seen each other since that night and it's what, like a week now?"

My eyes train down to the bar top. I don't want to tell them about my birthday night and that has me feeling guilty for hiding it from my best friends.

Monique doesn't look surprised and I wonder if Finn confided in Mike who then confided in Monique. That thought makes me frown even deeper. I haven't mentioned the present Finn gave me either. But pretty soon, I'm going to have to secure someone to come with me to the football game. I'm holding out even though I know it's pointless, and fucking mental, to do so.

"Well," Monique says, turning to face us. "Michael says Finn hasn't had a girlfriend in years, never dates and hardly ever has sex."

"What?" That's Chloe and me together.

"Yeah," she nods with big wide eyes. "He wouldn't tell me why or anything and said he's not celibate or a monk, but I think he's—"

"Vagina phobic," Chloe once again feels the need to add her two cents in.

"The only time I've ever seen him pick up a woman to bring home, he told her—more than once I think—that it wouldn't go beyond that night," Ophelia chimes back in. "She still went home with him because, well, look at him. He's fucking gorgeous and who wouldn't want a night with that, but still." Ophelia leans over, looking directly at me with a smile. Right. Who wouldn't want a night with him? I'm drowning in irony. "You're the first woman I've seen him show interest in since I met him."

"He's not interested," I say almost out of habit.

I feel eyes and looks being thrown all around me, but I choose to focus on my wine instead. Wine doesn't completely wreck your world with provocative words, earth-shattering kisses and thoughtful presents. In fact, the only thing wine does is make you feel good. And warm.

As long as you don't have too much of it. Then it might make you sick and eventually screw up your liver. Okay, I need to stop. None of this is productive.

"No more about Finn, please. I really don't want to talk about him. Ever again."

"I'll be right back," Ophelia says again. "This whole having to work during girl talk is becoming a nuisance."

"Michael told me he loves me." Chloe and I turn in synchrony to Monique who is beaming. "He's taking me to the Bahamas in February. I think he might propose to me then."

"You're not even living together."

She shakes her head with a smile. "No. But in two weeks, we will be. He asked me last night."

"Holy shit," I gasp. "Congratulations. That's amazing." I hug my very happy friend who lets out a little squeal of excitement.

"You bitch," Chloe says as she gets up and hugs her. "I'm so freaking jealous." I smack her arm. "What? Mo knows I'm over the moon for her." She turns to Monique. "You do know that, right?"

"Yes," Monique sighs. "You were just...being you."

"Exactly." She glowers at me. "She gets me. Oh god, please tell me you're moving in with him and he's not moving into your shoebox apartment."

Monique rolls her eyes. "Of course, I'm moving in with him. He's been an attending for years and has a really nice place not too far from the hospital. Anyway, I expect you ladies to help me move and then once I'm settled in, we'll throw a party or something."

"Is it weird that I don't feel like we're grown-up enough for this?"

"Yes," Monique, Ophelia and I all say in unison.

We leave the bar shortly after. Monique is anxious to get home to her new love. Chloe is meeting up with a guy she's been quietly dating. Ophelia had to work as the bar became increasingly crowded. And me? I'm walking in the direction of my building, but I'm sort of dragging my heels about it.

That box is still taking up residence on my coffee table. That perfect rose in a small bud vase next to it, even though I wanted to drown the thing in bleach. I couldn't. It's not the rose's fault.

What I really need is to pull myself out of him.

What I really need is a distraction.

What I really need is—to not trip over my feet as I walk. "Shit," I mutter, finding myself sprawled on the ground in the middle of the sidewalk as a million people walk past me, completely ignoring me. Fucking New York.

"Hey, you okay?" I glance up into warm brown eyes attached to a very handsome face attached to a very handsome body.

"Um…" I laugh. "Yes. Apparently walking is a skill I haven't quite mastered yet."

He chuckles, reaching his hand out for me to take. I do and when he hauls me up, he draws me in a little closer than what's socially acceptable. "I'm Mason," he says with a broad smile, showcasing his perfect white teeth.

"Gia."

His smile grows and I find myself matching it.

"How about I walk you wherever you were headed, Gia. Just to make sure you make it there without falling again."

"Sure," I say. "I'd like that."

Chapter Twenty-One

FINN

Five years ago

THE SOUND of the waves crashing against the shore fall in time to our rocking in the free-standing hammock strategically placed between the trees outside of our villa and the water. You'd think we were on some tropical island, but we're not. Kelly said she's always wanted to go to Italy so that's exactly where I took her.

We never got a honeymoon. She was pregnant with Logan when we got married and we never went anywhere to celebrate it. Logan. That's what we named our son. After his death, we hit a dark spot. A place where there was no light. We suffered through it together and I like to believe we've come out stronger on the other side.

I can't describe how it felt. There are no words which can comprise that level of devastation. We may not have gotten to know Logan, but that doesn't mean we love him any less than parents who get a lifetime with their child. At first, it just got harder instead of easier. The pain didn't dissipate with the passing of days. It was just too unexpected. Too sudden. Instead of Kelly's belly continuing to grow, it got smaller.

It's been almost nine months. We got married two weeks before he died on Christmas.

I feel like we're finally at a point where we can enjoy things again.

So I took us here, to Italy, during my August break. It's been ten days of traveling through the country and now we're relaxing near Tropea, my fingers gliding through her hair. "I love you," I say.

"Me too," Kelly says back. "This has been the best vacation of my life. Thank you for taking me."

I smile at that. "I'd do anything for you, baby."

"I know you would, Finn."

We fall silent, back into our rhythmic rocking.

After we lost Logan, Kelly quit her job at the law firm. She was planning on doing so anyway after he was born, but she just couldn't get out of bed for a while so that's what happened. Now that nearly nine months has past, she spends her days doing yoga and going out with friends she's met in her yoga class and learning new recipes which she likes to try out.

Me? I'm still in medical school. It felt impossible to start back immediately after break and though some of my professors were… lenient with me about it, it was a good distraction. So much so that I dove in full steam ahead.

Once I graduate and it's time for me to find an internship, I'm hoping we can try again. I'm hoping that Logan wasn't it for us.

We got matching tattoos on our backs of his footprints. We did it on our backs so that we wouldn't have to see them every day, but so that he's still a part of us. We really don't need the ink on our skin to feel him in that way, but I like that he's permanently etched on me.

We got to hold him, and while I'll always be grateful for that, I can't help the agonizing twist of my gut which comes whenever my mind drifts to him. But Kelly refuses to talk about Logan so I don't bring him up anymore. I guess it's just too painful for her. I get it. But I still wish I could mention him.

Sometimes I just need to talk about him. Know that he was real. Even if we lost him.

There's a lot Kelly doesn't talk about with me anymore. A lot she holds back. She lost a part of herself with him.

I did too.

"Do we have to go home?" Kelly asks on a sigh. "Can't we just stay here forever and live off your trust fund?"

I chuckle because I think she's kidding.

"I'm serious, Finn. I don't want to go back to New York. I don't want to live in reality. You have plenty of money. Enough that we could live off of forever and never have to work again."

"I'm in medical school, baby."

"Yeah," she says slowly, like she's thinking about the way she wants to phrase this. "But that could just be a hobby."

I inwardly sigh, because that is just a fantasy. Not reality. She can't run and hide from everything. Pain isn't location specific. It follows you no matter where you go. "We can't live here forever. Eventually we have to go home."

"I don't want to get pregnant again, Finn. I know you do, but I don't."

"We don't have to do this now, Kelly," I say to her, shifting so that I can see her face against the moonlight. I love the way she looks when she's illuminated by the moon. She's so beautiful. "I'm not in a rush. But eventually, I want us to try again to have a family."

A tear escapes her eye, rolling down her cheek. I reach up and wipe it away.

"I don't know if I can do it again."

"Just think about it. Like I said, we've got time and we don't have to figure it out now."

Kelly nods, leaning in to kiss me. I kiss her back. "I love you, Finn."

"I love you, Kelly." My kisses become more insistent. My hands more urgent. "I'll always love you. As long as we're together, nothing else matters."

"Yes," Kelly breathes against my lips. "Nothing else matters. Tell me you love me, Finn. Tell me you'll always love me. Always take care of me."

"Always," I promise. "Forever."

I make love to Kelly in that hammock. I show her that we're okay. That as long as we have each other, then we can get through anything.

Even our darkness.

Chapter Twenty-Two

FINN

Present Day

"YOU OWE me so big for this," I tell Mike who is making me move his girlfriend's heavy-ass boxes into his brownstone. On my birthday, no less. On fucking Halloween. One of the busiest nights in the ED. It's like an ED doctor's form of crack. Or candy since that's a more appropriate comparison. Crazy injuries and ridiculous costumes. I love it. In fact, I look forward to it every year.

But he asked me to take the day off so I could help him move her stuff in.

And since he's my best friend and he perpetually tolerates my bad moods, I said yes.

"Actually, we're even."

I pause on the steps of his brownstone and look up at him. "How the hell do you figure that?"

He smirks and I hate that deliberate grin of his. It never leads to anything good. "You'll see."

Just as the words pass his lips, the front door of his house swings open and I see Gia Bianchi talking to Monique I-have-no-idea-

152

what-her-last-name-is. "I don't see why you have to call it snooty-white-people cheese. And for the record, I take offense to that."

"Only rich white people buy it," Monique says with a shrug and Gia rolls her eyes.

"Fine," she huffs out. "I'll never buy you Robusto again. But you'll see when you try it that it's really freaking good and then you'll be sorry."

"Told you," Mike says to me and right now, I want to kick his smug ass. Because I gave up Halloween in the emergency department to move heavy crap and now I have to look at Gia while I do it. He thinks he's being funny. Or maybe he's giving me the push he believes I need.

But he's wrong.

Yes, I want Gia. That hasn't changed in the weeks since I last saw her. If anything, it's only gotten worse. Nothing makes you crazier than kissing the woman you're mad about, knowing it will never happen again. I blame the present I should have never given her. If she hadn't caught me in the hall stuck in my indecision, then she wouldn't have asked me to go with her to dinner. And if she hadn't asked me to dinner, I never would have found myself in that position. I guess it's not exactly Mike's fault. He doesn't know what happened with Gia that night. But that doesn't mean I can I just laugh this off as some inconsequential thing and ask her out.

Gia and Monique bounce down one more step before they notice us.

Monique smirks.

Gia frowns.

"Afternoon, ladies," I say. "Care to move out of the way so I can get this box inside without breaking my back?"

Gia steps aside, throwing her friend a glower similar to what I just gave Mike, and then I climb the steps up past her. She does her best not to look at me, but loses the battle and meets my eyes for the briefest of moments.

I haven't exactly been avoiding Gia, but I definitely haven't been seeking her out either. I go to a different bar. I don't eat lunch in the hospital cafeteria. I make sure that when I call for an OB consult, I demand a doctor and not a midwife. I'm an attending, so I pretty much get what I want.

I set the box down in the master bedroom because that's where it's labeled to go. When I turn back, Gia is standing on the threshold of the door, watching me with those big aqua eyes of hers. Eyes I still fantasize about gazing up at me while I'm on top of her, fucking her senseless. I nearly got that fantasy. *Nearly.*

"Sorry," she says. "I didn't know you were going to be here otherwise I wouldn't have agreed to help."

I hate everything she just said to me, but instead of telling her that, I nod.

"It's fine. Our friends are living together and we work at the same hospital. Seems likely that we'll run into each other from time to time."

"Happy birthday," she says, taking a hesitant step into the room, "I thought about getting you something, but–"

"No," I cut her off. "It's better you didn't."

"Right," she says and then she smirks at me with a glint in her eyes. "But do you think we can be friends? Or at least friendly?"

I take a step too. Hesitantly. But shit, this woman is like a magnet of perpetual pain and bliss. "As I recall, you were the one who said we weren't friends. Not me."

She smiles and my insides hurt. "Fine. Then I'm saying I'd like to be your friend. I'm saying I don't want it to be awkward as ass every time we're in the same room together."

"No awkward as ass. Got it."

She nods her head. "Awesome. So how've you been?"

Miserable. Lonely. Aching for you.

"Good. You?"

"Pretty good. I um…" she pauses, peeking over her shoulder and then takes another step toward me. "I've been sort of seeing someone."

"Sort of?" I try for a smirk, but know I don't even come close. This might be the worst conversation ever. All I want to do is tell her no. Tell her she can't sort of be dating someone when she should be with me. Not dating. Not sort of. Just with.

"Yeah," she laughs the word uncomfortably. "Well, not sort of. I'm seeing someone."

I turn away from her. Unable to stand it another minute, I pretend to busy myself with boxes that do not need my help. "That's great. I'm happy for you."

She sighs. I don't know what she was hoping for from me, but I'm hardly about to throw her a parade or a do a happy dance because she met someone. "I'm only telling you because I didn't want you to hear it from someone else. Like Mike."

"Thanks for letting me know."

"Finn?"

I turn to her. Her voice commands it and so I man the hell up and do it. Even if it might eviscerate me to look at her.

Gia takes three strides across the room until she's directly in front of me. I can smell her. Feel her warmth. See the different flecks of green and blue in her eyes. Admire the small freckle on the upper left crest of her cheek.

"I hope you find something good too."

Those words just officially killed me. On so many levels and in so many ways.

I already have, I want to tell her. But I keep my mouth shut.

"Are you taking him to the game?"

I don't know why I just asked her that. It was petty and petulant. I gave her two tickets. Not one. I knew the risk when I did it. But now…

"I haven't mentioned it to him."

That has me smiling. It's not serious, is what that says. Or maybe she likes holding on to my little present like it's a secret. That's just as good.

"So invite me."

She blinks up at me, her head tilting to the side. "You want to go to the game with me?"

"I thought you'd never ask."

She laughs, shaking her head like I'm too much. "That's not how I meant it and you know it."

"Really? I didn't catch that."

"Okay Finn," she continues that laugh. "Will you go to the game with me?"

"Sure, Gia. I'd love to go with you."

She sinks her teeth down into her full bottom lip, shifting her weight. "As friends though, right?"

"Isn't that what you said you wanted?"

She nods and it's a big nod. "Yes. That's what I want."

"Then we'll go as friends."

Words have never tasted so wrong leaving my mouth.

"Happy birthday," she says again, placing her hands on my shoulders and reaching up to kiss my cheek. My eyes close as her lips press against my skin. As her warmth invades all my senses. It's over far too quickly and when she rights herself, removing her hands from my body, I die in a way I haven't before. "You're thirty, right?" I nod. "It's a big one. We should go out and celebrate."

"You don't have to if you have plans."

"I don't tonight."

Shit.

"Okay then."

Shut up.

"Let's celebrate."

I'm so fucked.

"Great," she says with a smile. "It'll be fun."

Chapter Twenty-Three

FINN

"This is not what I had in mind when I agreed to celebrate," I say to Mike as I sit down in one of the stiff leather couches of the club he dragged us to. "Although, I will say, you dressed like a porn princess is certainly making a club on Halloween more palatable," I tell Gia as I make a show of looking her up and down.

She's wearing the tiniest of black dresses. In fact, I think if I were sitting across from her instead of next to her, I might know what color panties she's wearing from when she sat down. She's definitely showing off an insane amount of cleavage.

"Porn princess?" she laughs, tilting her head back. That's one of the things I like about Gia. She can laugh at herself and she doesn't take everything so seriously. Like I do. "That's great. I'll have to mention that one to Chloe."

"And in going back to your previous comment," Mike says. "What's not to like about this place. It's one of the premiere clubs in the city and we're in the *VIP* area."

"Do I strike as you the clubbing sort?"

"No, but I couldn't turn down free VIP."

I give him a half bow for that. "How did you manage this?"

J. SAMAN

Monique asks. She looks pretty too. She's all long legs with an athletic build. Totally Mike's type.

"I saved the life of the owner's brother."

I laugh, shaking my head. "Do tell."

"He came in with a GSW to the left femoral artery. A real bitch of a wound given its location."

"God, that's awful," Gia says, covering her mouth like she's actually upset by that. Damn, she's cute.

Mike shrugs. "Well, he lived and his brother told me that whenever I wanted to come down, to give him a call and he'd hook me up." Mike waves his hand around our seats complete with table service and private dance area. "And so he has."

"It's sort of freaky here though," Monique says, eyeing the crowd in their various costumes. "And really, despite what each of these women are wearing, I think the word slutty is at the front it. Slutty nurse—which I personally hate—slutty pilot, slutty vampire, etcetera."

"Certainly fun to look at." I grin at her.

Monique rolls her eyes at me. "Come on, Gia. Let's dance. Mike here can barely keep rhythm. He really destroys that whole black men can dance thing."

"Hey," Mike says, tickling Monique's side, eliciting his intended giggle. "I take exception to that."

"You *are* the exception to that," she teases with a grin. Leaning in, she gives him a kiss and then stands up, reaching out her hand for Gia. Gia stands too, throwing me a wink before sauntering off and treating me to a perfect view of her fantastic ass.

When I turn back to face Mike, he's giving me a look. A look I know well. After working with the man for three years, you get to know the many different expressions he can give. The one he's bestowing upon me now is not anywhere I want to go.

"What are you doing?"

"What do you mean?" I ask, playing dumb and not fooling him for a second.

"You know exactly what I mean. Gia," he says, leaning forward and inching his body to the end of the couch so that we can actually

158

hear each other without having to shout. "Monique told me you told Gia you're not interested, when we both know that's not true."

That's not what I said to her. Definitely not what I implied at least. Kissing typically doesn't mean not interested.

"Why are you pretending to suddenly be friends with her when you're clearly into her?"

"Stop," I say quickly. "You don't know anything."

"Bullshit," he snaps. "I know everything. You're into her. More than into her and you're pushing her away. How long are you going to torture yourself? It's been three *years*," he emphasizes and I feel sick.

"I'm not torturing myself."

"No," he points at me, "you are. Because suddenly you're friends, which is total crap. You don't do friends. Especially with women. Especially with women you want."

"What's your point?" I growl, beyond frustrated. Reaching out, I pick up the glass of vodka cranberry which was poured for me, and down it. The whole full glass of it.

"She was all about you, man. I know she was. But now she's dating Mason." Mason. He has a name. "And Mason is crazy about her. I met the guy. He's nice and attentive and he makes her happy."

"Great. That's what I want for her."

"Goddammit, Finn." Mike slams his hand against the glowing acrylic table. "What will you do when she marries him?"

"What?" I draw back, completely taken off guard by that. "She said they've only been together a couple of weeks."

"Yeah, but like I said, he's crazy about her. They're already pretty serious. Are you just going to let this happen? Let her go, because you refuse to start living your life again?"

I shake my head at him, my words failing before I can speak them.

"Don't let her get away, Finn. You'll regret it forever."

"Something else to add to the list."

Mike shakes his head at me, beyond exasperated. I'm right there too so I guess that makes us even. "Fine. It's your life and you know how I feel. But for the record, you're making a mistake. You deserve happiness and you're pushing it into the arms of another man with both hands."

Mike stands up, tossing down the rest of his drink the way I just did mine and then marches off in the direction of the girls, who are dancing in our private area. I get up too, because if he's going to dance with Monique, I can dance with Gia. I can do this. I can do friends. I can exist in a world where she's only partially mine.

And just fuck Mike. What the fuck? Why the hell would he say that shit to me? Marriage? Give me a goddamn break. Gia barely knows the guy. No way they're near that serious. Especially not with the way she still looks at me.

I take some semblance of relief with that. Not much. But some.

Gia smiles at Mike as he takes Monique into his arms and kisses her. Sure, I'm jealous of what they have. Sure, I'd love to have that with Gia. But I don't trust it. I know firsthand that it never lasts long. Everything you love can be gone in the blink of an eye.

Everything you think you know can be a lie.

None of that stops me from stalking up to Gia and taking her hand. It doesn't stop me from pulling her into my arms and it definitely doesn't stop me from bringing my mouth down close to her ear. "This okay?" I ask.

She blinks up at me with those wide cyan eyes and nods. Damn, this girl just does it for me. It would be so easy to kiss her again.

But then what?

We dance to a fast-paced song with slow-paced movements. Her head is against my chest. My arms are around her body. My fingers are caressing the fabric against her lower back. Her hand is placed on my chest. It's so completely perfect and yes, so very wrong.

It's loud in here. Annoyingly so.

"Come with me," I say into her ear. She nods. She lets me take her wherever I want.

She trusts me. And hell, I know she still wants me.

I move us so we're on the precipice of a dark alcove. The bass not so pronounced here. She's still partially in my arms, her body angled back so she can catch my eyes as my hands linger on her back.

I want to tell her so many things.

"Mike said your new guy is crazy about you," I say and wonder why I did. That wasn't one of the things.

Gia observes me, measuring my expression. But then slowly nods. "Yes. Mason is a great guy."

"How did you meet?"

Gia giggles lightly, an innocent smile on her lips. "I fell in the street. He helped me up and walked me home."

"So he saved you?"

She nods slowly and I hate that he's now her hero. That he got to be the one to pick her up and save her. Shit. It's like a sucker punch. Because despite all the crap I've put her through, I was always the one who was there when she needed me. Always there to pick her up when she fell.

"Are you happy with him, Gia? Is he what you want?"

Gia's eyes widen. Taken aback by my very direct question. In truth, I don't know why I asked it. If she says no, I'll be selfishly relieved but it won't change my disposition.

"I care about him a lot."

Her answer is evasive at best.

"What about you, Finn? Are you with anyone?"

"I think you already know that answer."

"Why?" she breathes, her eyes glassing over. I still manage to hurt her. Even when she's with someone else. Mike was right when he said I'm torturing myself. That I'm not friends with her. It's the depraved masochist in me. He likes to swim in his misery. Amplify it whenever possible.

And with Gia in my arms, that's exactly what I'm doing.

"It's a long story."

"I've got time."

I smile, tracing my fingertips across her soft cheek. She lets me and another piece of me dies with each passing stroke. "Maybe one day."

She huffs out a breath. But instead of pushing me away and storming off the way I expect her to, she presses her head against my chest, wrapping her arms around me once again as we gently sway to the music. Can't this woman ever do what I expect her to? What I need her to?

"Your heart is pounding, Finn." She sighs, deep breath in, deep breath out. "I'm persistent," she warns. "And not so easy to get rid of." Her chin rests against my chest as she gazes up at me. "Sort of like HPV."

I laugh, leaning down instinctively before I remember myself and draw back.

"One day, Finnigan Banner, I'll know all your secrets. And then you'll be stuck with me, whether you want that or not."

Don't make promises you have no intention of keeping.

Chapter Twenty-Four

GIA

My eyes remain focused on a small glow-in-the-dark star which is stuck on my ceiling. It's been here since I moved in and I never bothered removing it. It's lost almost all of it fluorescence, which sort of disappoints me. Not that it would be glowing right now. It's morning.

It's been one week since I last saw Finn. One week since we danced in the club.

One week since we declared that truce.

Honestly, I didn't expect him to say yes. I expected more of the same line he's been feeding me. I don't know which I was hoping for more. For him to say he still wants me but will never have me or that he's over me and is willing to try to be friends.

I guess I know which one it is now, don't I?

Only it still doesn't feel that way.

Finn looks at me in a way that speaks to more. And not just a little more. That look says he's desperate for me. It's an impossible image to shut off. To ignore. Especially when I've invested so much energy into him. So many of my thoughts.

All of this of course has me feeling guilty.

Especially as Mason lies here beside me, sleeping soundly. It's Saturday and I don't have to work today. And since Mason is your typical Monday through Friday, nine to fiver, he doesn't either. We have plans to spend the whole day together.

Doing what, I could not tell you.

It tends not to matter. We have fun no matter what. Mason makes me laugh and smile and everything with us is easy and effortless. Just the way I like it. He's smart and honest and forthright and sweet. He doesn't hide anything.

I like that too.

But I still find myself looking forward to that football game with Finn. I can still feel his warmth as he held me while we danced. He kissed my head. I don't even know if it was a conscious act or not. He pressed his lips into me, inhaled the scent of my hair and kissed me like I was something precious to him. I don't even allow my thoughts to venture to my birthday night.

I use his coffee mug every morning. That hot chocolate he bought me is long since drunk. That flower stayed in that bud vase until it's last dying day. And his card is tucked in the back of my underwear drawer.

I honestly cannot explain why I covet these things the way I do.

Maybe it's the challenge, the puzzle, which keeps me going.

Or maybe it's the looks and the kisses I'm unable to block out. That haunt me every time I close my eyes. Even when another man is beside me.

But that's all Finn will ever be to me. An unanswerable question mark.

Shaking my head from side to side, I focus on Mason. He's impossible not to adore. And I do adore him. He's quickly become my bright spot. The something to look forward to after work. He's even coming with me to meet my mother when I have dinner with her on Tuesday. I'm excited for that. I think she'll love him. And she no longer asks me about Finn so that's a bonus as well.

The alarm on Mason's phone blasts off with that annoying chirp he insists on using because evidently nothing else is capable of waking him. He groans, reaching over blindly and transporting his phone back into bed with him. He shuts it off with the swipe of his finger and groans again. "Why do I do this to myself?"

I giggle a little at that. "You're a glutton for punishment."

He rolls over so he's facing me before he wraps his arm around, tugging me into him so that we're face-to-face and body to body. "I must be if I'm willingly getting out a bed you're in, just so I can run."

I want to say he doesn't have to. That he can stay here with me, but I don't. I've tried that too many times only to be shot down every single one.

"Do you ever take a day off?" So far, every day we spend together he gets up early for a run. He also does this during the days we're not together. It's a bit much if you ask me, but since he didn't, I don't comment.

"No," he says, kissing my nose and then my lips. "I'm on a streak. Two hundred and ten days."

"Christ almighty. What do you do when it's snowing?"

"I still run. I only miss it if I'm too sick to move or if the weather is dangerous, which isn't all that often in the city."

"I'm impressed. I'm not nearly that driven. If it were me, I'd come up with a million excuses not to do it."

Mason shrugs, his brown eyes still half closed with sleep as a lazy smile bounces up the corners of his lips. "You could run with me, you know. It could be our thing."

"Because I like you as much as I do, I'm going to fill you in on a little secret." I lean in until my mouth is next to his ear and then I whisper, "I hate running."

He laughs, burrowing his face into my neck and tickling my ribs. "That's because you haven't run with me yet."

I roll my body left and right because even though I'm not all that ticklish, the sensation is still unpleasant. "No," I say, pushing him away enough to get him to stop completely. "Running just really isn't my thing. I was always that girl in high school who would walk the track while everyone else ran it, just to be obstinate. I'm more of a classroom athlete."

He laughs, running his nose along my collar bone, which elicits a very nice tingle. "A classroom athlete? Explain."

"Pilates, yoga and the occasional spin class."

"Ah. No wonder you have such a great ass," he muses, pinching my ass to prove his point. It has me grinding into him. But then he pulls away with a shake of his head. "If you do that, I'll never get out the door for my run." I pout. "Don't do that. I want to run."

Instead of be with me, I don't say. Instead I go for, "Okay, have a good run."

He leans in, mollifying me with a chaste kiss before getting up and changing into the running stuff he brought with him to my apartment last night. "Hey, why don't you meet me at that coffee shop that's a couple blocks from here? The one I met you at when you were working that time?"

"You have a real thing for their egg and cheese, don't you?"

He gives me a big grin and a wink, bending down to give me another kiss and then he's out the door. I sigh the second the door clicks shut and flop down onto my back, finding that rogue glow-in-the-dark star. I like that Mason is so driven and goal oriented and all that bullshit, but just once, I'd like to have morning sex with him. It's my favorite and something tells me that won't ever be part of our repertoire.

It's also making me feel a little guilty for not getting up and going to a class. I probably should. Evidently, I have a great ass which I need to maintain. Growling out my lazy frustration, I pull myself out of bed in dramatic flair, tossing the blankets off my body and huffing all the way to the bathroom.

But once I'm dressed in my new cute yoga outfit which I got on sale, I'm feeling better. The gym I belong to is actually a few doors down from the coffee shop we're meeting in and since Mason runs for a freaking hour and a half, I have plenty of time to do my class and cool down before I have to meet him.

Who the fuck runs that long? He must run like ten miles or something crazy like that. On workdays, he gets up at five a.m. so he has enough time to do it. Mason is a computer programmer, which I would typically associate with someone slightly nerdy, but there really is nothing nerdy about Mason.

In fact, he's more preppy pretty boy. Not generally my type, but I like it on him. Mason has salmon-colored shorts with small blue whales on them. And boat shoes, though I'm about seventy percent positive he doesn't sail. When I asked if he wore the shorts and shoes he said, of course, like, why wouldn't he. It's kind of cute and when I asked him to put them on for me with his whale-matching blue polo, he laughed and called me a noodle. *A noodle!*

I smile about that all through my class. I smile about Mason.

I smile about him the entire two-minute walk over to the coffee shop. The door chimes out a greeting and as I scan around the room, I find Mason sitting at a small table near the counter. He throws me a wave when he spots me. "Hey," he says. "I just ordered, so perfect timing."

His medium brown hair is damp and his cheeks are still a little flushed. His long-sleeved sports shirt is sticking to his chest in a very distracting way.

"How was your run?"

"Awesome," he beams. "My fastest mile yet. Seven minutes and twenty seconds."

"Damn, that's fast."

He nods, bouncing his eyebrows up and down. "You look like you hit the gym."

"I did. I caught a yoga class."

He laughs like I'm adorable for doing that and leans into me, kissing the spot directly next to my ear. "I think that's incredibly sexy. In fact, I think you're the sexiest woman I've ever known." He kisses that spot again and pulls back to catch my eyes. "Perfect in every way."

He kisses my lips softly, a smile lingering on them until I pull back and find Finn staring at us. At me. I swallow my tongue and turn a million different shades of red. He's wearing scrubs, his hair is a disheveled mess and his bright blue eyes are just a touch dimmer than normal. He looks like he's at the end of a shift instead of the beginning.

Even like this, he's still the most beautiful man I've ever seen.

"Gia Bianchi," he says my name in just such a way that it becomes personal without being obvious to anyone but me.

"Hi Finn," I say, my voice small and weak. Finn steps closer to our table so that someone can pass him and now he's practically looming over us. I feel Mason shift next to me and I realize his hand is on top of mine. I have the strongest urge to pull it away from him, but I don't.

I'm not hiding Mason from Finn.

"Finn, this is…my boyfriend, Mason Davis. Mason, this is Finn Banner. He's Monique's boyfriend's best friend."

Finn chuckles at that title and then says, "Ah, but I'm more than that now, aren't I?" I blink at him. "We're friends too, Gia. Don't play it off like we're not."

I want to be somewhere, anywhere other than here right now.

Mason looks up at Finn and then stands up to shake his hand. "I've heard a lot about you," Mason says and I wonder if that's true or not because I certainly have never mentioned Finn to him before.

Finn eyes him for a beat, but I can't tell what he's thinking. His expression is completely impassive. "Nice to meet you," Finn grins before he looks back at me. "Rare day off?"

I nod. "You look like you're just getting off."

Finn grins wider and I hate how I just said that. "Have a seat while you wait," Mason graciously offers and Finn nods his thanks, taking a seat in one of the empty chairs at our table. Next to me.

I think this may in fact be the most awkward and uncomfortable moment of my life.

"Yes," Finn says to me. "I'm on nights through next Saturday. But then I don't have to be back to work until the following Tuesday. I'll have all day *Sunday* and Monday off." He smirks at me and I know what he's referring to. Our football game. The football game I haven't mentioned to Mason yet. The football game I don't know *how* to mention to Mason.

How do you tell your boyfriend you're going to a football game with another man?

I honestly don't know, which is why I haven't said anything.

The lady behind the counter calls out Mason's name and he excuses himself to get up and grab our breakfast. "I'm working Friday and Saturday night this week too."

"Maybe we'll run into each other. On purpose for once."

He has a point. Why is it the only time you run into someone it's when you don't want to run into them? I mean, there's what, eight million people in this city? I get that we're close to the hospital, but still.

"Maybe," I say just as Mason sits back down with two egg and cheese sandwiches on an English muffin—even though I like mine on a bagel—and my cappuccino which I only started drinking after that night in the coffee shop with Finn. The word pathetic drifts into my mind, but I push it away. I've already had that fight with myself. More than once.

"Cappuccino?" Finn purrs knowingly. "No hot chocolate?"

Mason takes a bite of his sandwich and then looks over at me. "I didn't know you like hot chocolate. You always order cappuccinos when we're out."

I give Mason a warm smile, before turning back to Finn, my stomach in knots. "I only drink hot chocolate at night."

"I'll keep that in mind," Finn says, his hand skimming my knee from under the table, just as his name is called. "Enjoy your breakfast. It was nice to finally meet you, Mason." Mason nods at him through a mouth full of food, totally oblivious to anything and everything. "See you around, Gia."

Finn stands up, collecting his breakfast, but before he reaches the exit, he turns back and finds me. He holds me captive, rendering me powerless against the pull. His expression turns conflicted. Pained. And as is always the case with Finn, my heart bleeds out. What is it about us? What is it that makes us so right and so wrong? So perfect and so broken?

It's him, I realize. Not me. Because I would have given him everything. All of me. And no matter what I've done or how hard I've tried, he's never been willing to give me the same in return.

There is only so much a woman can take. I refuse to wait on something I instinctively know will never happen. And Mason and I could be so amazing.

Finn blinks, breaking our spell. He throws me a half-wave and then leaves. And I tell myself over and over again that it's a relief.

Chapter Twenty-Five

FINN

Four years ago

I'M EXHAUSTED. Completely and utterly wiped. Being an intern in the ED is grueling. Long days and even longer nights with very little sleep in between. But I love it.

I'm only a few weeks in, but it's incredible

After I graduated, I managed to secure an internship in the city. It meant Kelly and I didn't have to move which is something she said she really didn't want to do. Kelly is happy again. It took a long time for her, for us, to get there, but we have. I know we have. Things may not be perfect, but they're definitely close.

Whenever I'm not working, which isn't a lot, I do my best to be with Kelly. She's still not working, which is perfect because that means any down time I have, Kelly is there. So I take her places she wants to go. Like shopping. Kelly likes to shop a lot, but I don't care because it makes her happy and I like making Kelly happy.

Today I got out of work early. According my attending, Mike Sanders, I haven't left the hospital in almost twenty-six hours.

Honestly, it feels like longer. Mike made me go home and he didn't have to tell me twice. I practically flew out the doors.

On the way home, I pass by a flower shop and stop to look at one of the bouquets in the window which caught my eye. Kelly likes yellow. It's her favorite color which always struck me as an odd favorite color, but right now, looking at the yellow sunflowers in the window, I think it's the best favorite color ever.

Two blocks after the flower shop, I find a bakery. Kelly loves blueberry scones so I grab a couple of those for her too. Today is a good day, I decide. And even though I haven't slept in a very long time, I don't plan on doing that when I get home. I plan on making love to Kelly and then spending the day doing something fun. Maybe we'll go to a movie. Or a museum. Or walk through the park.

Might be a bit too hot for that walk though. Maybe I'll take Kelly to the beach. That's what I'll do. Kelly looks amazing in a bikini and it's the middle of the week so it won't be all that crowded.

I smile, thinking about Kelly in that red bikini of hers the rest of the walk home. And when I get to our building, I wave to the doorman and hit the elevator. Less than five minutes later, I'm unlocking the door to our apartment.

It's quiet. I don't hear Kelly anywhere and I wonder if she's out. I had this whole surprise-Kelly-thing going on in my mind, which is why I didn't text her to tell her I was coming home.

Shit.

That's not how this was supposed to go.

"Kelly?" I call out. No answer.

Sighing out, I walk into the kitchen and toss the box of scones onto the counter and go in search of a vase for the sunflowers. I'll put them on the coffee table, that way when she gets home and walks into the main living room, she'll see them.

I find a crystal vase which one of my mother's pretentious friends got us as a wedding present, and fill it with water. Unwrapping the cellophane from around the flowers, I drop them into the water, set them on the coffee table just so and then head for our bedroom.

Maybe by the time I'm done with my shower, Kelly will be home. I haven't showered in far too long either so that's definitely in order. Maybe it's better Kelly isn't home to see me like this.

I strip off my nasty scrub top, dropping it to the floor before I walk across our bedroom and open the bathroom door.

And then I freeze, because Kelly is sitting on the closed toilet, with her head bowed down over her bent knees.

"Kelly?" She looks up at me, her eyes rimmed in red. "Baby? Are you okay?"

She's surprised to see me standing here. Like she didn't hear me come in the apartment or call out to her or even open the bathroom door. "Finn," she says my name with a hitch in her voice. "Oh god, Finn. I uh...I didn't know you were coming home now."

"What's going on? Are you sick?"

She shakes her head, a tear gliding down her cheek as she stares at me. "No, I..." And then she looks down and I do the same, and that's when I see it.

The stick in her hand.

"Kelly?" I drop to my knees in front of her, staring down at that stick. "You're taking a pregnancy test?"

I don't know how to feel about this. I wish she had waited for me. Peeing on a stick to find out if you're pregnant is something that couples do together, Right? It's how we did it the first time. It's not something you do in the bathroom alone when you don't think your husband is coming home. She's crying now. A lot harder than she was when I first entered the bathroom and my heart breaks.

Kelly is scared. Of course, she's scared.

We already lost Logan and I'm sure she's terrified something like that could happen to us again.

"I'm so sorry, Finn."

I shake my head, removing the stick from her fingers. She lets me take it and when I see the word PREGNANT in small cap letters in the oval, I smile so goddamn big.

So. Goddamn. Big.

"Kelly, we're pregnant!" I laugh a happy bubble of excitement and then I wrap my arms around Kelly who is still crying. "Oh, baby. I know you're scared. I am too. But this is such a blessing. Everything is going to be fine."

She shakes her head against my neck. Maybe she's afraid I won't be home and she'll be stuck taking care of the baby alone? She has been complaining a lot about my hours and how she misses me.

"I get it, the timing isn't great with me being gone a lot, but I'll do everything I can to be here more. And my internship is only a year and then my hours should stabilize a bit. We always talked about having more kids—"

"Finn, you don't understand," she interrupts.

I pull back and cup her cheeks in my hands, searching her eyes. "Tell me, then. Whatever it is, we'll figure it out."

She stares at me for the longest of moments as more tears pour from those pretty eyes of hers. "I'm sorry," she finally manages. "I…" Kelly swallows hard and then wraps her arms around my neck, hugging me so tight. "I'm scared, Finn. I'm scared of so many things right now."

"I know, baby. I know. Me too. But I'm here and we're together and everything is going to be okay."

Kelly nods her head against me and when she finally manages to pull herself together, we kiss and we smile and I show her the flowers and the scones. "Thank you," she grins. "Blueberry is my favorite."

I smile. I haven't stopped smiling. "That's why I got them for you."

She nods. Takes a bite. Swallows it and says, "I'm sorry for hiding the test from you. I was scared and I didn't know how to face this. I think I've suspected it for a while. Things have just been so different. So…out of sorts."

"And now?" I ask.

"Now I have a lot to think about. But maybe I'm a little less scared. Maybe I can find my way through this and figure everything out," she says, but she can't quite meet my eyes.

Kelly and I kiss and I tell her I love her. She tells me she loves me too, even if she still won't meet my eyes.

Everything is perfect.
We're perfect.

Chapter Twenty-Six

GIA

"Will this night ever end," I whine, sitting behind the nurses' station with my feet propped up. I've been chatting with a few of the nurses for the last hour. They've been telling me about their husbands and kids, because there isn't a single pregnant lady in need of delivering a baby.

It's freaking unheard of and if it continues likes this, it's going to be the longest night ever.

I could probably go and sack out in the on-call room for a bit. Especially since Finn and I have the football game tomorrow. But I don't like to do that. If I fall asleep, I'm usually groggy when woken and that's just not safe for patients.

Not that we have any.

"You could catch up on your charting?" one of the nurses offers.

"Done," I say.

"You could read a journal? Catch up on your CMEs?"

"Done and done."

"Then you can go thank the gorgeous doctor who delivered this to you."

I glance up to see Rachel, one of the OBs, who is smiling from ear to ear as she reaches out her hand holding a very large to-go cup of coffee.

I can't stop the bubble of laughter as it climbs up my chest and out my mouth. I get up out of my seat and take the warm cardboard cup from her. "Is he waiting on me?"

"I don't think so. He just asked me to deliver this to you and then walked away as fast as he could like the floor was on fire."

I thank Rachel and move quickly to the door which leads out of the L&D floor, smiling as I hear Hannah, one of the nurses, laugh about how afraid men are of laboring women and babies.

Just as I reach the elevator, I spy Finn stepping on. "Hey," I call out. "Wait up." Finn sticks his arm into the closing doors and then they open for me with a loud angry ding. "Why the delivery and ditch?"

He smiles, but his eyes glance beyond me at the sign which says Labor and Delivery. "Not my department."

I roll my eyes at that and step on next to him. "But you brought me...what?" I look down at the cup in my hand.

"Hot chocolate."

I laugh. "Of course, but you do realize I'm in the middle of a nightshift and actually require caffeine."

He grins down at me, shifting ever so slightly to face me better. "That's why I had them add a double shot of espresso."

"And whipped cream?"

"You can't have hot chocolate without whipped cream."

"You're amazing," I say, taking a sip of my espresso-filled hot chocolate. "Yum. Where did you get this?" No way this came from the hospital cafeteria and the coffee shop off the lobby is closed at this hour.

"The coffee shop where I met your boyfriend last week." I peer up at him, trying to gauge his expression, but he's not giving me anything to work with.

"And how is it that you have time to walk over and get coffee?"

Finn takes a sip of his own large coffee with a smile. "It's Q in the ED."

"Ah," I say with a nod of understanding. "Us too."

In hospitals, it is against the superstitious laws to ever say the word quiet. It's considered bad luck. A jinx. Like saying good luck to a dancer before they go on stage instead of break a leg. It's simply not done.

"Then you have a minute to ride down the elevator and share your espresso-chocolate drink with me."

"Isn't that what I'm already doing?" I tease but then the doors open on the ground floor and we step out into the back end of the ED.

"What time am I picking you up tomorrow?"

Finn spins around on me, taking my arm and leading me down a vacant hallway. I feel like I shouldn't be here with him. That's it's too intimate of a setting. But then again, we're going to be alone all afternoon tomorrow.

"The game is at four-fifteen so how about two? Or is that too early? Will you need more sleep than that?"

Finn smiles down on me, edging the border of my personal space. "Two is a perfect." I take a sip of my drink and do my best to appear like he's not invading me. Like I'm completely unaffected by him. I figure this is just how it is with us and there isn't anything I can do about it. That it's just going to be my thing with him.

Finn is the emotional equivalent of an old tattoo. A permanent fixture, even if it's not the most prominent anymore. Even if it's slightly faded or maybe even partially covered by another one. A brighter one. It's still there. Forever a part of your skin.

That's Finn.

I tried getting rid of him, but found it was impossible. So now I live with it. Accept it for what it is. We fall silent and do that staring thing with each other which we've managed to perfect. The one that makes my heart beat just a bit faster. The one that makes my stomach swoosh.

"What did you tell Mason about tomorrow?" he asks, leaning into me just a touch more, those bright-blue eyes drifting all around my face.

"I told him I was going to see the Patriot's play the Jets."

He grins. "And who did you tell him you were going with?"

"You," I say.

That grin turns into a full-fledged smile. "And what did Mason have to say about that?"

I shrug because Mason wasn't happy about it. I never mentioned how I got the tickets. Or that they were even technically mine. I played the whole thing off like it wasn't a big deal and he didn't fight me on it, though I think he wanted to.

To be honest, I don't know why I asked Finn to come with me. Yes, he sort of asked himself along, but I could have said no. I should have said that I have a boyfriend. It was a moment of weakness, I think. It was the first time Finn and I had seen each other in a few weeks, since that ill-fated night in my apartment. And I was swept up in the idea that he and I could actually be friends.

It was idiotic.

Even now, standing here with him in the middle of the night, in a vacant part of the hospital, I know what I'm doing with him is wrong.

I can't make myself stop either.

Every little inch he gives me, I just want to take more, knowing full well it will never lead anywhere. It's a tease. A peepshow. But if you run your hand quickly enough through a flame, you don't get burned. That's what I'm banking on.

"He didn't like it, did he? You taking me to the game instead of him? Or didn't you tell him that's how this is happening?"

"Does the idea of Mason being unhappy about us going together make you happy?"

"I don't believe happy is the word I would use."

I want to ask him which word he would use, but I know Finn well enough to know he won't tell me. And really, what am I hoping his word would be?

"Mason knows nothing will ever happen with us," I say and instantly regret it. I don't know why I'm being petty with him. That's a lie. I know exactly why I'm behaving like this.

Finn steps into me, crowding me until my back hits the wall. He sets his coffee on the floor and then brackets me in with his arms. His face dips down so close to mine that his blazing eyes take up nearly my entire field of vision. His warm sweet coffee-scented breath fans against my lips.

"Is that what you told him?"

I nod. It's the truth, but I find myself daring him to contradict me.

"And what did he say to that?"

"Nothing," I say. "He didn't say anything."

"Does this feel like *nothing*, Gia?"

No. It feels like butterflies. It feels like heart palpitations. It feels like warm delicious tingles zapping each of my nerve endings in a synchronized dance. It feels exactly how it felt that night in my apartment and for that very reason, I need him to stop.

"Does it *matter*, Finn?"

He grins big and wide, his nose brushing against mine. Once. Twice.

"No," he whispers, his lips a half an inch from mine.

His answer is a relief and a punishment. But I refuse to let him control me any longer. Pushing against his chest so that I can breathe without tasting him, I duck under his arm, freeing myself. Finn steps back, his hands going to his hips as his eyes close, his face pinching up in regret.

He's shaking his head, chastising himself for…well, probably for everything.

I let him wallow in it. Succumb to it. He deserves it, and I think he knows that.

I turn away from him and walk back down the hall to the elevator, pressing the button and taking a sip of my now very cold drink. "Thanks for the espresso-chocolate. It was delicious," I tell him as I drop it into the trash bin. "I'll see you tomorrow at two."

The elevator doors open just as I say two, as if they knew I'd need to make an exit at that precise moment. Stepping on, I hit the button for my floor and close my eyes.

I can't look to see if he's there watching me. That man ransacks my heart. And day after day, I promise myself I'm done allowing it. That I'm finally letting him go. Because something dark broke that man. Something horrendous made him give up on love. And something tells me that will never change.

Chapter Twenty-Seven

FINN

"What are you doing here, Gia?" I ask, opening my front door and rubbing away the sleep from my eyes. I'm exhausted. In fact, I can barely open my eyes.

That is until I see her. She's leaning against my doorframe, her blue-green eyes are big and bright and lined in kohl. Her black hair is piled up on top of her head. Her lips are red. Motherfucking fuck-me red. And that dress. Jesus Christ, is she trying to kill me right now? She's wearing that red dress she wore at that party back in October. That strapless red dress which is beyond short with that amazing V down the center of her cleavage.

She entices the sleeping devil inside me, urging him to come out and play. She's a siren. A goddess. And so I'm so far past screwed at this point.

"What are you talking about?" she asks me. "You sent me a text, asking me to come over."

"Huh?" I tilt my head at her and she winks.

Gia steps inside and runs her fingers up my bare abs and chest. Slowly. She watches herself touch me with a wicked smirk on her lips and then when she reaches my neck, her eyes flutter up to mine. "I'm done with the games, Finn. I'm done with wanting you as much as I do and not being able to have you. I need you. Please give me what I need."

I kiss her.

My lips crash down on hers and I capture her face in my hands. The hot chocolate I bought her, wavers, threatening to topple over, so I take it and set it down on my coffee table. Because suddenly, we're at my couch. I don't care how we got here, I just know I need more of her mouth.

She moans against me, caressing my skin with her warmth. "Yes," she breathes.

And then I get serious. Positioning myself so that I'm hovering over her body, I meld my tongue against hers, groaning at the flavor.

Her hands grasp onto the muscles of my shoulders, pushing me away and pulling me closer in equal measure. I get her conflict. Understand her struggle. I am an asshole. I've been nothing less to her. She's right to question me. To push me away and demand answers.

But her will isn't strong enough to do any of those things.

Gia Bianchi wants me just as much as I want her and holy hell that makes me insane with a need that matches hers.

Sitting back on my couch, I pull her on top of me, her thighs straddling mine. Her dress riding up higher until her fantastic heat presses just where I need it to.

She moans into my mouth as she grinds against my achingly hard cock. Cries out as I rip the pins from her hair, making it tumble down her back in thick black waves. Groans as I yank down the front of her dress and cover her pink nipples with my mouth, licking, biting and flicking them with my tongue. Her tits are large and full and more than fill up my hands as I squeeze them. Fuck, she feels so good.

The remains of her dress are bunched up around her waist, her sweet pussy rocking into me in the most sublime of rhythms. My hands find her ass as we continue to dry fuck like teenagers in heat. She's wet. So goddamn wet for me that I can feel it through the thing material of her panties. The scent of her arousal permeates the air, driving me insane with a need I have never felt before.

"Gia," I growl, not even sure what I'm asking for when I say her name. It can't be for her to stop, even if it's madness for her to continue.

"Finn," she purrs my name. "Oh god, Finn."

And that's it. That's all it takes. Her swearing my name in combination with God's.

Flipping her body so that she's on her back again, I wrench her dress up, getting off on the sound of it tearing and then I lower my head into her panties. Also red, but they don't last long. They come off and then my mouth is on her pussy. Exactly where she wants it. I lick her, sucking on her clit with just the right amount of pressure and she whimpers, her back arching off the couch. My fingers glide into her incredible heat, pumping her in and out to the speed of my tongue. Her sounds instantly become the best sounds I've ever heard and the way she claws at my back and scalp, only spur me on. She tastes so good. So sweet and perfect.

God, how long have I wanted to taste her. To feel her like this. To have her come undone at my touch. Me. This woman is only for me.

"Come, Gia," I demand. "Come all over my face."

She does. She comes hard and loud. Her body writhing against me, her voice practically screeching as she tugs on my hair with surprising strength. It's not enough. Not nearly enough to keep her. To make her mine.

So I yank down my pants, and shatter every rule I ever created since the moment I met her. I enter her body and she invades my soul. I pump against her and she burrows a hole into my heart. I moan into her lips and she becomes part of my blood.

A part of me.

Gia becomes everything and I don't even think she realizes it happens.

But she does. Gia is feeling this too, because her eyes are locked on mine. Sweet beautiful tears falling from them as I fuck her with abandon. Nothing has ever felt this good before.

"I won't leave you, Finn."

My heart hurts.

"I love you, Finn."

I want to die.

"The past doesn't matter, Finn."

It's all that matters.

But I keep going because I can't stop. Because all I can think about is Gia. About how I want to cling to her promises. I'm so desperate for them to be true that I can't think straight.

But the moment it's over. The moment after she convulses around me and I come inside her without a condom on and the world is so goddamn perfect, I panic. My stomach twists and body aches to run and leave her here, half naked on my couch. I look down on her and she's smiling, but I can't think of anything other than all the ways she can destroy my very existence.

She's going to get pregnant.

She'll get pregnant and then I'll lose everything. I can't do it again.

I won't.

Gia has no idea. No clue how deep my darkness goes. How decimated a world can become.

Stupid fucking need. Look where you got me.

Inside the one woman who possesses the power to annihilate whatever's left.

I wake with a jolt. My body slick with sweat as I pant, trying to calm my racing heart. My ravaged heart. *What the fuck was that?* Dropping back down into my bed, I cover my eyes with my forearm. I have no idea what time it is. My room is dark. I have my thick, room darkening shades completely drawn.

But my alarm hasn't gone off yet, so it's not time to pick Gia up yet.

Shit.

After Gia got on that elevator last night, I pulled up the reservation for the car service on my phone. I stared at it for a very long time, debating everything. I should let her go be with this Mason guy and crawl back into the shadows of my life.

But I didn't cancel the car service.

And the irony of this, I can't even cancel with her because I don't have her phone number. I never got it. We've been perpetually running into each other.

Shit.

Getting up, I shower and dress for an evening outside in November in a windy-ass stadium in New Jersey. For an evening out with Gia Bianchi. The girl who I can't seem to stay away from. The girl who drives my overactive imagination wild.

Damn, that dream felt so real. *She* felt so real. So good.

The driver of the limo—okay, maybe I went a touch overboard—pulls up in front of Gia's building, and I hop out and buzz up.

"Oh Finn," she purrs into the intercom. "Always on time. You coming up or am I coming down?"

"Come on down, baby."

I say that and immediately pause. *Baby.* My chest clenches like a vice is squeezing it and I find I have to brace myself against the side of her building.

"Finn?" I feel Gia's hand on my back. "Finn? Are you okay?"

I look over at her, those aqua eyes and that raven hair and that...Patriot's football beanie on top of her head complete with red, white and blue pompom on top. And I laugh. I laugh so goddamn hard. Because she looks nothing like she did in my dream last night and I've never been so relieved by anything in my life. Yes, she's still beautiful, but it's so very different.

"Hey," she squawks, feigning indignation. "It's a football game in November, jerk face."

"Jerk face?" I laugh even harder.

"Yes. You're a jerk face for laughing at me." She unzips her coat and holds it open with a big bright smile. "Check this action out."

"Tom Brady?"

"TB12, baby."

I throw my arms around her without even thinking about it and I pull her into me. Hard.

Because I didn't laugh for three years. I cannot recall one single smile in those three years either. The first time I smiled was the day I sat next to her on that stoop. It was also the first day I laughed. It's how I knew she was different. It's how I knew I would think about her with a pang of regret after she got up and walked away.

And now?

Now I'm in love with her. It's not even a question in my mind.

She's absolutely everything which is bright in my bleak existence.

But I don't know how to go from that to this.

Because if there is one thing I've learned from the many heartbreaks I've endured, is that life doesn't care how much you've suffered.

There is no karma. No justice. No harmonic balance. No fairness and definitely no right versus wrong.

Nothing that says what I've been through won't happen again. In fact, I expect it would. Being born under a bag of shit doesn't disappear just because you've met someone who makes you feel alive instead of dead.

So I pull away from her, ignoring her bewildered expression at my sudden burst of affection and joy and go back to the waiting limo. "Jesus, Finn. You didn't have to get a limo. I would have been cool with a moped."

"Too cold for a moped. Get in, we're going to hit a shit ton of traffic."

Gia gets in, sliding against the smooth black leather seats, removing her jacket as she goes. Her eyes scan around the limo and then she looks up at the sunroof. "Did you ever see the movie *Big?*" I nod, knowing exactly where she's going with this. "You know that scene where they're riding around town, standing up and hanging out the sunroof?"

"Sure."

"I've always wanted to do it. But I don't think today is the day for that."

"I'll make sure we take another limo ride when it's not thirty degrees out."

She looks over at me with a smile. "I'm holding you to that. But only if after that you take me to your apartment so I can jump on a trampoline and sleep in your bunk bed."

"I always wanted bunk beds."

"Me too," she sighs, sagging back. "Being an only child sucks sometimes, you know?"

Not where I was growing up. A sibling would have just been another person for my father to beat the shit out of.

"Did you get enough sleep?" I ask, changing the subject completely.

"No. I freaking hate night shifts. They completely mess with my circadian rhythm. But no matter, I'll sleep tonight after the game and I don't have work tomorrow until noon."

"How'd you manage that?"

She gives me an incredulous look. "I took the morning off, Finn. What else is a woman to do?"

With her rhetorical question lingering in the air, she sinks down, propping her feet up on the bench seat perpendicular to us. Then she shifts until her head is resting against the edge of my arm.

I inwardly sigh. She audibly sighs.

"In case hell actually manages to freeze over tonight and the Patriot's lose and I'm too pissed off to say anything pleasant, thank you for the tickets." She angles her head so that her eyes catch mine. "This is the best birthday present ever. And for the record, you're a much nicer guy then you let anyone believe. But I'm on to you, Finnigan Banner. So no more trying to fool me with your asshole ways."

I lean down and kiss her forehead. I watch as she closes her eyes while I do it. I let my lips linger and when it gets to the point where I know I need to stop, I rest my head against hers.

My eyes close and my dream from last night is there. Right behind my eyes with visions of Gia, naked and desperate for me. God, how I want that with her. I blow out a heavy breath, a familiar ache pulling me back to reality. I'm doing everything wrong with her. And I don't know how to slow down. How to stop and push her away once and for all the way I know I should.

This is going to end ugly for us.

I'm going to hurt her. And there will be no coming back from that. For either of us.

Chapter Twenty-Eight

FINN

"Go!" Gia screams. "Run!" She's jumping up and down and tugging on my arm and her nose is red, as are her cheeks from the cold, and she's smiling so big and holy shit. Just holy shit. Because I don't necessarily care about football at all, but her excitement is contagious. "Touchdown!" Gia yells, doing a little dance and hugging me and laughing at herself. That's contagious too. "Go us," she sings, wiggling and dancing about. "We rule. We're the winners."

Now, we're not in Boston. We're in New York, well technically Jersey, but still. This is not a Patriot's crowd. But no one is yelling at her or giving her shit. In fact, they're laughing. Because she's just so goddamn cute. "You're a very gracious winner," I say and she laughs, nudging me with her hip.

"Never said I was. But maybe I should tone it down some?"

"Probably."

I'm smiling down at her. She's smiling up at me. She's staring at my mouth like she likes the way my smile looks. I'm staring at hers like I want to kiss it.

"Come here, Finn." She grabs my shoulder and yanks me down so that I'm close to her height.

"What the hell are you doing?"

She glances at me and rolls her eyes like it should be obvious. "I'm taking a selfie of us. I want a picture to commemorate our first Patriot's game together. And the win of course. Have to memorialize that."

She takes her phone out, extends her arm, presses her head against mine and then clicks away.

I can honestly say this is the first selfie I've ever taken, but then again, I don't get out all that much. "What's your number?" she asks, looking up at me expectantly.

"Why?"

"Jesus, Finn. What century are you living in? I want to text you the pictures. They came out really good." she flips her phone around so I can look at it. "See." I nod, because it is a great picture of us. But I don't want it on my phone, because if it's on my phone then I'll look at it. "And really, the fact that I don't yet have your number feels a little strange. So digits me, baby."

"What if I don't want you to have my number?"

She peeks up at me nonplussed. "Why wouldn't you want me to have your number? It's not like I'm going to go all geostalker on your ass. What did I tell you in the car on the way down about being an asshole?"

"Fine," I sigh, because she's right. I'm being ridiculous. I tell her my number and then she puts it in her phone and texts me pictures and an emoji of something which looks like chocolate soft-serve ice cream with a smiley face on it. "What's that?"

Gia bursts out laughing, "It's poop, Finn. Because that's what you're being. A poop."

"A *poop?*" I can't stop my smile.

"Yup. But since you brought me here and the Patriot's not only won, they kicked ass, I'm willing to be magnanimous and forgive you."

"Come with me," I say, twisting her body so we're facing the aisle and then I push her forward. "I want to get the hell out of here before we're stuck in traffic for ten hours."

"Party pooper," she says.

"I thought you weren't going to call me poop anymore?"

She laughs, turning her head over my shoulder. "Oh Finn, you made a joke. How adorable."

We reach the waiting limo and get in, both sighing out contentedly at the warmth of it. Gia takes off her coat and I do the same and she tosses her Patriot's beanie next to her coat and we settle in because we're not moving anytime soon.

"That was so much fun," she smiles sleepily. "Can we do it again next year? It can be our thing."

"Sure. I had fun too."

Gia grins as she closes her eyes, "I'm beyond thrilled to hear that. It's hard to tell with you sometimes."

I don't respond to that and Gia leans her head against my shoulder like she did on the way down, but this time, she's squirming around, unable to comfortably settle. "Here," I say, sitting back in the seat, propping my legs up on the other and positioning her head so that it's in my lap.

She blinks up at me, a little surprised, I think, but she doesn't pull away. And she doesn't stop me as I stroke her hair, marveling at just how soft and silky it is. Like flowing ink. "When was the last time you had a girlfriend?"

My hand freezes in her hair and for the longest time, I just watch at her. Her expression tells me she's nervous, that she knows she's skating on thin ice with this, but she doesn't retract her question. She's patiently waiting for my answer.

"I haven't had a girlfriend in six years." Technically Kelly was only my girlfriend for about a year before she became my wife. It was six years ago that I married her.

"Six?" she gasps.

I nod.

"You haven't been in a relationship in six years?" She's incredulous and I shake my head, correcting her misassumption.

"No. I haven't been in a relationship in three years." Her eyebrows knit together and I press my finger into the groove, flattening it back out. "I was married for three years." I don't know why

I just told her that. I don't particularly want her to know about my past. About Kelly.

Gia's mouth pops open a little. I believe I've stunned her speechless, which feels like a minor victory considering the subject matter. I wait for it with my heart stuck in my throat. The inevitable, *what happened*, question. But it never comes.

Instead a lone tear rolls down the right side of her face. She does nothing to brush it away and I do nothing, but watch it glide down her temple, only to be absorbed by her hair. "Are you happy with Mason?"

She nods. That's it and for some reason, that response bothers me. I want her to tell me she's blissfully in love with him. Hopelessly content. I want her to tell me that even though we have this unbelievable chemistry, that's all it will ever be.

"But he loves you," I say and comes out sounding defensive.

Now I get a shrug.

"What's your favorite color?" she asks and I smile at the change in subject matter.

"Aqua," I say, staring directly into her eyes. "Yours?"

"Bright blue."

I love that answer as much as I hate it. Especially since I know she's lying. Everything in Gia's world is lavender. Her phone case. Her freaking clogs. Her nails sometimes. It's why I made sure her birthday present wrapping, rose and mug were that color as well.

"What's your favorite food," I try, going for something safe.

"Clam chowder. The New England kind, not the Manhattan." Of course, it is. "And my grandmother's manicotti. Yours?"

"Sushi."

She laughs, shaking her head. "God, that's so pretentious."

I laugh with her because it sort of is. "Can't help that. Do you speak any other languages besides Italian?"

"Spanish. Do you speak any other languages?"

"French."

"French?" she snorts out. "Were you raised with a silver spoon in your mouth? Who the hell speaks French and has sushi as a favorite food?"

"I do believe I am not the only one to come from an affluent background."

Gia rolls her eyes at me. "That's another thing, the way you speak. You're very formal, Dr. Banner. It makes me want to ruffle your hair or pierce your tongue or something."

I smile, running my fingers across her cheek and through her hair. "Definitely no piercings, though if you had a tongue ring, I'd be all for a demonstration." She laughs and sticks out her tongue. No ring, but there is a scar. "You had one?"

"Yes. Rebellious stage when I was eighteen. I also got a tattoo."

"Where?" She points to the right lower quadrant of her abdomen, between her hip and pelvic bone. I don't ask what she has. Honestly, I'm a bit preoccupied with its location. But I'm afraid if I keep going, she's going to ask if I have one and then I'm screwed.

"Very sexy, kitten. Say something in Italian for me."

"What do you want me to say?"

I wink at her. "How about, I love, Finn. He's the greatest man in the world."

Gia laughs, shaking her head against my thighs as we slowly creep through game traffic. "No way. I'm not saying that."

"Oh, come on, Gia. Have some fun with me."

She rolls her eyes again and then says, "Amo Finn. È l'uomo migliore al mondo."

And because I'll never get another chance to say it. "Je t'aime aussi, Gia. Merci de me faire ressentir comme ça." She sucks in a shuddered breath, holding onto it before letting it out slowly. "Do you know what I said?"

She sniffles a little, her eyes becoming increasingly glassy. "The first part." She swallows. Clears her throat. "Not the second."

"Sucks for you. I know what you said."

She laughs, reaching up to wipe away at a falling tear. "Yeah, well, that's what Google is for, right?"

"Only if you know how to spell it."

"Asshole." She smacks at me. "Not fair. You tricked me."

"Just remember who said it first." I chuckle, enjoying the hell out of her angry glower.

"Doesn't count. You told me to say it."

"You're right," I concede, holding my hands up in surrender. "I did. I'm forever an asshole."

Gia watches me for a very long moment as something I don't understand crosses her features. She needs to ask me something, but is afraid to do so. "What?" I challenge. "Just ask me."

"Finn," she says my name so softly. Hesitantly. "What are we doing? Why does the thought of Mason being hurt with me going to the game with you, seem to please you? Why do you touch me and kiss my forehead and spend time with me? Especially after my birthday night."

I hate those questions. All of them. Why did she have to ask me that? Why did she have to go there after such a perfect day? Frustration slams in to my chest, as I run a hand through my hair and then down my face. "Because I'm addicted."

"Pardon?" That is not at all what she thought I was going to say.

"I'm addicted and you're...I don't know what exactly. Heroin? Alcohol? Both? Who the hell knows. But even though I'm not sampling the alcohol or shooting the drugs, it doesn't mean that I don't like to spend time in the bar. That I don't like to be around the drugs."

"I think I'm only partially following you."

Blowing out a loud growl, I say, "I like spending time with you, Gia. I think you already know that. In fact, I'm positive you do. But I told you it will never go beyond that."

"You told me all of this before. More than once actually. So what the hell are we doing here? Why do you bring me presents and dance with me and take me to football games?"

"I don't know," I huff out, really wishing she'd shut the fuck up already. "I tried, okay? I tried. But I'm not all that good at staying away from you. And maybe Mike's right about me. Maybe I like to cut myself just so I can watch it bleed, but that doesn't change the situation."

"Jesus, Finn. How the hell am I supposed to respond to that?"

I sigh. This is a losing battle with her. She's right. I know she is. I'm fucking with both of us, but I don't plan on stopping until she makes me. Maybe that's wrong, but it's all I've got and I can't go back to nothing when I've finally began to feel something good again.

"You're not, Gia. There is no response because there is no situation to respond to. You have a boyfriend, remember? You said friends, remember? I'm just trying to give you what you want. Make you happy."

"Because you're addicted." *To me*, she doesn't tack on, but we both know it's true. We both know that's exactly what I was saying.

I nod, my fingers wiping away yet another tear as it glides down her temple. "I think you're getting it now."

"No," she says with a shake of her head. "I *don't* get it. But you're not one for real explanations or detailed stories. And your truths that I believe you're very fond of, are perpetually sliced in half. I'm tired, Finn. You make me so very tired. But maybe I'm addicted too. Maybe that's the perfect way to explain this." She waves her finger back and forth between us.

I don't have an answer to that. If I were a better, stronger man, I'd cut her loose for good. But I'm not, so I return my hands to her hair and her eyes grow heavy. "Close your eyes, Gia. Get some rest." Shifting my position, I lean down and kiss her forehead. Being addicted to her sucks. "I'll wake you when we get home."

Gia sighs and as I draw back, her eyes flutter shut and her head tilts and she falls asleep just like that. With her head in my lap and my hands stroking her hair and my eyes glued to her face.

And when I know she's really out, I whisper, "Je t'aime."

Because even though she didn't mean it, I did.

Chapter Twenty-Nine

GIA

"Hey," Finn says to me with a big smile as I stroll up to him. "I didn't know you were going to be here."

I laugh. "That's a hell of a greeting there, Dr. Banner. That better not be a disappointed-to-see-me smile."

Finn laughs, pulling me in for a hug. He does that now. He hugs me. And he kisses me. On my cheek or my forehead–that's his personal favorite, I think–and sometimes, he likes to whisper secrets into my ear. Something changed between us after the game. After our conversation about being mutual addicted to the other.

He's no longer distant or careful with me.

Nor is he quick to push me away.

We spend nearly every day together. Not all day. More like small tidbits of time.

He stops by my floor–though he refuses to enter it–and brings me cappuccinos. Occasionally with hot chocolate, but mostly without. Or we just so happen to meet on a bench at the end of the hallway which leads away from radiology and eat lunch there together. And if we both have a rare weekday off, we do stuff. Together.

I don't know how it happened and I have zero explanation for it.

196

Finn is sweet and attentive and well…amazing.

"Never," he whispers in my ear. "I'm always happy to see you."

See what I mean?

But then he always does this: "Where's Mason?"

Stepping back, I take him in. He's so freaking hot tonight. He's wearing a dark blue sweater which makes his bright-blue eyes sparkle in contrast, and his hair is brushed the way I like it and he's got a decent layer of brown stubble lining his chiseled jaw, and his jeans are dark and low hung–and dear god–I think I'm blushing.

"He couldn't make it tonight. He had to work late on a project."

"C'est dommage."

"Yes, it is…dommage."

Finn laughs, pulling me into his side and kissing my forehead. "Even though I'm epically disappointed your lesser half isn't here tonight, I am relieved to no longer be forced to make small talk with the woman Mike brought to set me up with."

"What?" I step back, my eyes wide. "Mike brought a woman for you?"

It shouldn't bother me. It should make me feel…reassured that Mike is trying to set up Finn. Happy even. But it doesn't. It makes me sick. And that makes me feel guilty and this whole vicious cycle starts all over again.

Finn nods, taking my hand and guiding me through the large brownstone Mike owns, all the way to the back. "There," he says, nodding his chin in the direction of a very pretty strawberry blonde talking to Monique. "That's my forced blind date."

"She looks nice," I manage. Damn, jealousy is a real moth-erfucker.

"I'm sure she is. I'm sure she's very nice and smart and capable and yes, she's also decently attractive, but Mike should know better."

"How do you mean?"

"Don't play coy, Miss Bianchi, it doesn't suit you. I have no interest in being set up. But Mike already told her about me. I know he did because when I shook her hand, she blushed and looked away like a demure little doll."

"Maybe she was just caught off guard by your searing good looks and rugged masculinity."

Finn examines me as I bite my lip to try and hide my smile because I wanted that to come out serious, though I was being sarcastic, but now I can't stop my laugh. "Even though you suck at hiding your sarcasm—or your smile for that matter—I'm going to take that as a compliment from you, because I know you think I'm hot. But no, I don't think that was what her reaction was all about."

"Maybe you'll like her, Finn. Maybe she's the woman of your dreams and you're making the mistake of a lifetime by automatically dismissing her."

Finn turns to me, his eyes finding mine, locking me in. He takes a step, his arm and the side of his chest pressing into me ever so slightly. My breath hitches with the intensity in his expression. "No," he says softly, seductively. "She's not that one."

Oh. My. God.

"What are you two talking about in hushed tones?" Mike asks from behind us.

I spin around like a teenager caught making out with her boyfriend. But since I'm not, I recover quickly. "The woman you tried to set Finn up with."

Mike chuckles and slaps Finn on the back. "She's great, man. You'll really like her."

"Not my type."

"Oh," Mike says, his eyes bouncing down to me quickly before going back to Finn with a smirk on his lips. "And what exactly is that?"

"Not her," is all Finn says, jutting his thumb in the direction of the poor girl who actually looks really sweet. I can say that now that I know Finn isn't interested. If he was, I'd probably be hating on her. I'm just that mature.

"Fine," Mike groans. "But one day I'll convince you to rejoin the human male race."

"I wouldn't hold your breath. It's a party and I don't want to have to intubate you."

"That wasn't very funny," I deadpan and Finn pinches my side, making me squeal and jump because he always manages to hit that one sensitive spot.

"You could pretend to like my jokes."

I shake my head. "Your jokes are never funny."

Mike rolls his eyes at us. "We're just waiting on a couple more people and then we can eat. Thanks again, Gia for bringing some food. Monique was freaking out when she got stuck at work."

"No problem. I love cooking and I had Nonna Bianchi's recipes to work with."

"Nonna Bianchi?"

I narrow my eyes at Finn who is laughing at me, I think. "Yes. My grandmother, dick face. And you can laugh at me all you want, but wait till you try the food. That woman knew how to cook."

"Damn you're cute." Finn says and I can feel Mike smile and this is my cue to get the hell out of here, away from Finn who gives me looks and thinks I'm cute.

I roll my eyes at him, playing his words off like they're a joke. Like I don't feel them. "I'm going to go help Mo with food and meet Finn's date."

Spinning on my heels, I get my ass away from Mike's knowing smile and into the kitchen. Monique is talking to Strawberry Blonde and the more I observe her, the more infuriated with myself I become. She's very pretty and I have no doubt that if Finn gave her a chance, he'd be interested. Which is probably something I should have encouraged instead of discouraged.

I have Mason, and Finn doesn't want with me what I want with him, so I really need to let that one go. But honestly, I don't know if it would make a difference if I did. I think there is a very good reason why Finn doesn't date. I mean three years? That's just crazy.

You don't give up on love, on life, like that without a very good reason.

"There you are," Monique says with a big bright smile. She gives me an enormous hug, to the point that she's almost crushing me. She's wearing a stunning light green wrap dress and her black curly hair is pulled back into a low bun. She looks so unbelievably happy. Beautiful and happy. "You look beautiful," she says.

"Funny, I was just thinking the exact same thing about you."

"Gia, this is Alexandra Calhoun. She's a pediatric surgery fellow where I work. Alex, this is Gia Bianchi, a fellow midwife."

"So nice to meet you," she says with one of the most outstanding southern accents I've ever heard in my life.

"You too," I say with a smile. She's even prettier up close, even though she's definitely older than me. Older than Finn too I'd bet, maybe thirty-twoish. "Did you do your residency here in New York as well?"

She shakes her head. "No. I'm only in New York for my fellowship. I did my residency at Johns Hopkins."

"Wow," I say. "That's impressive." And it is. Johns Hopkins is one of the most sought after and demanding residency programs in the country.

She blushes, which I find to be a fascinating reaction considering she's a surgeon—a pediatric surgeon at that—and those people don't fuck around. They're hardcore, but this woman is soft and gentle. Kind of a contradiction.

I take back what I said about encouraging Finn to give her a try. He'd break her in two with his assholery.

"Gia, can you help me with this?" Monique asks me, pointing to the food, but I don't miss the timing. Finn just entered the kitchen with Mike and two other people I vaguely know.

"Sure." I smile at Alex. "Excuse me." I walk over to Monique who is standing in front of the oven, wearing hot-pink oven mitts.

"Is this ready?"

I peer down at the bubbling tray of chicken parmesan and nod. She knows it is. She was pulling me away from Finn. "Looks good."

"She's nice, right? And smart. You think Finn will like her?"

I shrug, busying myself with the container of baked ziti I made. "He said he wasn't interested."

Monique sighs, like this frustrates her. "That's because he's only interested in you."

"Is not," I say automatically.

"And you have Mason."

She's checking my reaction and all I can do is nod, but I can't

200

meet her eyes, because I'm a freaking weakling. "And I have Mason."

Monique smiles, mollified by my declaration and says, "Then let's eat."

I help bring everything out to the large dining room table they have set up, but just as I set the tray down, I feel a hand on my upper arm. "Looks amazing," Finn says, his thumb brushing up and down my bare flesh. "Why haven't you ever cooked for me like this before?"

I shrug. "Because you never asked me to."

He turns me to face him, tilting my chin up until our eyes meet once again. Damn if a flock of excited butterflies don't take flight inside me. Finn is that dip. That adrenaline thrill you get when you're in an airplane and you hit an air pocket, dropping five thousand feet before leveling off. Every. Goddamn. Time.

"Gia, my beautiful Italian goddess, will you cook dinner for me sometime in the near future?"

"Um…" I think I just forgot how to speak in coherent sentences. Or even how to formulate words. Instead I nod. And swallow. Hard. Because the look he's giving me right now has my toes curling and my eyes resisting the urge to roll back.

Finn smiles that smile I love so much on him and then he dips his head down, fanning his hot breath against my ear and whispers, "Breathe, Gia. Because if you become cyanotic, I'll opt for mouth to mouth with you instead of intubation."

He chuckles to himself like he's the funniest person in the world and then goes back over to Mike and some other doctor whose name I can't remember. And once he's gone, I suck in a very needed and audible breath. Finnigan Banner just managed to turn me into a puddle of pathetic, right here on the dining room floor.

And worse yet, I can't help but love it.

Chapter Thirty

GIA

The restaurant Chloe picked is just the right mix of unhealthy food and delicious drinks. It's the perfect spot for a snack with your girls. It's early afternoon now, but this time of year, it's practically dark. Picking up a piece of spicy chicken, I pop it into my mouth, chewing slowly while Chloe digests what I just told her.

"So is this George guy going to be there every time you see your mom now? I mean, coming for Thanksgiving is kinda a big deal," Chloe says as she shoves a nacho into her mouth and sips on her margarita.

"I know," I say thinking about Thanksgiving dinner yesterday. "My cousin said the same thing. George is a nice guy–don't get me wrong–but it I didn't realize he was already part of the family."

Today is the Friday after Thanksgiving, universally known as Black Friday. Every year, Chloe, Monique and I brave the crowds and go do some selfish shopping. I realize the 'holiday' was enacted so that you could do your Christmas shopping while taking advantage of all the sales, but we don't do that.

Instead we bought party dresses because Monique and Mike are having a Christmas party. Because they're living together in domestic bliss. Because they're in love.

I found a very pretty gold dress which looks fantastic against my skin color and it's just shimmery enough to be festive. After all our hard work, we're rewarding ourselves with snacks. And cocktails because—why not.

I'm working Christmas Eve day, but I'll go to the party after work and I have Christmas day off, which will help with post-party recovery. Even though I'm going stag to the party, I'm still looking forward to it. Mason is flying out to see his parents who live outside Denver. He's spending the week there and going skiing with them as part of their annual family vacation.

He didn't invite me along, which was fine. I think that was more his parents doing than his. Mason told me he brought home a girl once and his parents became extremely attached to her and then when they broke up, his mother was devastated. So I didn't get the invite. Not that I would have been able to go anyway. I would have never gotten the time off.

"I'm going home with Michael," –Monique always calls Mike, Michael– "for Christmas day. His mother called and invited me."

"Wow," Chloe marvels through a mouthful of food. "I bet he proposes to you that day."

Monique shakes her head, but her dark skin turns a little warmer. "No. I don't think it will be on Christmas." Yeah, she's hoping it happens on Christmas. "We just moved in together."

"So that means you can't get engaged?" I challenge.

"It just means I don't think it's happening over Christmas."

Chloe looks over at me, pointing a stern finger. "If you get engaged or move in with Mason, I might have to kick your ass."

"I love how supportive you are. Such a caring, nurturing friend." Monique snorts, but Chloe is undeterred. "Hey, no threatening me. I'm not moving in with Mason and we're definitely not getting engaged."

"Because she's in love with Finn Banner," Monique says with an impish grin. I think my eyes are, in fact, bugging out of my head and my jaw is on the floor.

"What nonsense are you spewing?"

Monique shrugs, but that grin remains. "Okay fine. You might not love him, but he absolutely loves you."

Chloe laughs at my expression and I throw her an eye which is meant to shut her up, but of course, because it's Chloe, only makes her laugh harder.

"Liar, liar, pants on fire," I say indignantly, but Monique is just shaking her head as she crunches down on a chip.

"I saw the two of you talking when you came for dinner last week."

I roll my eyes at that. "Well, since you saw us talking, that must clearly mean love is in the air."

"Don't be sarcastic, Gia. It causes wrinkles." I flip Chloe off and she blows me a kiss. "I want details. What is this about dinner conversation?"

"If you had come, you would have seen it."

"I was working. No need to get snippy with me."

Monique laughs. "Well, Finn and Gia were on one end of the table. And they were both leaning into each other and talking. Finn was smiling the entire time and he was laughing at whatever they were talking about."

"Yeah, I'm missing something here, aren't I?" Chloe asks, looking back and forth between Monique and me. I shrug, trying to play it off like I'm just as clueless as she is.

"Michael says Finn doesn't smile and he definitely doesn't laugh. At least he didn't used to. But he does both of those things with Gia. And he completely ignored a very pretty and interested pediatric surgery fellow. And," she says, pointing her finger in the air like she just remembered something, "he couldn't take his eyes off Gia."

I sigh. I don't want to hear any of this. I really don't. I've got a good thing going with Mason and Finn makes it known he's interested but will never act on that interest and I'm just…annoyed with it. And frustrated. And tired. Really freaking tired. I believe that's exactly what I told the man.

Trying to navigate the mind-fuck that is Finn, is exhausting.

Especially since he has taken to texting me in addition to our frequent meetings. And the majority of those texts are in French, so most of the time so I have to translate them. But I look forward to those damn texts. I covet them.

I'm spending all this time with Mason. We're getting so much closer. So much stronger as a couple and yet I have this platonic and not-so-platonic relationship going on with Finn. Something has to give and I know it needs to be my 'friendship' with him, but I can't make the cut. I can't sever the ties.

But where does that leave Mason and me?

How can I move forward with a man when I'm stuck in limbo with another?

"Can we just not do this? Talking about Finn is draining."

"Can we talk about the conjoined twins who Dr. Levine delivered the other night? Because that was fucking awesome." Monique and I both beam at Chloe with eager, inquisitive smiles.

"Conjoined where?"

"On their hip, which is super lucky for them because the separation surgery isn't supposed to be as bad there." Chloe goes on about the conjoined twins and we eat the rest of our snack and drink the rest of our cocktails and we don't talk about men again for the rest of the afternoon.

And I don't think about them either until I'm nearly at my building and I get a text from Finn asking me to meet him at Ophelia's bar. Standing in the middle of the sidewalk, I stare down at the text. I read it over and over again.

Then I call Mason.

"Hey," Mason answers on the first ring with a very audible smile in his voice. "How was shopping with the girls?"

Moving over to the side of the building, I lean against the brick, attempting to shield myself from the cold air. "It was fun. I got a dress."

"That's great. You'll have to try it on for me since I'll miss the big *reveal*." I laugh at the way he says reveal. Mason makes me laugh a lot. I love that about him. I wouldn't say I love *him* necessarily, but I'm sure it's only a matter of time. "You on your way back home?"

"I don't know. I was thinking about stopping in at Ophelia's bar. But if you're around, we could do something."

"Oh," he says and then pauses. "I'm going to meet up with a few of the guys to shoot some hoops and then I think we're getting dinner. You around tomorrow?"

I shake my head, unable to determine if I'm relieved or not. "No. I'm working until seven. I can do a late dinner though."

"Sounds perfect. I'll cook you something if you don't mind making the trip downtown."

"You've got a deal. Have fun with the boys."

"Say hi to the tattooed queen for me." I laugh, disconnecting the call. I didn't tell Mason that Finn was the one who invited me to the bar and I can't help the resulting twinge of guilt which accompanies that thought. But Mason knows I hang out with Finn. I typically tell him when I do and even though it's not Mason's favorite thing, he understands and accepts it.

So why didn't you tell him about it now?

Yeah, I don't have an answer for that. Maybe it's what Monique said to me at the restaurant? I don't know, but it's too late to call Mason back now and tell him, so instead I text Finn letting him know that I'm on my way and I start in that direction.

Twelve minutes later, I'm opening the door and waltzing inside. It's decently packed in here, but it doesn't take me long to spot Finn who is sitting at the bar, talking to Ophelia. Sliding into the vacant seat next to him, I tap him on the shoulder.

And when he turns to face me, his eyes light up. And he smiles, showing off all of his perfect white teeth.

Dammit.

"Hey," he says. "Glad you could make it."

"It was good timing," I explain. "I just finished up with Monique and Chloe."

"How was your holiday?" Ophelia asks.

"Not bad. Yours?"

"Really good," she gleams. "My little sister just had a baby so I got to spend a lot of time with them."

"Awesome," I smile, looking over to Finn who is no longer smiling. "What did she have?"

"A girl. So freaking cute. Her name is Olivia."

"Love that. Congrats auntie."

Ophelia grins at me. "What can I get you this time or is it bartender's choice?"

"The latter, please. Just nothing too strong. I already had a half a margarita."

"Coming up."

Ophelia winks at me and then goes off to make my drink. Spinning on my stool so I'm facing Finn, my legs dangle between us. "What about you? How was Thanksgiving with your mom?"

Finn glances over at me, setting his beer down as he does. His expression is...lukewarm at best. I wonder if being home yesterday was difficult for him. "We ate at the club. The food was the same as always, decent, but unimaginative. The rest was...boring. I see you got a dress," Finn bounces his head at the garment bag I draped over the back of my stool.

I nod. "Yup. I'll be pretty in gold. Are you coming to the party?"

"No," he says with an edge. "I won't be."

"Oh, are you working on Christmas Eve night?"

He shakes his head. "New Year's."

"Me too. Are you going away for the holiday?"

"No, Gia. I'm not." His tone is curt and that is so unlike him now, it takes me a second to readjust.

He doesn't want me to ask why he's not going to the party. It's written all over his stiff posture and tight expression. So, I don't. Finn has his limits. Sometimes he's more open than others. Like that day at the football game.

But today is undoubtedly not one of those days.

"Okay then," I shrug, turning back to the bar and grabbing my...I have no idea. "What is this?" I stare at it, scrunching my eyebrows.

Ophelia grins like the Cheshire cat. "It's a slow comfortable screw up against a wall."

I burst out laughing. "Is there such a thing?"

She shrugs. "Not in my experience, but I've always wanted to make one and no one ever orders them."

I take a sip and wince at the strength of it. "Holy hell, I can see why. I thought I told you not too strong."

"Did you miss the part where I said I've always wanted to make one?"

"Fine. I'll drink half of it. Go." I nod my head in the direction of the waiting line of people. "Do your one great. You're pissing off the customers."

Ophelia blows me a kiss and tosses Finn a wink and then leaves us.

"Where's your boyfriend right now, Gia?"

I can't help but scowl at that. Why did he invite me out if he's just going to be difficult? "Out with his friends. Would you like me to leave you alone to your shit mood?"

"I am in a shit mood." He runs his hand through his hair. "Honestly, I don't know why I came out. Why I asked you to meet me."

"Finn?" I reach out and touch his shoulder. He turns back to me and it looks like he's drowning. "Do you want to talk about it?"

He shakes his head no.

"Do you want to go ice-skating?"

A smile quirks up the corner of his lips. "Ice-skating?"

"Sure," I beam.

"I don't know how to ice-skate."

"Neither do I. We can fall on our asses together. It'll be fun."

"And break something and end up in the ED. No thanks."

"Wow," I shake my head at him. "You really are being a bear. Okay, no ice-skating and drinking beer doesn't seem to be doing it for you either. What about Netflix and Thanksgiving leftovers?"

"I don't have any leftovers."

"But I do. Some better than decent ones. Imaginative ones. Come on," I urge, tugging on his large muscular arm. Goddamn, Finn has some serious guns. When this man has time to hit the gym, I do not know. "I'll even let you pick what we watch."

Finn stands up after a couple more tugs and tosses forty dollars down on the bar even though I doubt these drinks cost more than fifteen combined. I love that about him. He can be so generous sometimes and I doubt he even thinks about it. It comes naturally when he allows it to. "Fine, but I'm warning you now, I'm not picking anything sweet or romantic or funny."

"Okay, we'll only watch things which are violent and serious. Possibly scary."

"Deal."

Chapter Thirty-One

GIA

"Finn," I start, looking over at him as he sits on my sofa in front of my television, my remote poised in his hand. "I know I said I was cool with you picking the movie, but I take that back now."

He doesn't acknowledge me, which is sort of exasperating if I'm being honest.

"No, seriously. I cannot watch *Clown*. Clowns scare the ever-loving crap out of me under the best of circumstances. Even when they're meant to be funny. This movie is not funny, Finn."

Finally, he glances in my direction, but he's still all somber and brooding. "That's the point, Gia. It's a scary movie."

I shake my head. "That's all well and good, but that doesn't mean I want to have nightmares like a fucking ten-year-old over it. Pick something else. Like *The Shining* or *Scream* or *Nightmare on Elm Street*. Something I've seen a dozen times and falls more within the realm of cult classic rather than Gia Bianchi torture device."

"Is the food ready yet?"

I sigh. Why did I invite him over? Why didn't I just let him sit in that bar and stew?

"You're not eating any of my delicious leftovers until you change the movie. I'm one hundred percent serious. If I have to, I'll kick your ass out over it."

He's doing his best not to laugh, but I'm actually not kidding. "Fine. I'll change it. But you do realize now that I know your weakness is clowns I can exploit it for my own personal enjoyment."

I pause, standing there and staring at him with wide eyes, one hand on my hip the other pointing a stern finger at him. "You're not just an asshole, Finnigan Banner. You're a sadistic asshole. What the hell kind of thing is that to say?"

He sighs, leaning back in my couch and scrubbing his hands up and down his face. "Yeah. Sorry. That was pretty fucked up of me. Maybe I should just go. Clearly I'm not in the right frame of mind to be around humans at the moment."

"Okay," I soften because I feel sort of bad for him. Clearly something is eating at him. "Put on *Young Frankenstein* because that movie is freaking hilarious. We're going to eat amazing food, followed by apple pie." He stares at me. Watches me. "With ice cream *and* whipped cream. And wine. I have a bottle of expensive wine which my cousin bought me. And you're going to chill the fuck out."

Finn stands up, the motion so quick and unexpected that I start. He strides over until he's crowding me. He always crowds me. Personal space isn't something he abides by. At least with me. "Why do you bother?"

I furrow my eyebrows, craning my neck so I can see him better. "What do you mean?"

"Explain it to me. What do you get out of this?" He waves his finger back and forth between us.

I have no answer to give him. We've already had this conversation. We're mutually addicted to the other, but I don't think that's where he's going right now. I think he's hit his limit.

"You have a boyfriend. You have a life. I'm an asshole. You said so yourself. So tell me why you brought me here."

"I don't know," I admit, stumbling over my thoughts a bit. "You are an asshole. And sometimes you irritate me to no end. And occasionally you're too honest without being honest at all. But I care about you, okay? I do. So now it's your turn. What do you get out of this?" I wave my finger back and forth between us the way he just did.

"Personal suffering and torment."

I take a step back, because holy crap, that hurt. "You texted me to come hang out. Why would you do that if I'm so insufferable?"

Finn grabs my face, drawing me closer, and tilting my head until his eyes bore into mine. "How can you think that? How can you can take those words and twist them into something they're not? I can't tell if you're intentionally being obtuse or if you really don't know."

I try to pry my face away from him, but to no avail. Finn has me in his grip and he's got a point to make which he's going to force me to hear. Whether I want to or not. He dips his head down until our eyes are locked and our faces are inches apart.

"I love you, Gia. I'm *in love* with you. It's why I seek you out. It's why I ask about your stupid boyfriend who is nowhere near good enough for you. It's why I kill myself day and in day out. I don't know how not to. I don't know how to let you go. And sometimes, I get to the point where it's too much. Like today. Everything is too much. I fucking love you and it's the last thing in the world I want to do."

I don't understand. If he loves me the way he says he does then why doesn't he *want* to love me? Especially when *I* want it so badly. "Then why–"

"Because I won't do it again!" he yells with so much force and conviction, I'm momentarily stunned.

What happened to you, Finn?

I shake my head in his hands, my eyes welling up the longer I gaze into his bright-blue eyes. This man loves me. But the thought of loving someone, of being with someone, pains him. Physically pains him. I can feel that pain leaching from him now. Rolling off him in waves.

Finn releases my face, turns, but instead of leaving the way I expect him to, he storms over to my window and slams the side of his fist into it, rattling the pane. Then he spins back around and drops to the floor. "Finn?" I call out.

No answer.

Because he's not there.

Finn is on the floor between my window and my couch. His knees are drawn up to his chest and his face is in his hands. And he's broken. Absolutely tortured. Just the way he said he was.

What happened to you, Finn?

I don't ask my question out loud and I don't flee into my bedroom the way my body is begging me to. Instead I slowly move across the room and drop down to my knees in front of him. My hands land on his knees and he jerks away. "Finn?" I say softly this time.

He shakes his head. His eyes closed. "I'm sorry, Gia. I'm so goddamn sorry."

That's all he says, but I think he believes that covers everything. All of the hurt he's about to give me.

He shakes his head again and then he laughs out humorlessly. "What the fuck? It's not even like you're the first one. I wasn't like this before." His eyes open and then they focus on mine. "What is it about you which makes you so goddamn special? Just go away, Gia. Cut me loose already."

I have no words. Only tears.

What did she do to you, Finn?

"I'm not leaving you," I tell him.

His eyes widen in horror. Then he smiles, but it's not a real smile. It's a Finn smile, I realize. "We'll see."

"Why did you come out there, then? Why did you come after me, if this is all there can ever be?"

I don't even know if I'm talking about that first time on the curb outside of the ED when my father died or that night on the balcony or the first night he brought me espresso-coffee or all those other times. We've had so many times. And yeah, some of them have been hard. Some of them have been downright awful.

But we've had so many good ones too. Some of the most memorable in my life. Finn makes me feel…hell, he just makes me feel. The good and the bad. The ugly and the beautiful. He gives as much as he takes, but what he gives is everything I need.

"Self-destruction and blind jealousy."

My head drops, my chin hitting my chest as I cry. I've never cried like this before. Never felt this sort of raw, vulnerable emotion. Never this sort of heartbreak. I've been waiting for this moment with Finn Banner for so long. And he didn't disappoint.

If he's not careful, he's going to get exactly what he wants from me.

"Is this what you want?" I sob.

"Not even close."

"I'll never forgive you."

"I don't deserve it anyway."

"Oh god," I wail.

His arms wrap around my body in a flash, and I topple backward against the force of his weight, his hand cupping the back of my head so I don't bash it against the hardwoods. His mouth is everywhere. My lips. My cheeks. My eyes. My nose. My ears. "I'm sorry," he says. "So fucking sorry."

I shake my head against him, wishing I were stronger. Strong enough to get up and force him out.

"I don't deserve you, but I want you, Gia. Want really doesn't even begin to describe my level of obsession."

I don't know how to do this.

"You can't do this to me again. Tell me you want me and you love me and then push me away."

"I panicked, Gia. I always panic with you. Everything is a gut reaction."

"No," I shake my head, my eyes still closed. "This was so much more than panicking."

I feel him pause over me and I risk opening my eyes. His bright-blue ones are inches from mine, but they're utterly defenseless. Beaten. "I love you," he says it so calmly I wonder if I imagined everything that just happened between us. "I can't make sense of anything other than that. But I can't give you what you need. I can only give you this."

His lips crash down on mine and then he kisses me with a force unlike any before it. His tongue invades my mouth and his hands occupy my hair and his soul dominates everything inside of me. But even as he kisses me, I feel how wrong this is to him. How conflicted and ill he is.

I am not this girl. It's why I didn't sleep with him the night of my birthday. I won't let myself fall victim to that level of hurt.

I push him back.

"That's not enough for me. I want more than this."

He shakes his head, but he doesn't say anything else.

I need to leave him. I need to scour the depths of my ravaged soul, pull myself up and off this floor and never look back. But I can't do that. Because I feel like there is so much more here. So much more to him and if he walks away now, I'll never know just how good it can be.

"Tell me," I demand. "Tell me what happened to you."

His expression is beyond shattered. But he doesn't answer me.

I scoot my body out from under his, yanking down the hem of my shirt as I go. I feel way too exposed right now. Clamping my legs shut, I twist them so that my knees are sideways on the floor and I'm sitting up facing him.

I stare at him. Pleading with him to open up to me.

More silence.

"See you around, Finn."

Standing up, I turn and walk toward my bedroom door. He doesn't come after me. He doesn't say anything to stop me. I pause on the threshold. Count to three.

Nothing.

Come after me, Finn.

He doesn't. So I open the door, walk through and shut it behind me, pressing my body against the cool wood.

Still nothing.

Come on, Finn.

He doesn't. He lets me hide away in my bedroom.

Why did he have to do this?

The front door to my apartment opens and shuts and I slide down, my head hitting my knees as I let go. I cry. I cry for him and I cry for me and I cry for us. Because I see all the beautiful potential he just let go. And all he sees is ugly pain.

Chapter Thirty-Two

FINN

Three years ago

KELLY IS eight months pregnant today. And she's not only still pregnant, but the baby is doing great. Grace. That's the name I picked out because she's a girl. Kelly is pregnant with a girl. Part of me is relieved that it's not another boy, because I wonder if we'd always compare him to what Logan could have been.

By the time we went to see the OB, she was already twelve weeks along.

Just goes to show you how busy and preoccupied I had been. I hate that. I hate that she suffered through her fears about being pregnant alone. That's why it took her so long to take the test. That's why she hid it from me.

Today is Christmas. And Logan would have been two years old today.

It's so bittersweet. I miss my son. Not a day goes by that I don't think about him. Wonder about him. Would he have had Kelly's blonde hair and brown eyes or my brown hair and blue eyes? What sorts of things would he like. Elmo? Mickey Mouse? What would be his favorite books? Favorite toys?

Kelly was upset with me that I had to work today. Last year, I was still in school and I was on break. So we sat together and mourned him. We couldn't do that today.

I tried to get the day off, but I'm an intern and it's practically impossible to take a day off, especially a holiday. But I was able to switch the last of my shift so now I'm on my way home to Kelly.

I bought her things. So many things. For her. Just for her.

I can't stop buying things for Kelly.

One of the things is a diamond necklace. I remember her eyeing it in a store window we passed on one of our walks a few weeks ago. So I bought it.

I want to buy things for Grace, but Kelly says no. She says it's bad luck.

Fine. I can wait.

I smile the entire ride up the elevator and once I'm unlocking the front door, I smile even bigger at the Christmas tree I put up. We didn't do one last year, but this year feels like hope.

That is until I hear the sound.

It's the sort of sound that has you freezing in your place so that you can ensure you heard it correctly. But once I do, I know something is wrong. Kelly is groaning. And screaming.

Oh God. *No!*

My keys slip out of my hands and my bag falls to the floor next to them. I sprint across the apartment until I burst through our bedroom door. And then I freeze again. Because Kelly is in fact screaming. But it's not in pain. It's in pleasure.

She is naked, her head thrown back, her eyes closed and her mouth agape. Her large round belly is slick with a sheen of sweat. Beneath her…well, I haven't even gotten that far.

Because my world just stopped.

My heart is breaking as I stand here watching my pregnant wife fuck another man in our bed on the anniversary of our son's death.

"Kelly?"

Her eyes open and her chin drops and her eyes find mine, wide and unblinking. "Oh no, Finn."

The guy beneath her jumps back, covering himself with my four-thousand-thread-count sheets. I can't look at him, though I'm positive in the brief half second that I did, I recognized him. "What the fuck?" I yell.

Kelly gets on her knees, covering her large naked body with the blanket and then her head drops. "I'm sorry, Finn, but it's probably better you find out about this now."

"Find out?" I'm baffled. None of this makes sense to me. "How long has this been going on."

"A year." She can't even meet my eyes. *A year?* How is that even possible? How is it possible for Kelly to have been fucking another man for a year and I not know about it? "I'm so sorry, Finn."

I want to tell her to stop saying she's sorry because the words are meaningless, but all I can think about right now is Grace. Yet, I can't bring myself to speak her name, so instead I stammer, "The baby?"

"Is not yours."

I jolt back. Like I've been shot. Because that is exactly what this feels like. Searing, agonizing pain right through the center of my chest, spreading throughout my entire body. "How do you know that? How can you possibly know that?" I scream at her.

"I had a test," she whispers contrite. "I had that needle test."

"A chorionic villus sampling?"

"Yes," she says slowly, her eyes finally brave enough to find mine.

How did I not know about this? How could she have hidden that from me all this time?

What the fuck is happening right now?

"So you've known about this since you were what? Fourteen weeks?" She nods and my vision sways in and out. Instinctively I reach back, grasping onto the door. I don't know how to make sense of this moment. All of my moments are with Kelly. "Grace," I say her name and my heart splinters, shattering into a million tiny pieces. "You let me name her, Kelly. You let me go with you to every doctor's appointment I could. I sat there for the ultrasound and held your goddamn hand when we found out she's a girl. I painted her room. I built her crib. You let me fall in love with that baby, with being her father, and you knew she wasn't *mine?*"

Kelly is crying now. And the piece of shit who was fucking my wife in my bed on the day my son died is just sitting there, silently watching us.

He's the father of my baby.

I want to kill him, but he's not the problem. Kelly is. Because she just took everything I've ever loved away from me. Everything I had left. I had nothing before her. She gave me herself and then Logan and Grace. And now they're all gone and I have nothing again.

"How could you do that to me?"

"I'm so sorry," she says again.

"Stop fucking saying that!" I bellow at the top of my lungs. "How could you lie to me for eight months? For a year? How could you let me believe she was mine? That *you* were mine?"

"I didn't know how to tell you," she sobs. "You were so excited about the baby and every time I tried, I just…lost my nerve."

Lost her nerve? What the motherfuck?

"When were you going to tell me? After she was born and I was holding her in my arms? Were you going to wait until the moment you saw just how much I love her and then kill me for good?"

Kelly had done so much to heal me after my childhood. After my father. Our marriage had been my rock. My one stronghold against it all. The one thing I clung to. Especially after we lost Logan. And now?

Kelly just cries and cries and the guy actually moves to comfort her. Like she's the one who needs it right now. He's one of the lawyers she used to work with, I realize. And this almost makes me want to laugh. Because this piece of shit is the father of my child. He's getting my wife and my baby and I'm losing everything.

I lost my son. I'm losing my wife and my daughter.

Kelly lied to me for a year. She's been screwing another man for a year. She became pregnant with his baby and allowed me to believe it was mine.

I have nothing left in me.

Thank you, Kelly. Thank you for reminding me that love is a fallacy, happiness an illusion and trust a misconception.

I will never make the mistake of believing in any of them again. Never.

Chapter Thirty-Three

FINN

Present Day

I LEAVE GIA'S APARTMENT, hating myself just a little more with each step I take. I have no answer for why I provoked that fight. No reason for why everything in my mind went south the moment she stepped into Ophelia's bar. She's right, I invited her there.

But the second she stepped into that bar, and I felt the familiar ache in my chest at seeing her, it all just became too much. The time of year. The Christmas party dress she bought. The fact she's with another man who isn't me. The fact I know she wants to be with me and isn't because I don't know how to trust anyone anymore.

Every little piece of it began to pile up on top of me until I was buried under it. Under the avalanche. All I could think about as she approached me was standing up and pulling her into my arms and kissing her until she had no choice but to belong to me. The need was crushing.

But it was more than that.

It was paralyzing.

I trust Gia. I believe that she cares for me. I believe that she may in fact love me.

But so did Kelly.

I never doubted Kelly's love for me. Even after it all ended. I knew she had loved me at one point. But I also knew she had stopped. Somewhere along the way, after we lost Logan and I started my internship and life generally sucked for us as a couple, I lost her.

But it's not like Kelly ripped out my insides in your typical fashion. She did it with flair. With charisma. She made sure the job was done right.

After I walked out of our apartment, with nowhere to go and a great big vacuous hole in my chest, I promised myself I was done. I mean, what the fuck good had love ever done for me? My father was a world-class bastard. Not just physically abusive, but mentally. Psychologically. He'd find just the perfect way to make you believe that he actually gave a shit before he'd rip the rug out from under you. And my mother? Please. She was just as bad. Sure she didn't hit me, but she didn't stop him and she never cared when I was bleeding and crying on the floor.

In fact, sometimes, she just walked away. Pretended like she never saw me like that.

So when Kelly came along, I absorbed all the love she was offering me, like a sponge. I needed it. I craved it. I went to tremendous lengths to keep it. Because at the end of the day, it felt like all I had. Like her love was the dividing line between being an actual human with real human emotions and wholly indifferent to that spectrum.

I never wanted to be the latter.

The moment I checked myself alone into that hotel room, I felt it. I felt myself becoming something dark. Something cold-blooded and hateful. Sure, I promised I'd never love again. That's sort of the thing to do when you're in that situation. When your wife uses your heart as a trampoline.

But I honestly hoped I wouldn't keep that promise. I hoped that one day, I'd find someone I was capable of loving. If for no other reason than to keep me alive.

Then I met Gia.

The moment I saw her, I knew. I just fucking knew. She was that person. And in that moment, I was grateful for her. It's why I went outside to talk to her. It's why I was sweet and sympathetic and even flirty despite the inauspicious circumstances of her father's death.

But hell, it was the first time any light had dared to venture into my dark world in such a long time. It's why after she walked away, I thought about her. Imagined her.

Then she walked back into my life like a shining star, bright and fiery hot and so goddamn spectacular that there is no other word to describe her. I couldn't stay away. And shit, did I try. In so many ways and so many times. I fell in love with Gia without even having to try. It was easier than falling.

Falling in love is a misnomer. When you fall, you hit the ground. Gravity takes over. It's pure physics. There is no hitting the ground with her. There is no bottom with this. No end. No base.

I told Gia that I love her. I don't think she was all that shocked really, but I still said it. And I kissed her. Again. I kissed that sweet, luscious mouth which tastes like home and feels like heaven. Then I lied to her when I told her that's all I would ever give her. Like we could just have sex and nothing more.

Fucking asshole!

I knew that would end it for her. I knew that would be the deciding moment where she finally got rid of me. I did it to force her hand, because there was no way I was ever going to be strong enough to tell her goodbye. She makes me so weak and yet so strong.

She's built me back, piece by piece. Even if those pieces still have holes in them, I'm more complete with her than I've been in three years. Hell, in my entire life. The love I have for her is blinding.

But do I want to be blind again?

I missed so much. All of the warning signs with Kelly.

All the different ways she deceived me.

Turning the corner, I run my fingers through my hair, tugging on the end and growling out. People passing by must think I'm crazy, but I could give a shit what anyone thinks of me. Except Gia. What have I done to her? I should go back. I should go back and fix this because she's never going to speak to me again.

And then what will I do?

Could I do this with her? Could I try for her?

Christ, I want to. I haven't wanted to try anything with anyone in three years, but I want to with her. She might just be worth the risk.

Because when I'm with her, I forget the rest. I forget the pain and the past. I forget she has the power to annihilate me. I get swept up in her and nothing else matters.

What the hell have I done?

I'm going back. That's it. *Man the fuck up, Finn.*

And suddenly, that thought has me smiling. It fills me with a sense of calm. A sense of…right.

Spinning back around, I slam directly into someone. The force of the impact knocks them off balance and they begin to teeter back. Instinctively I reach out to grab them, grasping onto their arm and pulling them back up.

"I'm so sorry," I apologize quickly, but when I focus in on the person I just smacked into, my hand instantly drops back down to my side. My stomach sinks.

"Finn?" Kelly says, her brown doe-like eyes wide. Startled. Apprehensive.

We stare at each other for a moment and I realize the last time I saw Kelly was when she was naked, fucking another man in our bed on the anniversary of our son's death. But then I notice the movement by her side and my eyes cascade down to see a little girl. Long white-blonde hair and big brown eyes and red chubby cheeks and a pink dress and I'm choking on my grief.

"Mommy?" she says, clearly uneasy with who this man is that is now staring at her.

"It's okay, Gracie," Kelly soothes, pulling her in closer to her side.

Gracie. Grace. Kelly named the daughter that is not mine, Grace. The name I picked out.

I wonder if she's sleeping in the room I painted. In the crib, I built. In the apartment, I once owned. But I imagine she's too old for that crib. She's close to three. And now that I turn my attention back over at Kelly, I notice she's pregnant. Maybe about six months along. My eyes instantly water, but I can't look away from them.

How could you do this to me, Kelly? How could you take this away from me?

"How are you, Finn?" Kelly asks softly, unable to handle my silent staring anymore. "You look well."

Is that a joke? I can't tell if that's a joke or not. All I can focus on is the pain.

I want to run from it. Hide from it. Like I used to do when I was a little boy and my father would come home drunk from the club and beat me because I was there.

Forcing myself to pry my eyes away from the little girl who is not mine, I look at Kelly. She has tears in her eyes too. She swallows hard and shakes her head. "I'm so sorry," she whispers and I choke down the tormented spasm strangling me.

Kelly squeezes Grace's chubby hand a little tighter like she's afraid I might try grab her and run off, and then she steps around me and walks away as quickly as Grace's small legs can go.

I don't know how long I stand here, picturing them in my head. Hours maybe, because now it's very dark out and the streets are thinning out and I'm completely frozen through. Blinking back into focus, I notice I'm two buildings down from Gia's.

Gia.

My eyes glide up the brick façade of her building and I wonder what she's doing. She could be with Mason now for all I know. Even if she's not, it doesn't matter. I was a fool to imagine I could try for something real with her. I want to trust her. But I don't. Running into Kelly just brought it all home for me. Everyone I have ever trusted has lied to me. Anyone I ever put myself out there for, has let me down.

I think I'd rather take a bullet to the head than put myself in that position again.

I lost Logan. And then I lost Kelly and Grace. If I lose Gia after having her, well, that will be it for me. I know it will. I'll never make it back from that. I'll end up like my father.

An angry alcoholic who only found joy in hurting others.

I refuse to turn into that. And I refuse to hurt Gia any more than I already have.

So I leave Gia's street and I flag down a passing cab and I go home.

But I'm not even safe here. The moment I walk in my front door, I spy Gia's Christmas present sitting on the island in my kitchen. I bought her an Apple Watch because she doesn't have a watch and she was complaining she should probably get one. I got her one with a lavender sports band for work and a pretty leather band which I think she'll like for when she's out.

But I didn't stop there because her iPhone is old and she's too lazy and indifferent to get a new one. But I wanted her to have a new one because I want her to have the best of everything. Even if that will never include me.

I was eager to see the expression on her face when I gave it to her, but now I'm thinking it's best if I send it. I can't return it. I want her to have it too damn badly. Have this small piece of me, like the mug I gave her for her birthday which she uses for her coffee.

I need to sever all ties and go back to my small world which Gia Bianchi is not a part of.

I knew how to do that life. How to live in a world with nothingness and emptiness. I can do it again. A place where I'm untouchable.

Chapter Thirty-Four

GIA

My eyes close slowly, my exhaustion catching up to me the way it's apt to do when you've been working too much and sleeping too little. I swear, I could fall asleep right here in line.

"You want your usual, Gia?" Josephine, the barista in the small coffee shop off the main corridor of the hospital asks me.

"Yes please," I say through a yawn. "It was one hell of a shift."

She smiles at me, no doubt having heard the same words from many others who frequent this shop. Moving back so I'm not in the way while I wait, I accidentally step on someone's foot. Turning around, I apologize to the woman and then shift off to the side. My eyes flutter shut as I lean my head against the wall of the shop.

Tonight is Christmas Eve which also means it's Monique's and Mike's Christmas party.

Chloe is coming too so it should be fun, but I think at this point, I'd much prefer to go home, have a bath and a glass of wine and go to sleep. I can't though. I promised I'd go. Which means, I need to suck it up and deal. Hence the caffeine.

"You look tired," Finn says, but I refuse to open my eyes to him until I can get control of the sudden pounding in my chest his voice elicits. I inwardly sigh. I wish he would have continued on without talking to me. Finn is much easier to manage if I avoid him and he avoids me.

"I am," I reply. "But thanks for pointing that out. You do know when people say you look tired, they're basically telling you that you look like shit."

Finn chuckles and I ignore the way that sound makes me feel. The way I get chills from it every damn time like a Pavlovian response or something. It's been fucking weeks, you'd think by this point I would be further along than I am with this whole getting-over-Finn thing. But I have yet to reach a steady state with this.

"You don't look like shit. Just tired. Beautiful and tired."

I sigh, because that's just infuriating. *Pick a side, Finn and stick with it.*

Slowly opening my eyes to him, I want to sigh all over again, but for a different reason. It's been over three weeks since I've seen him and it's like no time has passed. My feelings and emotions are still what they were when he walked out of my apartment that day. I want to be angry at him for this, but I've been finding that emotion nearly impossible to conjure up.

I'm more sad than anything else and a lot of that sadness is *for* him.

"Gia," the barista calls out my name, but before I can move to get my coffee and get the hell out of here, Finn steps forward and retrieves it for me, holding it and me hostage. I'm tempted to leave them both here, but I need that freaking coffee, dammit.

"You're not typically an evening coffee drinker," he says, handing me my to-go cup. "Hot chocolate?"

Does he have to smirk at me? Maybe I should ask him to stop doing that. It's distracting and counterproductive.

"No. Coffee. Just plain old coffee." Not even cappuccino.

"How come, Gia."

"Because, *Finn,* I'm going to the Christmas party in a couple hours and as you were so gracious enough to point out, I'm tired."

"And beautiful," he says, stepping into me. "I believe I said you were also beautiful."

"Stop flirting. You're not allowed to flirt with me anymore."

"How's Mason," he asks, and right now, I want to punch him in his nose. On that small bump which gives him just the right amount of character. I bet it was broken once before and that's why it's there, so if I punch him directly on that spot, I'm liable to break it again.

"He's in Denver," is all I say because I really wouldn't know how Mason is, because I haven't spoken to him since I broke up with him weeks ago. I hated to do it, but it needed to be done.

It just drove home how unfair life is. How unjust it can be. Mason cares about me. He loves me, a fact he threw out when he was asking me not to end things. He was my boyfriend and had zero issues committing to that. He was all for it.

Finn is perpetually the opposite of this. Yes, Finn said he loves me, but he doesn't want me the way Mason does. He doesn't want that love to proliferate. He doesn't want commitment.

But the fucked-up thing is, I want Finn. But I can't have Finn and Mason deserves so much more than second best. Than being the consolation prize. He deserves someone who is one hundred percent invested.

I am not that person.

And sure, I could have stayed with him. Ridden things out. Hoped that Mason eventually eclipsed Finn. But I won't use him like that. It's not Mason's fault.

It's mine.

If I had never accepted that birthday present, things would be different. If I had never begged him to come to dinner with my mother and George. If I had never asked him to be friends or gone to the ballgame or flirted or returned his texts or had lunch with him every damn day, none of this would have happened. I would have met Mason and I would be happy because he's the type of man any woman would be happy with.

But that's not what happened and truth be told, I've only missed Mason a little. Not a lot. Not enough that I would ever consider going back to him. But it didn't end well. It was messy. And sad.

I've missed Finn a whole hell of a lot more. Why? I have no clue.

"You've been working a lot," he says, taking another small step into me, playing with my personal space the way he always does.

"How do you know that?" I clip out, wondering why I'm still entertaining this conversation and yet, at the same time, knowing the exact reason why.

Finn smiles, his fingers brushing an errant piece of hair off my face and tucking it behind my ear. I shudder at his touch and cringe at myself for reacting like that.

"Because I check up on you. How else do I know when to leave your cappuccino or hot chocolate?"

"I should go," I say, taking a step back and bumping into the freaking wall and nearly hitting the fire alarm in the process. "I have the party to get ready for. You're not going, right?"

Finn shakes his head slowly. "No. I won't be there." His expression turns impossibly dark.

What happened to you, Finn? How did she ruin you? Why did you have to ruin me too?

"Well then, have a good Christmas."

He looks down at the floor, breathing hard, that dark look only growing more ominous, before he manages to find my eyes again. "You too, Gia. Sorry I'm going to miss seeing you in your gold dress." He leans in and kisses the corner of my lips, pressing his forehead against mine and then he's gone. Like he was never there.

But I still feel him.

I wonder if that will ever go away. If time really does heal all wounds, it doesn't seem to where Finn is concerned.

I walk home in a daze which neither my coffee nor the cold night air helps. The dull ache in my chest is growing more pronounced with each step. The sensation of his touch, his kiss, lingers.

Fucking, Finn. Asshole. Bastard.

That helps a little.

When I reach my front door, I find a package waiting in front of it with a sticky note on top from one of my neighbors.

Intercepted UPS for you. Merry Christmas—Eliza

I have no idea what's in the box, but I pick it up and bring it inside, setting it down on the counter in my kitchen. Walking into my bedroom, I strip off my nasty scrubs and shower off way too many hours spent in the hospital.

My gold dress is hanging on the outside of my bureau. I stare at it for a minute and wonder what Finn would think of me in it. Then I give myself a mental smack and get to my hair and makeup. Gold eyes to match my gold dress and very minimal lips and cheeks. My hair I'm leaving down, but I use the curling iron to give it some soft waves.

And once I'm fully dressed, I stare at myself in the mirror. I wish I felt as good as I look, because my reflection is pretty damn good. My heels click against my wood floors and just as I'm about to grab my nice coat and head out, I spot that package sitting on my counter and my curiosity gets the better of me.

Opening it up, I find a large white card covering a brand-new iPhone and Apple Watch. I don't have to open the card to know who these are from. Sometimes I can't stand how thoughtful he can be. Like those freaking coffees and hot chocolates he still delivers and the birthday present and the fact that he always picks up a tab whenever we went out, leaving a ginormous tip. If I ever had a bad day, he'd call to make sure I was okay, even if he was in the middle of a shift.

And now the new watch and phone.

The bastard even got me a band for work and a band for going out and a pretty lavender phone cover, to match my pretty lavender band, because he knew I lied when I said that bright blue is my favorite color. He knows that it's lavender. He's always known.

I haven't bought him a present. Why would I? Our friendship is long since over. But honestly, even if I was going to get him something, he's impossible to shop for. He has everything and wants for nothing. What do you get a man like that? My plan had been to cook him a really amazing dinner, because I know that's the one thing he's missing and he asked me to that night at Mike and Monique's.

No one ever cooks for him. No one ever takes care of him.

I wonder if his wife did that for him. Put him first.

I know he came from an abusive home. That his mother isn't the warmest or kindest woman on the planet. I know he's an only child. I know he was married for three years and hasn't been with anyone since, and I know something happened to make him give up on love even though he said he loves me.

Oh, Finn. What happened to you?

And why despite the fact that he ruined me, do I find myself feeling sorry for him?

Yeah, I have no answer for that one.

Finn loves me and he's throwing away a shot at something incredible. And I don't know why. He's never told me. He's never opened up to me about it.

I don't know what to do.

Do I call him and thank him? Text him? Send it back?

No, I won't send it back. I might not understand what's going on with him, but he obviously put a lot of thought into this gift and wanted me to have it.

Which is exactly why I should send it back.

Setting my new toys down on the counter, I order up my Uber and head out into the cold, dark, Christmas Eve night.

The party is in full swing by the time I arrive and it's decorated to the nines. Twinkling lights and scented candles and beautiful wreaths. But the showstopper is the Christmas tree. It looks like something out of a magazine.

I could never create something like that. My tree—if I did one—would look like something a second grader put together and that's if I did a decent job.

I spot Monique and Mike over in the corner, talking with a few other people so I head in that direction. "Hey," she says, her dark eyes lighting up when she spots me. "There you are. You look gorgeous." She gives me the up and down once over.

"Thanks," I say, giving her an air kiss so I don't get my lip gloss all over her. "You do too and your place looks phenomenal."

Monique looks over to Mike who bows proudly. "I did good, huh?"

"You did good, Mike." I pat him on the shoulder.

"Can I get you something to drink?" he asks, waving his hand over toward the bar.

"Sure, thanks."

Mike walks with me over to the bar and begins to pour me a cup of some sort of red punch, but before he can hand it to me and leave me to my own devices, I blurt out, "What happened to him?" Mike stands up tall, but if he's surprised by my question, he doesn't show it. "I mean," then I sigh, deflating just a little, "he loves me, Mike. He told me he did. And here's the kicker, I love him too. But he won't be with me and I know he hasn't been in a relationship in three years and I want to know why. I don't think I can move on until I know it's never ever going to happen, and maybe if I know why he is the way he is, I'll understand and stop holding onto something I've needed to let go of for months."

Mike smiles at me and it's really not the reaction I was expecting from him. "He told you he loves you?"

I nod. "Yeah, but he followed it up with another riveting speech about how he'll never be with me."

"Did you tell him you loved him back?"

"Well no, but I don't think that's the hold up."

"No," he says, rubbing his smooth jawline, "it's not, but it's really not my story to tell."

"But you know it, don't you?"

"Yes," he says slowly and then he takes my arm, guiding me through the main room past the kitchen where Chloe is. She gives me a bewildered look as I pass her, but doesn't comment. We step out onto the back deck, into the freezing night and I wrap my arms instinctively around myself to ward off the chill. Mike turns to me, his expression bleak. I'm instantly anxious as to where this is headed. "He told you he was married, right?" I nod. "Did he ever tell you more about Kelly?"

Kelly. I guess that's her name. Somehow, I imagined it to be more sinister than sorority girl. Something like Maleficent or Wicked Queen.

"No. Just that he hasn't had a relationship since her."

Mike nods, his dark eyes piercing into mine for a very long minute before he speaks again.

"Gia, Finn hasn't had the charmed life everyone who looks at him believes he has. He had a rough upbringing and then his father died and he met Kelly. I'm not going to tell you everything. As I said, it really isn't my place. But I will tell you Finn lost a piece of himself and then the rest was taken from him. He's experienced more pain and loss than anyone ever should, and then some. Some men just don't come back from that. I'm not sure I would."

Chapter Thirty-Five

FINN

"Why are you here?" Ophelia says to me as I slide into one of the wooden bar stools across from her. "Shouldn't you be at the party with everyone else?"

I shake my head, because no, I shouldn't be there. I should be exactly where I am. About to drown my many sorrows in a vat of scotch. Because tomorrow is the worst day of the year and this bar isn't open then, which means I'll have to suffer through it alone. But I can't tolerate doing that right now. And I can't tolerate being around happy people at a Christmas party. I certainly can't tolerate being around Gia in her gold dress, so here I am.

"Johnny Walker Blue. Four fingers, no ice and you can probably just leave me with the bottle."

Ophelia gives me the long once over and I wait patiently while she decides if she's going to aid me in my journey to total self-destruction.

Ophelia is pretty. I've always thought so. If I could have gotten away with fucking her and never having to see her again, I might have done that once upon a time. But I like this bar. It's close to my condo and it's close to the hospital. And it's comforting in an inexplicable way.

So I never tried it.

"Coming up," she finally says. "But you do know it would be like a fourth of the price to just go out and buy the bottle in a store, right?"

"Does it look like I care if I spend five hundred dollars on scotch right now?"

"No," she says, leaning across the well of the bar so that she can put her elbows on the wood and level me with her eyes. "Money has never been your issue."

I laugh humorlessly at her choice of words. "You got me there."

"I'm not stupid enough to think this is all about Gia. I knew you before I knew you with her. But you should know she broke up with that Mason guy weeks ago. So, if by some weird miracle this drinking binge is about her…" she trails off with a shrug.

"My son would have been six tomorrow."

It's the first time I've said those words out loud. To anyone. The impact of them slams into me with so much force that it knocks the wind out of me and I have to clutch onto the edge of the bar for support.

Ophelia nods at me, the corner of her mouth pulling down.

I can't even bring myself to mention Kelly or Grace. That wound is still too new. Especially after seeing them only a few short weeks ago.

"Okay then, Johnny Walker Blue it is." She goes to the back only to return a few minutes later with two crystal glasses. Not glass. Crystal. She sets them down on the counter, one for me and one for her from the looks of it. Ophelia grabs the mostly full bottle of Blue from the very top shelf and proceeds to pour us each a healthy glass. She holds up her tumbler and I hold up mine and we lock eyes. "My big sister would have been thirty-two tomorrow. Car accident."

I nod. "Car accident."

"Fuck Christmas."

"Fuck Christmas."

We drink to that. Both of us slamming down the entire drink in one gulp. She winces, blowing out a huge breath of alcohol-tainted air. I swallow mine down just to feel the burn and acknowledge the pain.

Ophelia takes her glass and sets it on the back counter of the bar. Maybe for later. Maybe because it's a special glass which can't go in the dishwashers here. Whatever the reason, she leaves it there and leaves me without another word to go about my drinking. I guess everyone has their own heartache. Their own secret pain they don't wear on their sleeve for others to witness.

Lifting that heavy bottle, I pour myself a moderately full glass, because I'm not in the mood to keep refilling it, and then I take a sip this time. Closing my eyes, I allow myself to picture Logan. To remember how he felt in my arms when I held him that one time. What it felt like to kiss him goodbye before they took him from us.

Then I think about Grace. That beautiful little girl who was the spitting image of her mother. There was none of that piece of shit who is technically her father, in her. For some reason, I find some comfort in that. Especially since brown hair is a dominant gene and that guy definitely had brown hair.

And Gia. Why did Ophelia have to tell me she broke up with Mason? That doesn't help me right now. I've already done so many things wrong where she's concerned. Hurt her in so many ways. I don't want Gia to be single. To be alone. I want her to be happy. That's all I've ever wanted for her.

Taking another sip, I lean back and allow the flow of alcohol to color my blood with heat. My eyes close and my mind wanders. "I should kick your ass, Banner," Mike says and I wonder if I'm more drunk than I thought.

My eyes open slowly and I turn my head. Mike is dressed in black sacks, a black jacket and a white button down. And a bright red tie. I guess I'm not imaging him. "You going to court?" He just glares at me and I throw Ophelia a look, but she tosses her hands up in surrender and shakes her head as if to say, *it wasn't me.*

"My girlfriend is pissed at me. I left our house, our first Christmas party, to come and see you."

Leaning my elbow against the bar, I position myself so I'm facing him better. "Go home, then. I certainly never asked you to find me and I sure as shit don't need a babysitter. I'm perfectly capable of getting drunk and tucking myself into bed. Maybe someone else's bed if I'm really lucky."

"You stupid fuck," Mike snaps and this surprises me because Mike is not known for his aggression or language for that matter. Only with me it seems. "You're sitting here wasting yourself in a bottle of scotch when you could be with Gia."

"Don't," I warn, sitting up straight and using my three extra inches as an advantage. "Go. Home. I'm not fucking around. I will not have this conversation with you. Not tonight."

Mike slouches down and looks over at Ophelia who has been furtively watching us out the corner of her eye as she serves up other people's drinks. Mike raises one finger and then points to the bottle. She nods and then a minute later, she's bringing him a glass. "Ice?"

"Sure."

"You good here?" she asks both of us, but her eyes are on me.

"Yeah," I say, even though I know we're not. "We're good."

She walks off, back to work as things begin to pick up and I'm left with Mike and a bottle of scotch between us. Mike pours himself a glass and then raises it up at me. "What are we drinking to?"

"To Logan," I say and Mike gives me a pleased grin.

"To Logan."

We both take a sip and I have to wonder at just what the hell he's doing here.

After several long silent minutes, he finally says, "Do you remember that little girl who came in after that apartment fire? It was your second year of residency. One of the worst days I've ever had as a doctor. Three people died on my table and ten more were sent up to the burn unit including that little girl."

"Yes," I say, lost in that memory. I still think about that little girl. Certain cases, certain patients, just stay with you. "Both of her parents died in that fire. They threw her out the window because they knew they weren't going to make it out."

Mike nods, his eyes boring into mine. "She fell two stories, shattered both her ankles, her left ulna and had third degree burns on over thirty percent of her body."

"Shit, that was awful."

"Do you remember what you said to her when she told you she was scared and in pain?"

I look over at my friend and shake my head. "You said, if you're scared and in pain, it means you're still alive. It means you're still fighting. You told her it takes a very brave person to keep fighting even when they're scared and in pain."

"Mike—"

"Tonight, is the first time I've heard you say Logan's name since the day you told me about what happened with Kelly and the baby. And that was the only time you've ever spoken about that."

I shake my head, turning away from him, my hands closing around my crystal glass. My throat constricts making it nearly impossible to swallow. To breathe. My chest feels like it's being crushed by a vice.

"I've never mentioned anything about this before tonight, because you've lived through a hell I've never known. A hell most haven't. I always kept it to myself, because I figured you knew better than I what your world was like and what you could handle. But I was wrong, Finn. I did you a disservice by staying quiet all this time. And I'm sorry for that. I'm sorry I wasn't a better friend to you."

"I can't do this, Mike. I always appreciated you kept your opinions about my life to yourself. It's why we've stayed close as long as we have. And I was just saying that to comfort her. She was alone and her parents were dead and she just needed someone to listen and tell her it was going to be okay. That little girl could be worse off now than she was then."

"No," he says and then shoves his phone in my face. There's a picture on it of a young Hispanic girl with braided pigtails. She's smiling, missing a tooth on top. And even though the little girl in my memory was covered in burns and gauze and blood and smoke, I know this is the same girl "She's in third grade now. A straight-A student and top speller in her elementary school. Her foster mom adopted her and they live on 123rd street."

I have no words. My mind tumbling in a million different directions as I stare sightlessly into the amber liquid in my glass.

"You can't change the fact your son is dead or that Kelly deceived you or that Grace isn't yours. Life has been real shit to you. I will not dispute that. But Gia loves you. She told me so tonight."

Shit, that makes me ache and smile and ache all over again.

"Gia is not Kelly. Gia is not your mother or even your father. She still cares despite everything you've put her through. She's the one, Finn. That might sound like a cliché, but it's true. She's it. You'd be a fool not to fight for her."

Mike picks up his glass, tosses back the rest of it, slaps me on the back and then walks out.

You'd be a fool not to fight for her.

His words recycle themselves through my mind on constant repeat, swirling around the way the scotch swirls in my glass. Suddenly, I'm struck with the most bizarre form of irony. All this time, I've acted on the principle that if I lose Gia, the way I lost Logan and Grace and even Kelly, then that will be it for me. I'll officially be done. Because there really is only so much a man can take.

So I pushed her away, effectively losing her.

Yet somehow that felt more palatable. Being the one in control seemed to make all the difference. But I realize I never had control. It was always an illusion. Because I'm still the one sitting here alone, hurting, when I could be with her. It sounds easier than it feels. I've been emotionally paralyzed for a very long time.

The idea of going to Gia, of asking her to be mine, terrifies me. A million terrible things could happen to her or us. And I'm powerless to stop any of them. How do I make sense of that? How do I compartmentalize such a prominent part of me? I've been ruled by this pain and fear for as long as I can remember. Even before we lost Logan, it was there.

I'll always grieve from the losses I've sustained. There will always be a scar. Jagged and poorly healed.

But maybe not having Gia is worse than all that?

A fool not to fight for her.

Yeah, he's probably right about that.

Chapter Thirty-Six

GIA

This is the second Christmas since my father died and to be honest, it doesn't feel any easier than the first one. It might actually be worse because this year, I'm alone. My mother is on a cruise with her man friend, George, and sure, I could've gone up to Boston to be with my aunts and uncles and cousins, but it's not the same.

Christmas will never be the same as it was.

It's the ripple effect. One small stone in a pond eventually causes a tsunami.

But I'm making the most of it, even if I am by myself. Monique is with Mike and his family and Chloe is with her parents in Brooklyn and I'm here, picking at the manicotti I made, drinking expensive wine and watching *A Christmas Story* for the millionth time.

It's a pity party, if ever there was one.

After I spoke to Mike on the deck last night, I left the party. I just couldn't be there when I had so much on my mind. On my ride home, I decided I need to just let it all go. I don't know what I was expecting him to say to me. It's not like he was going to tell me something and then I would suddenly fall out of love with Finn.

It's going to take time.

Bumping into him and having him bring me coffee isn't going to help that.

I considered switching hospitals, but I love my job and where I work so that's not going to happen. Honestly, I think I need to have a conversation with him. Tell him he needs to back off and leave me alone. It's the only way I'll be able to move on with my life. I manage when I don't see him. I get through my days and even my quiet nights, but every time he interferes with that, it sets me back.

Lifting my glass of red wine to my lips, I startle at the sound of my phone pinging with a text, nearly dropping the glass and spilling the expensive wine all over myself. Instead of all that drama, a few drops escape hitting the floor. Rolling my eyes at myself, I pick up my phone and grin when I see the text from Chloe.

Chloe: *What are you doing? Stop drinking wine and watching A Christmas Story in your pajamas. It's pathetic. Get dressed in something warm, brush your hair and put on some makeup. We're going out.*

I can't stop the bubble of laughter as it climbs its way out of my chest. God, am I that freaking predictable?

Me: *I thought you were at your parents?*

Chloe: *Such drama. I can't take it anymore. Seriously. I want to go to the winter village at Bryant Park. Meet me there in twenty.*

Even though I'm beyond tempted to just stay in and sulk in my pajamas with my wine, I text her back telling her that I'll meet her in thirty. Twenty minutes just isn't possible. I need a shower. I look like *Night of the Living Dead* right now.

My hair is piled on top of my head in a messy bun of sorts and even though I washed my face last night, I'm sure I still have some remnants of my makeup under my eyes. I'm wearing an old worn t-shirt and yoga pants and a sports bra. I get a smiley emoji and as I step into my hot steamy shower, I realize I'm smiling too. This is exactly what I needed.

Finding an Uber on Christmas is a lot easier than anticipated and in under thirty minutes, I'm strolling through the park, admiring the soft glow of the holiday shops as they light up the night. The Christmas tree which separates the shopping area from the ice-skating rink is huge and beautiful with multicolored lights and a giant sparkling star at the top.

I can't find Chloe anywhere even though it's not all that crowded so I dig my phone out of my purse and call her. "Where are you?" she asks without so much as a hello.

"I'm near the tree," I say glancing around like she's going to materialize at any moment. "Where are you?"

"I got held up, but I'm on my way. Go rent yourself some skates and I'll be there in ten."

"Skates?" I half laugh, half shriek the word.

"Yes, Gia. Ice skates. I want to go ice-skating."

That reminds me of the day after Thanksgiving when I suggested the same thing to Finn. Not the fondest of memories. "I don't know how to skate, Chloe. I will bust my ass all over the place. Can't we just grab some fattening dessert and shop around?"

Chloe sighs into the phone like I'm messing up all her plans. "No. We cannot. I've been dying to go all season and today is the perfect day for it. Just humor me this once and after, I'll make sure you get your dessert."

"Fine," I huff. "But you have to hold my hand and when I fall, you're not allowed to laugh."

"Promise. I'll be there soon. Go grab some skates. I brought my own pair so I'm all set." I get the hang-up beeps and I can't suppress my eye roll at my friend. Of course, she has her own goddamn skates and I'm forced to rent. And fall. Because that's exactly what I'm going to do. Tomorrow I'll be nursing a bruised ass, but what the hell. I'm here.

And when in New York…

Making my way around the perimeter of the rink, I find the skate rental area and get in line. This is going to take hours and suddenly I'm wishing I had just stayed home. But the line progresses faster than I anticipate and before long, I'm renting skates and tying them on. Chloe is still not here and she doesn't pick up her phone when I call her, but at this point, I don't have a choice but to get on the ice and try and skate and hope she shows up soon.

The moment I step onto the ice, my feet slip out from beneath me and I begin to fall backwards. Probably because you're not supposed to step onto ice, you're supposed to glide.

A small startled yelp escapes my lips, just as someone catches me from behind, wrapping their arms around me and pulling my back snugly against their chest before righting me just as quickly. And when I turn to see who my savior is, I gasp instead of yelping again. "Just in time," Finn says with a warm smile, his bright-blue eyes sparkling against the bright white of the ice.

His hand reaches up to brush a few strands of hair from my face, tucking them securely behind my ear. I don't know what to say. What to think. I'm so confused. People are whizzing past us, skating and laughing and I'm stuck between Finn's arms and running—or skating—the hell out of here. "What are you doing here?"

"Ice-skating," he says with a smirk. "This was your idea, remember? We'll fall together, you had said." His expression grows genuine and my stomach flips, doing summersaults around and around.

"Did you follow me here?" I accuse.

Finn chuckles, shaking his head. "No," he says, gliding into me, crowding me until I have to crane my neck to see him. And when I do, I begin to slide back again. My footing on this ice is anything but steady. Finn reaches out, grasping onto my biceps to stop the motion, holding me against him. "I enlisted the help of your friends to get you out of your apartment and to meet me here."

"You what?" I squeal. "That's impossible. Chloe wouldn't—"

"I knew you would never agree to meet me if I asked you to," he interrupts. "So I got Chloe's number from Monique who was only too happy to oblige me. Chloe was a different matter. I had to beg her for assistance in this little subterfuge."

None of this makes any sense to me. "Why, Finn? What are you after now?"

He grins, his eyes growing soft and warm. He cups my face with one of his cool hands and says, "You, Gia. I'm after you."

Tears threaten to fall, stinging the backs of my eyes and I push his hand away. "I can't do this with you anymore, Finn. You can't buy me coffee or hot chocolate. You can't invade my space or touch me. You can't buy me presents. I need you to leave me alone. For good this time."

He shakes his head, refusing to budge or pull away from me, his expression growing demanding. I look away, out into the field of skaters dancing across the frozen surface. I can't take this anymore. It just hurts too damn much. He may say he's after me, but it won't last. He'll tell me all the things I need to hear and then in the next breath, he'll tell me we can't be together.

"I can't do that, Gia. I love you and I need you." A hiccupped sob burns its way past my lips and he slides me back into his arms. "I want to tell you I'm sorry," he says, lifting my chin until my eyes meet his once again. "But in my experience, the words mean nothing. There's no responsibility or commitment behind them. It certainly doesn't erase the pain and distrust I've caused."

Suddenly, Finn slides back, giving me the space I need to breathe. The space I need to think. He's breathing so hard, it's audible. His chest rising and falling, his breaths fogging out into the frigid night as white plumes of vapor. I can practically hear his heart pounding. Mine is just as loud.

"This is so hard for me," he continues, his voice tremulous. "Practically impossible. But you're worth it, Gia. Everything I'm terrified of seems to disintegrate when I look at you. I'm ready to do this with you, if you'll still have me. It won't be easy. I've got some serious issues I need to work on. I'm about as fucked up as it gets when it comes to this sort of thing. But I'm ready to give you everything. My past, maybe not all of it right now, but I will eventually. My present and hopefully, if you'll take it, my future."

I shake my head, unable to make sense of any of this. Helpless tears fall down my face, that I instantly reach up to wipe away. I don't want to be helpless right now. I don't want to be the puppy who continues to seek out love and affection only to be repeatedly smacked over the nose for it. Instinctively I step back, needing more distance from him, but my feet begin to drift out from under me again, because we're still wearing fucking ice skates standing on a sheet of frozen water. Finn laughs a little as he too begins to sway.

"Maybe the ice-skating wasn't such a brilliant idea. I was trying for romantic. Trying to get you to fall with me." He lowers himself to his knees, reaching for me and pulling my body into his. Wrapping his arms around my waist, he holds me against his warm body so there is nowhere I can go. "I've messed this all up with you a million times over and in a million different ways. I know you don't trust what I'm telling you is for real this time. But I'll make it up to you, Gia. I'll be everything you deserve. Just say you'll give us a chance. Please," he smiles reverently up at me, squeezing me just a bit tighter.

I shake my head, staring straight into his blue eyes. God, those eyes. How many different ways have they both excited and haunted me? "You've really fucked with my head."

"I know, and I'm so goddamn sorry for that. But my world doesn't revolve around the sun unless you're in it. Without you, all I see is darkness. I'm literally on my knees–that are incidentally freezing cold and soaking wet–begging you. Be mine, Gia Bianchi. Because I don't think I can live without you anymore."

I sigh, my hand coming up to run along the bristles of his stubbled cheek. Finn leans into my touch, his eyes closing against the sensation before he opens them again, pinning me with an unwavering steadiness. How could I say no him? I don't even want to try.

"Evidently, I'm a glutton for punishment, because I still love you despite my best efforts and better judgment. So yes, Finn. I'll be yours if you'll be mine. But if you fuck this up again, I'll kill you and make it look like an accident."

The most brilliant smile lights up his face and in the next second, his mouth is on mine. His lips forceful and dominant, his tongue commanding as he absorbs every breath and gasp and moan and sigh from me.

"Oh my god," a woman squeals with such a piercing shrill that we can't help but pull away and look over at the elderly woman holding what I assume is her husband's hand. "Danny, I think they just got engaged. How romantic," she simpers. "It reminds me of when you proposed to me under the tree at Rockefeller Center."

I peer up at Finn who is now standing and smiling, laughing despite myself. "Don't get any ideas, Dr. Banner," I warn.

"Wouldn't dream of it, Miss Bianchi," he says and then winks. "But I think we need to get out of here before we actually do fall and break something."

I nod in agreement. I've had just about all the ice-skating I can take.

Chapter Thirty-Seven

GIA

Ever so carefully, with Finn's hand holding mine, we step off the ice, take off our skates and return them. I don't ask where we're going as Finn leads us out of the park and back to the street. He flags down a cab and helps me inside the warm interior which smells like pine trees thanks to the plastic air freshener hanging from the rearview mirror.

Finn gives the driver my address and as we set off, he wraps his arms around me like he can't handle the distance a minute longer. "Are you hungry?"

I shake my head no.

"You're very quiet, Gia. Talk to me. What's going on through that beautiful head of yours?"

"I'm nervous," I admit, because I am. I feel like there are so many unknowns when it comes to Finn. For instance, I still don't know his history. What his admitted serious issues even are. What if they're too much for me? Or they become too much for him. Again.

"What are you nervous about?"

"Everything."

The word hovers in the air between us. Swirling around, filling the silence with a heaviness which wasn't there seconds ago. I hate that I just killed our moment, but I can't help it either. I'm not one of those women who can just jump blindly into something because the man I love tells me he loves me and he's ready. I know I just need time. I know I just need some reassurance. Something more than flowery words and soul-busting kisses.

"Me too," he says softly and something in his quiet confession has me smiling. It makes me feel like we're in this together. Like it's okay if we don't have it all figured out right now.

We will.

Of that I have no doubt.

Because this is Finn. And this is me. And we're us. We're in this together now. I can feel that radiating from him. Yeah, we're scared. He's got something dark about him. That sort of thing doesn't just go away because he tells me that he loves me. But despite his reservations and mine, he's in this with me.

He pivots on the seat to face me with that smile I love so much spread across his lips. That smiles tells me everything I need know. That smile really does say this is forever. That smile says we've got this.

How long have I wanted this man? God, it feels like forever.

My fingers find the stubble of his face. I think that might be one of my favorite things to touch. Well, so far anyway.

Our eyes lock as his mouth captures mine once again. His lips are velvety soft and he taste likes the cold night air and something deliciously warm. Something that hints at the burning desire just under the crest of this sweet kiss. He takes his time with me. Familiarizing himself with every inch of my mouth. Letting me know he's in no rush. That we have all the time in the world.

I love that. But it's not enough. All it's doing is driving me wild. Making me crazy with an urgency I haven't felt since my birthday night in my apartment. "More," I whisper and he groans into me. His hands fist in my hair and our bodies are pressed as close as physically possible without me being in his lap in the back of the cab. Any miniscule amount of space just feels like too much.

We're like two teenagers in heat trying to beat the clock.

"Gia," he breathes against me and I shudder. He grins against my lips. "Have I ever told you how sexy I think it is when you do that?"

"Mmmmm," I breathe into him. I think I'm done with coherent thoughts to rhetorical questions.

"It drives me fucking insane. It makes me want to do all kinds of dirty things to you."

I'm about to ask him what sorts of dirty things. Or better yet, I'm about to ask him to show me, but the cab stops and we're forced to pull away with breathless grins.

Finn pays the cab driver, no doubt overtipping him. "Come here," he says to me, taking my hand and tugging me into his side. He holds on to me, waiting patiently while I unlock and open the two doors which lead into my building.

The moment we step into the elevator, he's all over me. Bull-dozing me into the back wall and ravaging my mouth like a starving man. His hands are everywhere. One in my hair again and the other gliding along my back, down past my ass to the back of my thigh before he raises it up, hitching it around his waist and pressing into me.

I moan at the contact, throwing my head back, and giving him perfect access to my neck. The elevator dings, but he doesn't pull away from me. Instead he lifts me up into his arms and carries me, wrapped around him, down the hall to my door. "Keys," he raps, taking them from my hand and kissing me as he fumbles to unlock my door, compressing me into the wood as he does.

The door is open and the keys are out of the lock. He carries me to the kitchen and sets me down on the counter, his body is pressed between my spread thighs. "I have more to say," he speaks urgently against me before suddenly pulling back to catch my eyes. "A hell of a lot more to tell you."

"You will," I pant, staring up into his hooded eyes. Damn, that's hot. "You're going to tell me whatever you have left to say later. But it's not later yet and if you stop kissing me now, I'll never forgive you."

"Can't have that. I just got you back." Finn's lips crash to mine as he undoes the zipper of my jacket. And once that's on the ground, he rips off my sweater, smiling at my sports bra that I never removed from earlier. "Well, that's convenient," he says, staring down at the front zipper.

I laugh, and Jesus shit does it feel good. Everything about this just feels so…right. So long in the making, but now that it's here, it's infinitely better than anticipated. His fingers reach up to the small plastic tab, his gaze vacillating between my breasts and my eyes. And when he has the zipper undone and the bra parts, he grins the grin of the devil.

"Oh Gia," he says with a slight shake of his head. "You're so goddamn beautiful. Better than any fantasy I could ever come up with. I fucking love you and your perfect, delicious tits." I can only moan, throwing my head back as his mouth covers my nipple, his other hand kneading and squeezing me just right.

His fingers undo the button and zipper of my jeans, gripping onto the edges and yanking them down past my knees and tossing them behind him onto my kitchen floor. Finn gives me a wink which has my pulse exploding and then he drops to his knees, his face inches from my panty-covered pussy.

"Good thing you're tall."

Finn laughs as he reaches out, grasping onto my hips and sliding me to the very edge. "I won't let you fall. Well," he amends with that sexy-as-sin glaze in his eyes, "at least not until I'm ready for you to." He grins, looping his finger through the thin sides of my panties and slides them down my legs. His mouth finds me, licking and making me cry out embarrassingly loud. He does it again and again and then stops, gazing up at me. "I love how your breath pauses every time. Right before my tongue does this." Then he licks me again, this time with more pressure and I think I might pass out. That's how good this is. His tongue and fingers making me arch my back as I scream out obscenities mixed with his name.

They're all combined into one.

Because…*Oh. My. God!*

And when I'm panting and praying and crying and laughing, Finn stands up and kisses me, making sure that I taste everything he just did to me. My fingers find the buttons of his shirt and after undoing three of them, I become frustrated. Needy. Impatient. I yank on the two sides of his open shirt and I tug until buttons go flying and both Finn and I are laughing.

I don't care. I've been dying to explore every inch of him since I woke up with him in my bed. Probably before that. Most definitely before that. My palms glide across the hard, smooth and muscular expanse of his chest, my lips matching the stride of my hands step for step. Finn groans and the sound of it only spurs me on.

His pants and boxer briefs hit the floor around his ankles, he covers himself in a condom and then he's inside me. Finally. We're one and nothing has ever felt so good. So perfect. So...*Yes!*

His mouth searches mine, but he doesn't kiss me. He rests lips against me, as he moves inside of me. As we make so many sounds together. As we desperately cling to each other. As our eyes watch the other.

And when we explode, we do that together as well.

Finn's forehead rests against mine as we both try and subdue our rapid breaths and erratic heartbeats. Our smiles are unstoppable. "You're incredible," he says, rubbing the tip of his nose against mine. "And definitely worth the wait." He takes me in his arms and helps me down off the counter. "Can I keep you like this for the rest of the night?"

I giggle, burying myself into his chest. I love the way he smells right now. I love that he's here, in my apartment. I love everything about this moment.

"No. You can't." I say, enjoying the displeased expression on his face. "I'm hungry and we need to talk."

"Yes. We do," he says, his expression growing sober. His hand reaches up, the tips of his fingers gliding across my cheek. "Can I stay with you tonight?"

I nod. I'm dying to fall asleep with him in my bed, his arms wrapped around me. I'm dying for morning sex with him. I'm dying for all of this with him. "Yes. I'd love that."

Finn takes my hand, leading me over the sofa and pulling me down next to him so our bodies are once again connected. But that's it. His eyes hit the coffee table in front of us, sightlessly staring as he tries to figure out how to start. My heart beat kicks up. I can feel myself starting to tremble with the building suspense. I'm sitting there, waiting on him, trying to be patient, but the tension is mounting as the silent seconds tick by.

Finally, he sucks in a deep shuddered breath, his hands clasping mine as his eyes regain their focus and turn to mine, "I want to tell you everything, Gia. But I'm just not ready for that yet. A lot of it, I still don't know how to talk about. But I can tell you some of it."

He sucks in another deep breath, and I squeeze his hands, letting him know that whatever he has to tell me, is okay. I'm here. I told him once that I wouldn't leave him and as I stare into his beautiful blue eyes, I know with absolute certainty that nothing he can say to me now will change that.

"I met Kelly, my now ex-wife, when I was in medical school. The day of my father's funeral, actually." He smiles at that, but it's the saddest smile I've ever seen on him. "Happiness and love were two things I never really experienced before I met her, and as a result, I did whatever it took to perpetuate them. I did love her," he says, watching my expression as he does. "I won't deny that, but after meeting you, and being with you, I realize it was always...inadequate. Lacking that crucial indescribable piece which would make it real and whole."

I lean in and kiss the corner of his lips. He smiles down on me, some of the light returning to his eyes. He tells more about Kelly. About how they found out about her being pregnant the day he asked her to move in with him. The way his mother never liked her and how he probably should have listened when she told him she was a wolf in sheep's clothing. He tells me about Logan and I weep silent tears for his unfathomable loss. He goes on to explain how Kelly deceived him in the most egregious of ways and because of that, he hasn't wanted to put him in that position again.

But that's where he stops. He doesn't continue. He doesn't get into specifics about what Kelly did. Not yet anyway. I know he will when he's ready. But there is still one thing that I don't quite get.

"What made you change your mind then? About us, I mean."

Finn releases my hand and cups my face. His nose dips down,

brushing against mine. "You did." His lips press to mine, before he draws back so to see me. "You never gave up on me, Gia. You loved me no matter what. You have no idea what that means to me." Another kiss. "A good friend reminded me that it takes a brave person to continue to fight, even when you're scared and in pain. That I'd be a fool not to fight for you. He was right."

I climb into his lap and take his face in my hands. "Thank you," I say. "I know it wasn't easy to tell me about Kelly or about Logan." I lean in and kiss him before I drop my forehead to his. "History doesn't always repeat itself, Finn. Sometimes it's like a lightning strike. I know there's a lot more you haven't told me, but I won't be another storm for you to weather. I'm the sunshine you feel when it's all done."

Chapter Thirty-Eight

FINN

I wake with a start. A jolt of my heart, and before I know what I'm doing, I'm sitting upright in bed. It's still dark out as my mind races, trying to make sense of the dream that now seems like more of a nightmare.

Gia.

My head automatically drops toward the sleeping, still body beside me. Her dark hair is splayed across the white pillow it's resting on as she lies on her stomach. A breath of light streams in through the curtains framing the window, glimmering against the smooth skin of her back.

She is a vision, and as with every time I look at her, my chest clenches.

But that dream.

The dream that felt so real.

All because it is a nightmare I have lived before. Only this time, it was Gia who I lost.

Before I can stop myself, I reach out, snaking my arm around her belly and dragging her into me. She stirs with a small groan as I plant my face in her hair, breathing in her calming scent.

"You okay?" she rasps.

"Yes," I tell her, though I'm shaking my head.

I am and I'm not. Neither are a lie.

This makes the third time in the month Gia and I have been together that I've woken like this. That I've dreamt of losing her.

"I love you," I mumble into her, holding her just a little closer. A little tighter.

She twists in my arms, her blue-green eyes peeking open, blinking against the minimal light as she tries to focus. "Another nightmare?"

I nod and she leans in, pressing her lips to mine. "I'm not going anywhere, Finn. You're unfortunately as stuck with me as I am with you."

I chuckle at her sarcastically grim tone and kiss her back. Hard. My tongue sweeping into her mouth for a taste. How I went so long without Gia, without allowing myself to take the leap with her, feels crazy to me now. Months of tortured agony I put both of us through.

And for what?

Now it all feels so hard to remember.

I roll us until I'm hovering over her, my hands bracketing her head. Gia is gloriously naked. So am I, for that matter since this is how we fell asleep.

I stare down into her eyes, my fingers tracing the lines of her face. "Move in with me," I ask before I can stop it.

I want this with her. A forever. I'm done waiting. Done being so fucking scared all the time.

Her eyes widen in surprise, though I don't know why. In the last month, the only nights we've spent apart were when we were working.

"Are you just saying this because of the dream?"

I shake my head. "No. I've actually been thinking about it for a while now."

"Finn."

I smirk when she doesn't follow my name up with anything else. "Is that a yes?"

"I. Um," she sighs breathlessly. "Yes. I'll move in with you."

I raise an eyebrow. "You really don't sound sure."

"I am. It's just that your hard cock is poking me in a very sensitive spot. It's distracting me from this very sweet and romantic moment."

"Your pussy is like a magnet for him. He can't help it."

She laughs, reaching up to run her fingers through my hair. "Good. Then he'll always know his way home."

"Home. So that's really a yes?"

She nods, her eyes sparkling, her lips spread in a breathtaking smile. "It's a yes. For sure."

My matching smile is unstoppable and I kiss her again. A little deeper this time. Showing her just how happy her yes makes me.

"I was kind of thinking we should buy a new place. Something together. Something that's us instead of you moving into my place or me moving into yours."

"Okay. But I'm not letting you pay for the whole thing. I have my own money too, Doctor Banner," she warns with a reproachful tone.

"You're adorable when you're feisty. We'll fight about it later. Until then, I think my cock would really like to go home now."

She spread her legs wider for me, wrapping them around my back, and pushing me toward her. "I love you," she says, and my smile is instant. I will never tire of hearing those words from Gia.

"Love you," I reply as I sink into her soaking wet heat. Always so ready for me.

My lips capture hers in a scorching kiss, my tongue sweeping through her lips, dancing with hers. It's wild and messy. Unrestrained.

I groan into her as I pick up the pace, holding her thigh against my hip as I piston in and out of her.

So tight. So wet. So warm. Nothing has ever felt better than being buried inside Gia. She *is* my home in every way.

"Closer, Finn. I need you closer. Deeper."

Wrapping my arms around her, I lift her up, moving us until I'm sitting with her straddling my thighs. Gia tosses her head back as I thrust her down on me, a long, loud moan fleeing her lips.

"Fuck," I bellow through a strained groan. "Jesus, Gia. Your pussy is gripping my cock so tight."

"Fuck me, Finn. Fuck me."

Christ. This woman…

I start pumping harder now, a bit faster as I push up into her while she simultaneously drops down on me. Her fucking amazing tits bounce and sway, and my face dips, capturing one perfect, pink nipple into my mouth.

She cries out at this, her hands gripping my hair, tugging on the ends as I devour her. The only noise in the room are her whimpers. The wet sound of my cock as I pound in and out of her.

"You're so perfect," I growl into her chest, pulling back and staring into her eyes. "Nothing has ever felt better."

Her forehead drops to mine, our eyes holding as I continue to screw her like tomorrow is never coming. Her eyes start to roll back into her head and I reach down, finding her swollen clit and rubbing it the way I know she likes. Firm, but tender circles, and she detonates.

Comes on a loud scream, her nails finding purchase in my shoulder blades. I grunt, going faster now until sparks dance behind my eyes, and I follow her over the edge, growling out my release with a harsh expletive.

Her upper body collapses against mine, and I fall backward, taking her with me to the middle of the bed. She lies boneless on my chest, her breathing ragged, matching my own.

"You've destroyed me," she whispers after a few minutes. "Ruined me. Body and soul."

"Thank God. I'd hate to be the only one ruined."

I feel her smile against my sweaty chest. Running my fingers through her inky hair, I brush the stuck threads back from her tacky skin.

"Good thing we don't have a shift in the morning," she muses on a sleepy yawn.

"Tomorrow we're going condo shopping. And getting both of ours ready to sell."

Another yawn and she mumbles, "Whatever you say. I don't care where we live as long as I'm with you."

I press my lips into her hair. *My thoughts exactly.*

Epilogue

FINN

One year later

It's a cliché. I can't help that. And typically, it's not my style to fall into those. But this day represents so many different things for me now and I can't think of a better way to do it. A better woman to do that with. Because the moment I saw her, walking into my ED with that ridiculous black gown on, I knew she was going to change my life. I knew she was going to be the one to bring me back to the land of the living.

It just took a really long time to accept it. To trust it.

To *want* to trust it.

But I do now and here we are. Christmas Day. Again.

I won't lie and say I'm not terrified, because I am. There are so many unknowns. So many things could go wrong and take all of this built-up endurance and smash it into nothing. I have no control over that and I am a man who likes control.

But who the fuck cares?

She's the ride. The high. The life that pumps through my blood and tells everything else they're wrong. That they have no idea. Gia walks up to me, that smile which I dream about, on her full red-tinted lips.

She's beautiful.

So much more now. Unfathomable that it's even possible.

"You're a good sport," she says to me, wrapping her arms around my stomach and leaning into my side. "I know you hate this."

She's right. I do hate it. Family gatherings can go screw themselves. "Just remember that later, when you're exhausted and I want sex."

Gia laughs, rolling her eyes at me.

Those pretty aqua eyes.

The ones that remind me of the waters off the coast of Exuma in the Bahamas. That's exactly why I took her there for vacation.

"I'm always up for sex. You're the one who's going to have to turn me down soon."

"Never," I say as I kiss her lips.

Those pretty lips.

The color of the dress I bought her for tonight. Crimson. It is Christmas after all.

My hands glide along her body and I find myself wishing my mother wasn't here. Or her mother. Or her mother's new husband, George. Or our friends. Because, Gia.

Gia. Gia. Gia. It's all about Gia. It will always all be about Gia.

And…it's time.

"Okay, settle down," I say to everyone in that asshole way I've perfected over the years. They groan at me. I'm annoying them, interrupting their lively chatter. But I don't care. This is the moment. "Seriously, Gia and I wanted to thank you all for coming to celebrate this miserable holiday with us."

That actually gets a few chuckles if you can believe it.

Gia throws me a look and I shrug. It's not like it isn't true. Well, partially true. This is the anniversary of the day Gia and I got together, so I guess that makes it better.

"Gia, love," I say, turning to look her square in the eyes. Goddamn, that's a sight that will never get old. "You're the best thing that's ever happened to me. You not only tolerate my insanity, but you accept me for who I am. You're the light to my dark. The fire that keeps me burning. I am yours as you are mine and I am going to love you forever. I knew it the moment I saw you. The moment I sat next to you on that stoop outside that emergency department."

Gia is crying now. Those beautiful tears she cries.

Those exquisite tears which make me want to hold her that much closer.

Smiling, I lower myself to one knee and everyone in the room gasps.

But not, Gia.

No, my girl laughs at me, shaking her head and covering her mouth. "God, you're an asshole."

I nod, because I am. The perfect asshole. And she's my perfect counterpart.

"You're my soulmate. The woman I'm meant to spend forever with. Gia Bianchi," I grab her hand, gazing up into her eyes. "Will you tell your mother and my mother they're going to be grand-mothers?"

No one makes a sound. Except Gia who laughs and forces me to stand. "You're going to be grandmothers," she says through her laughter and tears. "And you're going to be uncles and aunts," she says pointing to Monique, Mike and Chloe. Chloe's boyfriend looks a little sick, but I don't think Gia was including him in this moment.

"But…" That's my mother and I can't help my grin.

"Don't worry, Mother. I married her. I talked her into it when I took her to the Bahamas last month," I say, this time looking right at Gia. "In fact, that's what I had planned the whole time. It's not my fault she sneak-attacked me with the pregnancy thing."

It's true.

I had planned on asking her to marry me there, but I also wanted to do it there. I didn't want a big wedding and I knew Gia felt the same. I figured it was the perfect solution to that. The day after Thanksgiving last year was a total disaster for us. That's when everything fell apart. I wanted to change that for her. For us. So I bought her a ring and I had the whole trip to the Bahamas planned out.

But the moment we landed, she turned to me and said, "I'm pregnant."

And I said, "Awesome, then you won't say no when I try to give you the ring that's been burning a hole in my pocket."

She said yes, in case you missed it. Because Gia loves me and I love her and we're going to have a baby. Amazing how the pendulum can swing back around.

We have no plans to find out the gender. We're excited to be surprised. Very few surprises in life are good, but this is one of them.

At least that's what Gia keeps reminding me. I wasn't so sold on the surprise notion.

"You're married and having a baby?" Chloe shrieks a bit incredulous. It has been a month since we got back after all. But I needed to wait before we told people. At least through the first trimester. Stepping forward, her mouth slightly agape, she points a very stern finger at Gia. "And you didn't *tell* me? You didn't even invite me to the wedding?"

Gia shrugs nervously, chewing on the corner of her mouth. She's got a lot of ground to make up with her friends, because Monique has a very similar expression on her face. "I have pictures," Gia offers sheepishly.

"Oh, hell no," Monique says as Mike puts a hand on her shoulder, giving her a light squeeze. "I expect more than pictures. I expect details. I expect stories."

"Promise," Gia laughs, hugging her friends, who giggle and squeeze her tighter than I would like considering our baby is growing inside her body.

"Grandma?" her mother says, glancing down at Gia's still mostly flat tummy. The dress hides it well. Only she and I know that bump is there. The most beautiful bump I've ever seen. "Gia, you didn't let me make my only daughter a wedding?"

I think her mother is upset.

"Sorry, Mom. It all happened so fast," Gia says, still chewing on her lip as she reaches out for my hand.

I take it, holding her close to me.

"I'm so happy for you, honey," her mother says and Gia bursts into tears. Her hormones are all over the place. "But I'm still making you a party," she warns. "And you're letting me go with you to pick out a dress. You will not take this away from me, Gia," her mother scolds, before she reaches for her and wraps her in a huge hug. "Your father would be so happy. Il tuo papà ti sta guardando."

I have no idea what she just said, but now Gia is a mess, hugging her mother fiercely and sobbing into her neck. Then her mother hugs me and the three of us are hugging. It's a new experience if I'm being honest.

"I'm delivering the baby," Monique yells out and then her and Chloe get into it, calling dibs on the birth of my child.

Mike steps forward and hugs me the way guys do, complete with back slaps. "I knew it all along, man."

"Always taking the credit," I tease. But really, I thank him. I thank him without words when they seem to fail me. I thank him for what is probably the hundredth time. It's because of him I'm here with her.

My mother gives me a stiff nod and a half smile, because that's as much emotion as she capable of. It's enough. She likes Gia. She even invited her to the club as a lunch guest. That's a pretty big honor coming from my pretentious mother.

Everyone lingers a bit longer, but I consciously made the decision to tell them at the end of the night for a reason. Because I have plans for Gia.

Once everyone leaves, I drag her into our bedroom. She's exhausted. The first trimester of pregnancy hit her hard and hasn't seemed to abate in the second. Lots of nausea and vomiting. So I strip her down, run her a warm, but not too hot, bath, loaded with bubbles and help her in. Gia groans when she hits the water.

"I need to clean up."

"No," I say. "I'm on top of it. You get to relax." She smiles the smile of a wife who is very happy with her husband. I love that smile. It might in fact be my favorite of the ones she gives me.

I leave her to soak and clean everything up. Our friends and family really know how to make a mess and it takes me longer than I would like. By the time I return, I can't tell if Gia is asleep or awake or somewhere in between. Lowering to my knees, I move over to the edge of the large tub I had installed for her when we bought this condo.

She opens one eye. "I'm relaxing, Finn."

"I can see that, love. But I have something for you."

Gia shifts in the tub to face me, water sloshing all around her gorgeous naked body. "But I have everything I need."

"No," I say. "But close."

"Okay, Finn. Explain to me what exactly I'm missing."

"This," I say and then I hand her the dark red box. Her eyes widen and her mouth pops open and when she opens the box and sees the tiny baby bracelet with the name *Natalie* engraved on it, she starts to cry again.

"You, asshole," she yells, splashing water at me. "We were going to be surprised."

"Yeah, but it's a girl, Gia. And I had to look. No way I couldn't. There was a very obvious lack of male parts on that ultrasound. Natalie," I say again. "It's a very pretty Italian name and it was Nonna Bianchi's first name, so it's perfect."

She shakes her head, those beautiful tears falling down her cheeks again.

"Thank you for making me a little girl."

"No," she says. "We did it together. We made her together. We made this together." Her fingers thread through mine and I think I'm forgiven for peeking even though we agreed on surprise. I lean in and kiss her lips, playing with her wedding ring she finally let me put on her finger. "And besides, you know as well as I do, she's only a little girl because of you."

"Maybe," I muse. "But if we're lucky, she'll be so much more."

The End

Liked Finn and Gia's story? <u>Sign up for my Newsletter</u> and get a FREE copy of one of my books!

I sincerely appreciate that you take the time to read Beautiful Potential. I would love it if you'd leave a review. Keep reading for a sneak peek at Reckless Love and The Edge of Temptation!

Other works by J. Saman:

Wild Love Series:
    Reckless Love
    Love to Hate Her
    Hate to Love Him
    Crazy To Love You

The Edge Series:
    The Edge of Temptation
    The Edge of Forever
    The Edge of Reason

Start Again Series:
    Start Again
    Start Over
    Start With Me

Las Vegas Sin Series:
    Touching Sin
    Catching Sin

Other works by J. Saman:

Darkest Sin

Standalones:
Love Rewritten
Beautiful Potential
Forward - FREE

End of Book Note

End of Book Note

Thank you so much for reading this book!

Well, what can I say. Finn, right? Yeah, he had his ups and downs. I found myself both loving and hating him. There were times when I wanted to smack him upside the face for the things he put Gia through. Then there were times I swooned along with Gia.

Love is real shit sometimes. I think we forget that. I think we read these books and see these characters and forget that not everything about it is easy. That after the declaration is made, there is still work to be done.

That's what I wanted in this one. I wanted there to be recognition that all the fear and anxiety and mistrust doesn't get washed away with simple words. Even if those words have profound meaning. I love you is not a panacea. It does not erase our pasts or our mental hang-ups.

After I finished this book, I had a small epiphany. It seems like love not conquering all, is a common theme in my books. In Start Again, Kate had to figure her own crap out before she could be with Ryan, even though she loved him. Start Over, well, Luke was a mess.

He had a ton of issues and Ivy, being the strong chick that she was, went off to live her life. Their love didn't fix their insurmountable obstacles. Same with Start With Me as Claire had some crazy life stuff she needed to navigate in order to move past the "I will never be in a relationship" thing with Kyle.

In Forward, Lara does love Tom. There is no denying that. But their love wasn't enough to breach the divide. In LR, well, I don't know. Xander and Abby just had issues.

I loved Gia. I hope you did too. She was fun and spunky and tough while still having a soft squishy side. There was so much about her that I admired. So many things that I found real in her character. I sort of wish she was real because I think she'd be an awesome friend.

One of my beta readers suggested that I remove Grace from the plot all together. That Kelly cheating on Finn was enough of a betrayal. And I toyed with that. I thought a lot about it. And then I realized that her cheating on him and their marriage ending, wasn't enough to put him into a place where he literally shut himself off emotionally. In the chapters with Kelly, he's so sweet and warm and affectionate. Yeah, he's still Finn. He's still sort of a jerk, but he clings to her love because it's the only thing he has.

And when she takes everything away from him, all that love, all that trust, all that future and possibility, he turns into the Finn we see throughout most of the book. I don't think losing Logan and then having his wife cheat on him was enough to get him to that point. A marriage can very easily fall apart after a tragic loss and I think he would have been able to accept that eventually. I think Grace was the key.

So yeah, I kept her. I hope you don't think it was too much. If you do, well, I made a choice and I stuck with it and I hope you can appreciate that. I also threw in a Lara Gould (from Forward) cameo, because in my mind, it was her hospital and her ED and I love her.

I hope you enjoyed this one. I'm working on a few other things at the moment, so stay tuned. More to come.

You can find me on my website, Facebook, Twitter, Instagram, Goodreads. If you're interested in getting emails from me that include promotions, giveaways, freebies and new releases, please sign up for my newsletter.

XO,

J. Saman

Keep reading for a sneak peek at Reckless Love and The Edge of Temptation.

Reckless Love

PROLOGUE

Lyric

I CAN'T STOP STARING at it. Reading the two short words over and over again ad nauseum. They're simple. Essentially unimpressive if you think about it. But those two words mean everything. Those two words dive deep into the darkest depths of my soul, the part I've methodically shut off over the years, and awaken the dormant volcano. How can two simple words make this well of emotions erupt so quickly?

Come home.

I don't recognize the number the text came from. It shows up as Unknown. But I don't have to recognize it. I know who it's from. Instinctively, I know. At least, my body does, because my heart rate is through the roof. My stomach is clenched tight with violent, poorly concealed, sickly butterflies. My forehead is clammy with a sheen of sweat and my hands tremble as they clutch my phone.

It's early here in California. Not even dawn, but I'm awake. I'm always awake, even when I'm not, and since my phone has, unfortunately, become another appendage, it's consistently with me.

It's a New York area code.

Goddammit! I suck in a deep, shuddering breath of air that does absolutely nothing to calm me, then I respond in the only way I can.

Me*: **Who is this?***

The message bubble appears instantly, like he was waiting for me. Like there is no way this is a wrong number. Like his fingers couldn't respond fast enough.

Unknown: ***You know who this is. Come home.***

I don't respond. I can't. I'm frozen. It's been four years. Four fucking years. And this is how he reaches out? This is how he contacts me? I slink back down into my bed, pulling the heavy comforter over my head in a pathetic attempt to protect myself from the onslaught of emotions that consume me. I tuck my phone against my chest, over what's left of my fractured heart.

I'm hurting. I'm angry. I'm so screwed up and broken, and yet, I'm still breaking. How is that even possible? How can a person continue to break when they're already broken? How can a person I haven't seen in four years still affect me like this?

I want to throw the traitorous device into the wall and smash it. Toss it out my window as hard as I can and hope it reaches the Pacific at the other end of the beach, where it will be swept away, never to return. But I don't. Because curiosity is a nefarious bitch. Because I have to know why the man who was my everything and now my nothing is contacting me after all this time, asking me to come home.

Unknown*: **I'm sitting here in my old room, on my bed, and I can't focus. I can't think about what I need to be thinking about. So, I need you to come home.***

I shake my head as tears line my eyes, stubbornly refusing to fall but obscuring my vision all the same. Nothing he's saying makes sense to me. Nothing. It's completely nonsensical, and yet, it's not. I still know him well enough to understand both what he's saying and what he's not.

Me*: **Why?***

Unknown*: **Because I need you to.***

Me: *I can't. Too busy with work.*

That's sort of a lie. I mean, I *am* headed to New York for the Rainbow Ball in a few days. But he doesn't need to know that. And I do not want to see him. I absolutely, positively, do not.

Unknown: ***My dad had a stroke***

My eyes cinch shut, and I cover them with one hand. I can't breathe. A gasped sob escapes the back of my throat, burning me with its raw taste. God. Now what the hell am I going to do? I love his father. Jesus Christ. How can I say no to him now? How can I avoid this the way I so desperately need to? *Shit.*

Me: ***I'm sorry. I didn't know. Is he okay?***

Unknown: ***He'll live, but he's not great. He's in the ICU. Worse than he was after the heart attack.***

I shake my head back and forth. I can't go. I can't go home. I was there two months ago to visit my parents and my sister's family. I have work—so much freaking work that I can barely keep up. I don't want to see him. I won't survive it. I'll see him, and I'll feel everything I haven't allowed myself to feel. I'll be sucked back in.

Things are different now.

They are. My situation has changed completely, but I never had the guts to call him and tell him that. Mostly because I was hurt. Mostly because I felt abandoned and brushed off. Mostly because I was terrified that it wouldn't matter after all this time apart. If I see him now, knowing how much has changed…Shit. I just…Fuck. I can't.

I don't know what to do.

I'm drenched in sweat. The blanket I sought refuge in is now smothering me. I'm relieved his father is alive. I still speak to him once a month. Wait, let me amend that—he still *calls* me once a month. And we talk. Not about Jameson. Never about him. Only about me and my life. I'm a wreck that Jameson is contacting me. I can't play this game. I never could. It was all or nothing with him.

Unknown: ***I miss you.***

I stare at the words, read them over again, then respond too quickly, ***Liar.***

Unknown: ***Never. I miss you so goddamn much.***

I think I just died. Everything inside me has stopped. My heart is not beating. My breath has stalled inside my chest, unable to be expelled. My mind is completely blank. And when everything comes back to life, I'm consumed with an angry, caustic fury I never knew I was capable of.

Unknown: *Are you still there?*

Me: *What do you want me to say?*

Unknown: *I don't know. I'm torn on that. Please come home.*

Me: *Why?*

Unknown: *Because I need you. Because he needs you. Because I was always too busy obsessing over you to fall for someone else. Because I need to know if I'm making a mistake by hoping.*

I shake my head vigorously, letting out the loudest, shrillest shriek I can muster. It's not fucking helping, and I need something to help. Clamoring out of bed, I hurry over to the balcony doors, unlocking them and tossing them open wide.

Fresh air. I need fresh air. Even Southern California fresh air. A burst of salty, ocean mist hits me square in the face, clinging to the sweat I'm covered in. It's still dark out. Dawn is not yet playing with the midnight-blue sky.

I stare out into the black expanse of the ocean, listen to the crashing of the waves and sigh. I knew about him. I would be lying if I said I hadn't Facebook-stalked him a time or twenty over the years. Forced myself to hate him with the sort of passion reserved for political figures and pop stars. But this? Saying he misses me?

Me: *Seeing me won't change that. But if you're asking, you are.*

He responds immediately, and I can't help but grin a little at that. *You still care about me, Jameson Woods.* When I catch the traitorous thought, I shut it down instantly. Because if he cared, if his texted words meant anything, then I wouldn't be here, and he wouldn't be there, and this bullshit four a.m. text conversation wouldn't be happening.

Unknown: *I'm not asking. Seeing you might change everything. But more than that, I need you here with me. My father would want to see you. Come home.*

I hate him. I hate him. I hate him!

Me: *I can't come home. Stop using your father to manipulate me.*

Unknown: *It's the only play I have. You can come home. I know you can. Are you seeing someone? Before you respond, any answer other than no might kill me right now.*

I growl, not caring if anyone walking by hears. How can he do this to me? How can he be so goddamn selfish? Doesn't he know what he put me through? That I still haven't found my way back after four years? I shouldn't reply. I should just throw my phone away and never look back.

Me: *No. And you're a bastard.*

Unknown: *YES. I Am! Please. I am officially begging. Really, Lee. I'm not even bullshitting. I'm a mess. Please. Please. Please!!!!*

Me: ...

Unknown: *What does that mean?*

Me: *It means I'm thinking. Stop!*

My eyes lock on nothing, my mind swirling a mile a minute.

Lee. He called me Lee. That nickname might actually hurt the most. And now he's asking me to come home. Jameson Woods, the man I thought was my forever, is asking me to come home to see him. And for what? To scratch a long-forgotten itch? To assuage some long-abandoned guilt over what he did? Why would I fall for that?

I sigh again because I know why. It's the same reason I never bring men home. It's the same reason I haven't given up this house even though I don't fully live in it anymore and it's far from convenient. It's the same reason I continued this conversation instead of smashing my phone.

Jameson Woods.

The indelible ink on my body. The scar on my soul. The fissure in my heart.

Unknown: ...

I can't help the small laugh that squeaks out as I lean forward and prop my elbows on the edge of the railing. The cool wind whips through my hair, and I hate that I feel this way. That I'm entertaining him the way I am.

Me: **What does that mean?**

Unknown: **It means I'm getting impatient. Please. I need you to come home. I know I'm a bastard. I know I shouldn't be asking you this. But I am.**

Unknown: **Aren't you at least a little curious?**

YES!

Me: **NO!!!!!!! And bastard doesn't cover you.**

Unknown: **Please. It's spinning out of control, and I need to see you. I need to know.**

Me: **You already know.**

Unknown: **About you?**

Me: **Yes, or you wouldn't be texting me at four in the morning.**

Unknown: **It's seven here. Does that mean you'll come?**

Me: ...

Unknown: ...

Me: **Yes.**

My phone slips from my fingers, clanging to the hard surface of my balcony floor. My phone buzzes again, a little louder now since the sound is reverberating off the ground. I don't pick it up. I don't look down. I don't care if he's thanking me or anything else he comes up with. I don't care. I don't want to know.

Because I'm busy getting my head on straight.

Locking myself down.

I'm worried about his father and I want to see him, want to make sure he's okay with my own two eyes.

I'll go home and I'll see him. I'll see him, and I'll do the one thing I was never able to do before. I'll say goodbye. My eyes close and I allow myself to slip back. To remember every single moment we had together. To indulge in the sweet torture that, if I let it, will rip me apart piece by piece. Because I know what I'm in for, and I know that once I step foot off that airplane, nothing will ever be right again.

WANT to find out what happens next with Lyric and Jameson? Grab your copy of Reckless Love today!

The Edge of Temptation

CHAPTER 1

Halle

"No," I reply emphatically, hoping my tone is stronger than my disposition. "I'm not doing it. Absolutely not. Just no." I point my finger for emphasis, but I don't think the gesture is getting me anywhere. Rina just stares at me, the tip of her finger gliding along the lip of her martini glass.

"You're smiling. If you don't want to do this, then why are you smiling?"

I sigh. She's right. I am smiling. But only because it's so ridiculous. In all the years she's known me, I've never hit on a total stranger. I don't think I'd have any idea how to even do that. And honestly, I'm just not in the right frame of mind to put in the effort. "It's funny, that's all." I shrug, playing it off. It's really not funny. The word terrifying comes closer. "But my answer is still no."

"It's been, what?" Margot chimes in, her gaze flicking between Rina, Aria, and me like she's actually trying to figure this out. She's not. I know where she's going with this and it's fucking rhetorical. "A month?"

See? I told you.

"You broke up with Matt a month ago. And you can't play it off like you're all upset over it, because we know you're not."

"Who says I'm not upset?" I furrow my eyebrows, feigning incredulous, but I can't quite meet their eyes. "I was with him for two years."

But she's right. I'm not upset about Matt. I just don't have the desire to hit on some random dude at some random bar in the South End of Boston.

"Two *useless* years," Rina persists with a roll of her blue eyes before taking a sip of her appletini. She sets her glass down, leaning her small frame back in her chair as she crosses her arms over her chest and purses her lips like she's pissed off on my behalf. "The guy was a freaking asshole."

"And a criminal," Aria adds, tipping back her fancy glass and finishing off the last of her dirty martini, complete with olive. She chews on it slowly, quirking a pointed eyebrow at me. "The cocksucker repeatedly ignored you so he could defraud people."

"All true." I can't even deny it. My ex was a black-hat hacker. And while that might sound all hot and sexy in a mysterious, dangerous way, it isn't. The piece of shit stole credit card numbers, and not only used them for himself but sold them on the dark web. He was also one of those hacktivists who got his rocks off by working with other degenerate assholes to try and bring down various companies and websites.

In my defense, I didn't know what he was up to until the FBI came into my place of work, hauled me downtown, and interviewed me for hours. I was so embarrassed, I could hardly show my face at work again. Not only that, but everyone was talking about me. Either with pity or suspicion in their eyes, like I was a criminal right along with him.

Matt had a regular job as a red-team specialist—legit hackers who are paid by companies to go in and try to penetrate their systems. I assumed all that time he spent on his computer at night was him working hard to get ahead. At least that was his perpetual excuse when challenged.

Nothing makes you feel more naïve than discovering the man

you had been engaged to is actually a criminal who was stealing from people. And committing said thefts while living with you.

I looked up one of the people the FBI had mentioned in relation to Matt's criminal activities. The woman had a weird name that stuck out to me for me some reason, and when I found her, I learned she was a widow with three grandchildren, a son in the military, and was a recently retired nurse. It made me sick to my stomach. Still does when I think about it.

I told the FBI everything I knew, which was nothing. I explained that I had ended things with Matt three days prior to them arresting him. Pure coincidence. I was fed up with the monotony of our relationship. Of being engaged and never discussing or planning our wedding. Of living with someone I never saw because he was always locked away in his office, too preoccupied with his computer to pay me even an ounce of attention. But really, deep down, I knew I wasn't in love with him anymore.

I didn't even shed a tear over our breakup. In fact, I was more relieved than anything. I knew I had dodged a bullet getting out when I did.

And then the FBI showed up.

"I ended it with him. *Before* I knew he was a total and complete loser," I tack on, feeling more defensive about the situation than I care to admit. Shifting my weight on my uncomfortable wooden chair, I cross my legs at the knee and stare sightlessly out into the bar.

"And we applaud you for that," Rina says, nudging Margot and then Aria in the shoulders, forcing them to concur. "It was the absolute right thing to do. But you've been miserable and mopey and very . . ."

"Anti-men," Margot finishes for her, tossing back her lemon drop shot with disturbing exuberance. I think that's number three for her already, which means it could be a long night. Margot has yet to learn the art of moderation.

"Right." Aria nods exaggeratedly at Margot like she just hit the nail on the head, tossing her messy dark curls over her shoulders before twisting them up into something that resembles a bun. "Anti-men. I'm not saying you need to date anyone here. You don't even have to go home with them. Just let them buy you a drink. Have a normal conversation with a normal guy."

I scoff. "And you think I'll find one of those in here?" I splay my arms out wide, waving them around. All these men look like players. They're in groups with other men, smacking at each other and pointing at the various women who walk in. They're clearly rating them. And if a woman just so happens to pass by, they blatantly turn and stare at her ass.

This is a hookup bar. All dark mood lighting, annoying, trendy house music in the background and uncomfortable seating. The kind designed to have you standing all night before you take someone home. And now I understand why my very attentive friends brought me here. It's not our usual go-to place.

"It's like high school or a frat house in here. And definitely not in a good way. I bet all these guys bathed in Axe body spray, gelled up their hair and left their mother's basement to come here and find a 'chick to bang.'" I put air quotes around those words. I have zero interest in being part of that scheme.

"Well . . ." Rina's voice drifts off, scanning the room desperately. "I know I can find you someone worthy."

"Don't waste your brain function. I'm still not interested." I roll my eyes dramatically and finish off my drink, slamming the glass down on the table with a bit more force than I intend. *Oops.* Whatever. I'm extremely satisfied with my anti-men status. Because that's exactly what I am—anti-men—and I'm discovering I'm unrepentant about it. In fact, I think it's a fantastic way to be when you rack up one loser after another the way I have. Like a form of self-preservation.

I've never had a good track record. Even before Matt, I had a knack for picking the wrong guys. My high school boyfriend ended up being gay. I handed him my V-card shortly before he dropped that bomb on me, though he swore I didn't turn him gay. He promised he was like that prior to the sex. In college, I dated two guys somewhat seriously. The first one cheated on me for months before I found out, and the second one was way more into his video games than he was me. I think he also had a secret cocaine problem because he'd stay up all night gaming like a fiend. I had given up on men for a while—are you seeing a trend here?—and then in my final year of graduate school, Matt came along. Need I say more? So as far as I'm concerned, men can all go screw themselves. Because they sure as hell aren't gonna screw me!

"You can stop searching now, Rina." This is getting pathetic. "I have a vibrator. What else does a girl need?" All three pause their search to examine me and I realize I said that out loud. I blush at that, but it's true, so I just shrug a shoulder and fold my arms defiantly across my chest. "I don't need a sextervention. If anything, I need to avoid the male species like the plague they are."

They dismiss me immediately, their cause to find me a "normal" male to talk to outweighing my antagonism. And really, if it's taking this long to find someone then the pickings must really be slim here. I move to flag down the waitress to order another round when Margot points to the far corner.

"There." The tenacious little bug is gleaming like she just struck oil in her backyard. "That guy. He's freaking hot as holy sin and he's alone. He even looks sad, which means he needs a friend."

"Or he wants to be left alone to his drinking," I mumble, wishing I had another drink in my hand so I could focus on something other than my friends obsessively staring at some random creep. *Where the hell is that waitress?*

"Maybe," Aria muses thoughtfully as she observes the man across the bar, tapping her bottom lip with her finger. Her hands are covered in splotches of multicolored paint. As is her black shirt, now that I look closer. "Or maybe he's just had a crappy day. He looks so sad, Halle." She nods like it's all coming together for her as she makes frowny puppy dog eyes at me. "So very sad. Go over and see if he wants company. Cheer him up."

"You'd be doing a public service," Rina agrees. "Men that good-looking should never be sad."

I roll my eyes at that. "You think a blowjob would do it, or should I offer him crazy, kinky sex to cheer him up? I still have that domination-for-beginners playset I picked up at Angela's bachelorette party. Hasn't even been cracked open."

Aria tilts her head like she's actually considering this. "That level of kink might scare him off for the first time. And I wouldn't give him head unless he goes down on you first."

Jesus, I'm not drunk enough for this. "Or he's a total asshole who just fucked his girlfriend's best friend," I protest, my voice rising an octave with my objection. I sit up straight, desperate to make my point clear. "Or he's about to go to prison because he hacks women into tiny bits with a machete before he eats them. Either way, I'm. Not. Interested."

"God," Margot snorts, twirling her chestnut hair as she leans back in her chair and levels me with an unimpressed gaze. "Dramatic much? He wouldn't be out on bail if that were the case. But seriously, that's like crazy psycho shit, and that guy does not say crazy psycho. He says crave-worthy and yummy and 'I hand out orgasms like candy on Halloween.'"

"Methinks the lady doth protest too much," Aria says with a knowing smile and a wink.

She swivels her head to check him out again and licks her lips reflexively. I haven't bothered to peek yet because my back is to him and I hate that I'm curious. All three ladies are eyeing him with unfettered appreciation and obvious lust. Their tastes in men differ tremendously, which indicates this guy probably is hot. I shouldn't be tempted. I really shouldn't be. I'm asking for a world of trouble or hurt or legal fees. So why am I finding the idea of a one-nighter with a total stranger growing on me?

I've never been that girl before. But maybe they're right? Maybe a one-nighter with a random guy is just the ticket to wipe out my past of bad choices in men and make a fresh start? I don't even know if that makes sense since a one-nighter is the antithesis of a smart choice. But my libido is taking over for my brain and now I'm starting to rationalize, possibly even encourage. I need to stop this now.

"He's gay. Hot men are always gay. Or assholes. Or criminals. Or cheaters. Or just generally suck at life."

"You've had some bad luck, is all. Look at Oliver. He's good-looking, sweet, loving, and not an asshole. Or a criminal. And he likes you. You could date him."

Reaching over, I steal Rina's cocktail. She doesn't stop me or even seem to register the action. I stare at her with narrowed eyes over the rim of her glass as I slurp down about half of it in one gulp. "I'm not dating your brother, Rina. That's weird and begging for drama. You and I are best friends."

She sighs and then I sigh because I'm being a bitch and I don't mean to be. I like her brother. He is all of those things she just mentioned, minus the liking me part. But if things went bad between us, which they inherently would, it would cost me one of my most important friendships. And that's not a risk I'm willing to take. Plus, unbeknownst to Rina, Oliver is one of the biggest players in the greater Boston area.

"I'm just saying not all men are bad," Rina continues, and I shake my head. "We'll buy your drinks for a month if you go talk to this guy," she offers hastily, trying to close the deal.

Margot glances over at her with furrowed eyebrows, a bit surprised by that declaration, but she quickly comes around with an indifferent shrug. Aria smiles, liking that idea. Then again, money is not Aria's problem. "Most definitely," she agrees. "Go. Let a stranger touch your lady parts. You're waxed and shaved and looking hot. Let someone take advantage of that."

"And if he shoots me down?"

"You don't have to sleep with him," Rina reminds me. "Or even give him your real name. In fact, tell him nothing real about your-self. It could be like a sexual experiment." I shake my head in exas-peration. "We won't bother you about it again," she promises solemnly. "But he won't shoot you down. You look movie star hot tonight."

I can only roll my eyes at that. While I appreciate the sentiment from my loving and supportive friends, being shot down by a total stranger when I'm already feeling emotionally strung out might just do me in. Even if I have no interest in him. But free drinks . . .

Twisting around in my chair, I stare across the crowded bar, probing for a few seconds until I spot the man in the corner. Holy Christmas in Florida, he *is* hot. There is no mistaking that. His hair is light blond, short along the sides and just a bit longer on top. Just long enough that you could grab it and hold on tight while he kisses you. His profile speaks to his straight nose and strong, chiseled, cleanly shaven jaw. I must admit, I do enjoy a bit of stubble on my men, but he makes the lack of beard look so enticing that I don't miss the roughness. He's wearing a suit. A dark suit. More than likely expensive judging by the way it contours to his broad shoulders and the flash of gold on his wrist that I catch in the form of cufflinks.

But the thing that's giving me pause is his anguish. It's radiating off him. His beautiful face is downcast, staring sightlessly into his full glass of something amber. Maybe scotch. Maybe bourbon. It doesn't matter. That expression has purpose. Those eyes have meaning behind them and I doubt he's seeking any sort of company. In fact, I'm positive he'd have no trouble finding any if he were so inclined.

That thought alone makes me stand up without further comment. He's the perfect man to get my friends off my back. He's going to shoot me down in an instant and I won't even take it personally. Well, not too much. I can feel the girls exchanging gleeful smiles, but I figure I'll be back with them in under five minutes, so their misguided enthusiasm is inconsequential. I watch him the entire way across the bar. He doesn't sip at his drink. He just stares blankly into it. That sort of heartbreak makes my stomach churn. This miserable stranger isn't just your typical Saturday night bar dweller looking for a quick hookup.

He's drowning his sorrows.

Miserable Stranger doesn't notice my approach. He doesn't even notice me as I wedge myself in between him and the person seated beside him. And he definitely doesn't notice me as I order myself a dirty martini. I'm close enough to smell him. And damn, it's so freaking good I catch myself wanting to close my eyes and breathe in deeper. Sandalwood? Citrus? Freaking godly man? Who knows. I have no idea what to say to him. In fact, I'm half-tempted to grab my drink and scurry off, but I catch Rina, Margot, and Aria watching vigilantly from across the bar with excited, encouraging smiles. There's no way I can get out of this without at least saying hello.

Especially if I want those bitches to buy me drinks for the next month.

But damn, I'm so stupidly nervous. "Hello," I start, but my voice is weak and shaky, and I have to clear it to get rid of the nervous lilt. Shit. My hands are trembling. Pathetic.

He doesn't look up. Awesome start.

I play it off, staring around the dimly lit bar and taking in all the people enjoying their Saturday night cocktails. It's busy here. Filled with the heat of the city in the summer and lust-infused air. I open my mouth to speak again, when the person seated next to my Miserable Stranger and directly behind me, gets up, shoving their chair inadvertently into my back and launching me forward. Straight into him.

I fly without restraint, practically knocking him over. Not enough to fully push him off his chair—he's too big and strong for that—but it's enough to catch his attention. I see him blink like he's coming back from some distant place. His head tilts up to mine as I right myself, just as my attention is diverted by the man who hit me with his chair.

"I'm so sorry," the man says with a note of panic in his voice, reaching out and grasping my upper arm as if to steady me. "I didn't see you there. Are you okay?"

"Yes, I'm fine." I'm beet red, I know it.

"Did I hurt you?"

Just my pride. "No. Really. I'm good. It was my fault for wedging myself in like this." The stranger who bumped me smiles warmly, before turning back to his girlfriend and leaving the scene of the crime as quickly as possible.

Adjusting my dress and schooling my features, I turn back to my Miserable Stranger, clearing my throat once more as my eyes meet his. "I'm sorry I banged into you . . ." My freaking breath catches in my lungs, making my voice trail off at the end.

Goddamn.

If I thought his profile was something, it's nothing compared to the rest of him. He blinks at me, his eyes widening fractionally as he sits back, crossing his arms over his suit-clad chest and taking me in from head to toe. He hasn't even removed his dark jacket, which seems odd. It's more than warm in here and summer outside.

He sucks in a deep breath as his eyes reach mine again. They're green. But not just any green. Full-on megawatt green. Like thick summer grass green. I can tell that even in the dim lighting of the bar, that's how vivid they are. They're without a doubt the most beautiful eyes I've ever seen.

"That's all right," he says and his thick baritone, with a hint of some sort of accent, is just as impressive as the rest of him. It wraps its way around me like a warm blanket on a cold night. Jesus, has a voice ever affected me like this? Maybe I do need to get out more if I'm reacting to a total stranger like this. "I love it when beautiful women fall all over me."

I like him instantly. Cheesy line and all.

"That happen to you a lot?"

He smirks and the way that crooked grin looks on his face has my heart rate jacking up yet another degree. "Not really. Are you okay? That was quite the tumble."

I nod. I don't want to talk about my less than graceful entrance anymore. "Would you mind if I sit down?" And he thinks about it. Actually freaking hesitates. Just perfect. This is not helping my already frail ego.

I stare at him for a beat, and just as I'm about to raise the white flag and retreat with my dignity in my feet, he swallows hard and shakes his head slowly. Is he saying no I shouldn't sit, or no he doesn't mind? Crap, I can't tell, because his expression is . . . a mess. Like a bizarre concoction of indecision and curiosity and temptation and disgust.

He must note my confusion because in a slow measured tone he clarifies with, "I guess you should probably sit so you don't fall on me again." He blinks, something catching his attention. Glancing

past me for the briefest of moments, that smirk returni
lips. "I think your friends love the idea."

"Huh?" I sputter before my head whips over my sh
catch Rina, Aria, and Margot standing, watching us with equally
exuberant smiles. Margot even freaking waves. Well, that's embarrassing. Now what do I say? "Yeah . . . um." Words fail me, and I
sink back into myself. "I'm sorry. I just . . . well, I recently broke up
with someone, and my friends won't let me return to the table until
I've re-entered the human female race and had a real conversation
with a man."

God, this sounds so stupidly pathetic. Even to my own ears. And
why did I just admit all of that to him? My face is easily the shade
of the dress I'm wearing—and it's bright motherfucking red. He's
smirking at me again, which only proves my point. I hate feeling like
this. Insecure and inadequate. At least it's better than stupid and
clueless. Yeah, that's what I had going on with Matt and this is not
who I am. I'm typically far more self-assured.

"I'll just grab my drink and return to my friends."

I pull some cash out of my purse and drop it on the wooden bar.
I pause, and he doesn't stop me. My fingers slip around the smooth,
long stem of my glass. I want to get the hell out of here, but before I
can slide my drink safely toward me and make my hasty, not so
glamorous escape, he covers my hand with his and whispers, "No.
Stay."

Want to find out what happens next with Halle and Jonah? Find out
now with The Edge of Temptation.

Made in the USA
Las Vegas, NV
19 November 2022

59814484R00173